RAPHAEL
by R. A. MacAvoy

A masterful blending of high adventure and moving
throughtful drama, *Raphael* is the culmination of a magnificent
fantasy epic by one of the most heralded new writers of our
time.

Praise for R. A. MacAvoy's previous works:

TEA WITH THE BLACK DRAGON
A 1983 Nebula Award Nominee

"A refreshing change from the more familiar epic or heroic fantasy. I recommend it highly."

—*San Francisco Chronicle*

"A very different fantasy . . . It's a wonderful book, with beautifully drawn characters and a tremendously varied and unexpected background. I wish I'd written it."

—Elizabeth A. Lynn

DAMIANO

"MacAvoy, who more than fulfills the promise of her last year's *Tea With the Black Dragon*, has mastered all the skills needed to write good historical fantasy, and adds a marvelously spare, clear prose style."

—*Chicago Sun-Times*

"A treasureable read. Roberta MacAvoy is undeniably a writer to watch for."

—Anne McCaffrey

"A large-souled adventure, formidably funny, knowing and word-wise."

—*The Philadelphia Inquirer*

DAMIANO'S LUTE

"I found *Damiano's Lute* very absorbing. The author's ability to bring to vivid life the background of this period of history, and yet interweave it with the type of fantasy which was actually accepted in that day of positive faith is truly amazing."

—Andre Norton

W9-AOJ-095

RAPHAEL

R. A. MacAvoy

BANTAM BOOKS
TORONTO • NEW YORK • LONDON • SYDNEY • AUCKLAND

RAPHAEL

A Bantam Book / September 1984

ISBN 0-553-24370-5

Published simultaneously in the United States and Canada

Bantam Books are published by Bantam Books, Inc. Its trade-
mark, consisting of the words "Bantam Books" and the por-
trayal of a rooster, is Registered in U.S. Patent and Trademark
Office and in other countries. Marca Registrada. Bantam
Books, Inc., 666 Fifth Avenue, New York, New York 10103.

PRINTED IN THE UNITED STATES OF AMERICA

O   0 9 8 7 6 5 4 3 2 1

For Qui

First came the seen, then thus the palpable
Elysium, though it were in the halls of hell,
What thou lovest well is thy true heritage
What thou lovest well shall not be reft from thee.

Ezra Pound
Pisan Cantos (81)

1

Two young people sat quite comfortably on the grassy bank of a stream, leaning against a willow whose ancient body seemed designed for leaning. Plangent water reflected the little green leaves of the willow, including even the tiny round crystals of dew which hung from the leaves, with only artistic distortion, while below the line of the water cool fish brooded, wearing coats of bright enamelwork.

On either side of the stream a lawn spread out, tended by cloudy sheep. Other beasts, too, roamed at their graceful will across the landscape: the ox and the wide-horned aurochs, the slouching camelopard, the corkindrill—each animal as fat as a burgher and similarly complacent. None were ragged, none scarred. None raised its elegant head except in wonder at the sweetness of the air.

Of course there were birds, and even in the lacy mass of the willow they sang, regardless of the presence of two or three sleek and platter-faced cats who meditated while resting upon the largest branches, their white, gray, or many-striped tails curled below them like fishhooks trolling the air.

Although there were aurochs and a camelopard, and it has been said that these are wary beasts and unsocial, this park which contained them had not the appearance of wilderness. Beyond the copse of fruiting trees on the far side of the river rose a white palace of intricate shape and exquisite proportion, though through distance and the balmy air its exact lineaments were confused. Another, more homey sort of house rose closer to hand, on the bank of the stream itself. This edifice was square, three stories tall, and also white—sparkling white—except for a roof of red tile and certain tasteful borders of red and gold about the windows.

These windows were large, as though the house had been
built without care for winter, and they yawned wide and
shutterless, as though no thief had ever been born. From
these windows hung pots of divers herbs. A pretty gravel
path wound away from the tower and kept company with
the stream for a while, before humping itself over on a
painted bridge and heading toward the ambiguous palace.

The two young people who lounged beside the path (and
beneath the birds, and the cats, and the willow leaves all
hung with dew) were both decorative and restful to the
eye—of a piece with the rest of the scene. One was a small
and delicately made maiden all dressed in white save for a
red kerchief which she wore around her neck, hanging
down in back. Her hair was not flaxen, but as white as her
dress—and yet there was no mistaking this child for an old
woman. Her pleasant triangular face was as innocent of
wrinkles as it seemed of thought. Her eyes were soft and
brown. With a yawn and a stretch this child rolled away
from the tree and began rooting about in the grass in the
most unladylike fashion, on all fours, apparently searching
for something, while she turned those strange, heavy
pupiled eyes on her companion with a mixture of fawning
and mischief.

He, too, had large brown eyes, and he was also dressed in
white, though upon his glimmering garment there were
certain touches (as there were in the square tower) of scarlet
and gold. He was not pale, however, but swarthy, and his
hair was a mass of lazy curls. He continued to lean against
the willow tree while his hands played over the strings of a
perfectly plain, perfectly perfect lute. He happened to be
seated (in seeming content) on a dead branch, which he
took care should not be visible to the girl.

The music he made was like the light which bathed and
enfolded this garden without a wall: impossibly rich and
simple, too fine-textured for the world of days. And he
didn't play alone, for his melody was answered by a descant
from the winged sky, while below the grass murmured a
sweet continuo.

It was a piece without beginning or end, and a glance at
the rapt face of the musician communicated that he was well

satisfied with the work. But at some time during that long morning, the musician raised his head and left the music to continue without him. His eyes, like those of the girl, were drowned drunk as though they witnessed something beyond sky, river, leafy tree, and rippling grasses.

As though they witnessed glory.

His eyes were so because he, she, the corkindrill, and all of those who strolled, slouched, soared, or sang their perfection in that crystal air, were the dead—the blessed dead—and this was their realm.

And in truth there was neither stream nor willow, nor leaves of the willow nor dew to hang from its leaves, nor tower nor palace nor pretty gravel paths winding between them.

There was only peace here: great peace, bought with pain, perhaps. Redeemed by love, most certainly. Peace, at any rate, and it had shattered the bonds of time.

But this particular blessed soul (the one with the lute) raised his head and the beautiful drowned eyes squinted, like those of a nearsighted man trying to focus at a distance.

"What is it, Dami?" asked the white girl, and she plumped herself down in front of him.

For some moments he did not respond, but stared past her, and past the stream and the copse of fruit trees and the white palace beyond, into unimaginable or unremembered distance. Then he met her gaze, while his fingers evoked a trickle of emotion from the lute strings.

"I felt, little dear," he said slowly, "as though someone had floated here on the wind from far away, offering me all of heaven and earth to follow him."

She scooted closer, until her soft and innocent (though not particularly clever) face rested mere inches from his. "What did that feel like?"

He sighed. "It felt like a stomachache."

Macchiata snorted and sat back heavily on the grass. "But, Master—Master! You dont HAVE a stomach!"

She peered at him sidelong, grinning, and sought again in the grass around the willow. At last she found the branch Damiano had concealed, and she pulled it out from under his legs.

"Hah! There it is.

"Come on, Dami," she wheedled winsomely. "Throw the stick for me again."

He looked into her eyes. "Are you pining for your natural form, little dear? Would you like to be a dog once again?"

Macchiata slipped his gaze and looked hungrily at the branch in her master's hand. "Not pining. I like my girl shape. Especially the hands, which make it easy to pick up sticks.

"Please, Dami. PLEASE throw it again."

The greatest of the archangels, Lucifer by name, had a palace as grand as that behind the orchard in Tir Na nOg—the Isle of the Ever Young—though Lucifer's watchful fortress was neither white nor charmingly situated. Atop the square box of it was a small, high chamber possessing four windows. These reached from the floor to the vaulted ceiling, and they stood always open.

One of these windows looked grudgingly toward the clean north, just as one beheld the generous south with due suspicion. The third window kept a wary eye against the wisdom of the east while the last window denied all hope of the west. Despite this eclectic airiness, the atmosphere in the chamber was a bit stuffy and it smelled like a dead fire. A single grayish, dirty fly droned in frustrated circles though the air of the chamber, as though despite all the windows it could not find a way out.

Within the arches of this high room stood only a table and a chair. On the table was placed a small replica of the palace itself, which was as intricate as its original—as squatly heavy and as drear—and only less fearsome because of its size. At the very top of the model perched a tiny cupola of four windows, within which rested two tiny atomies of furniture: a table and a chair. The chair in the model, like that in the original, was empty.

But the owner of the palace (and the model) was returning, ploughing his way through the sky on wyvern's wings. He came not from the north or south or from any other clear direction, but in great, frustrated circles, and he stopped to pant on the black iron roof of this highest chamber before slithering in.

As the light of one window was darkened for a moment by his serpentine bulk, the fly found its way cutely into the model of the palace, where it settled itself upon the matchstick perfection of the tiny table in the highest chamber.

Lucifer sloughed off his hideous wyvern shape and appeared with a sneer upon his elegant carnelian features. He despised ugliness almost as much as he distrusted beauty, but since his own angelic wings had shriveled long ago, he had to take some other shape if he were to fly. He threw himself into the hard chair and scowled out each window in turn.

A long climb and a bootless errand in a place which could not be seen out of any of his watch windows. A place beyond the limits of his dominion. Lucifer was in a foul, foul mood.

Curse the deaf, dimwit shade!

If only Lucifer COULD curse him, or indulge himself in any deed on physical or spiritual plane which could do damage to the object of his dislike. But he could no more sting the little creature than he could sting God Himself, who held it in His infuriatingly careful hands. He could only call it names out loud, not the worst of which was "dago." He stared at his new toy palace, unseeing.

Someone new entered the chamber through the hatch in the floor which led into the rest of the palace. This someone was a small demon, raspberry-colored and raspberry-shaped, with two long feet and a very small head. Observing that its master had returned, the demon waddled over to the table and pulled itself up with its very agile and workmanlike hands.

A single glance at the Infernal Face led it to slip once more to the floor, where with a muted, worried buzzing it started to waddle its way once more to the door hole.

But Lucifer reached out and snatched up the thing, which was named Kadjebeen, plumping it ungently down on the tabletop.

The demon, thus presented, had a strong resemblance to that sort of fat-bottomed toy which has lead weights built into the round wooden base and which cannot be knocked

over, no matter how hard or how many times one hits it
Lucifer was very aware of this resemblance, for he had used
the little demon in this manner many times. Now he did
not strike it, except with a glare.

It had feet longer than its legs. This was perhaps necessary in order to keep its rotundity in balance when it
walked. It was not strictly necessary, however, for its feet to
curl up in ornamental curlicues at the toes like Turkish
shoes. This was a piece of pure individuality on the demon's
part, and Lucifer—who was in many ways responsible for
the rest of the demon's appearance—ground his predatory
teeth at it.

The demon cringed. "Y—Your Magnificence's new palace image is finished," it announced, its voice the timbre of
a tree frog's. "D—does Your Magnificence approve?"

Lucifer let his eyes slip for a moment to the marvelous
model on the table beside the demon. Then his baleful gaze
returned. "There's a fly in it," he stated flatly.

The demon rolled his eyes. (He could do this very well,
because they were on stalks.) He examined the work of his
hands carefully, and he, too, noticed the insect. He stuck
one of his spider-thin fingers into the cupola window and
made shooing gestures. A bad-tempered buzz responded.

But Lucifer was no longer paying attention to the image.
He had sunk back into his throne with an almost adolescent
sullenness, and was biting his fingernails.

"Something isn't right, in all this," he grumbled between
his teeth. "From the very beginning, every carefully
thought-out plan I made regarding that—that Eyetalian—
went awry."

The demon knew better than to ask questions of its master; it merely held one rococo toe in each nervous hand and
pulled on them alternately.

"It wasn't my failure, either," continued the twisted angel, as he brooded and destroyed his cuticles. "I led him to
me with perfect logic and baited every trap with his heart's
desire. I should have had him a hundred times." He shot a
pointed look at his servant.

"Not that Delstrego had any importance in himself, mind
you. No more than any of that . . . that mortal tillage of
mine. But such as he was, he was Raphael's weakness."

Lucifer straightened in his chair and dropped his fist to the table. His face was a sculpture of cold hate, at which the demon stared in a terror of admiration. "Raphael's weakness," repeated Lucifer, gaining fury as he spoke.

"Oh, my sickly sweet, sainted brother!"

The Devil flung himself to his feet. The table was jarred and the intricate, careful palace model skidded over its smooth surface. The raspberry demon flailed and caught it just before it went over.

"Don't do that, please, Your Magnificence!"

"Raphael! Raphael!" hissed Lucifer. His face went from coral to blotched snow and rubies. "After Michael, I hate you more than any created being! And since you've never had the Sword-Angel's hard-headed good sense, you have let events carry you to ME.

"And you did it all by yourself." And at some sudden memory, Lucifer snickered, as his anger was cut with ugly hope. He stopped before a heavy metallic tapestry which hung between north and east, and he fingered it, following its embroidered story with his eyes.

"Once you were no more than a mirror for Him, like that other sheep, Uriel: beautiful, blank, and . . . and quite safe from influence.

"Now you've become nearly as much a slave to the earth as some sylph of earth's air, brother. You bob right and left as the winds take you, and there is no one down there—absolutely no one, you will find—who can protect you."

And with these words, and the more complex thoughts which went behind them, Lucifer's mood flipped over, from immediate disappointment to eventual success and he looked inward upon a balmy future steeped in revenge.

"You see, Kadjebeen, my playing at dice for the soul of the little witch man wasn't a loss, after all. No—for every time he escaped me, it was by some great expense of Raphael's, until now, after only a little time at the gambling wheels of earth, my brother is near bankrupt."

Lucifer giggled then, and in a moment he had himself convinced that he had never been interested in Damiano Delstrego's soul at all.

"My only mistake," concluded Lucifer, raising his eyes and pointing at the raspberry demon, Kadjebeen, who still sat on the table, clutching his cunning image between his curly feet, "was in trying to use the man as the final bait to my trap now that he is dead and therefore untouch—or rather, I mean, without importance to me. Though as a gesture it would have had such artistic merit . . ."

Kadjebeen folded his hands and stared at his model, lest he be accused of acquiescence in the idea that Lucifer had made any mistake at all. And that he was wise to do so was proven in the next moment, for Lucifer smote his palm with a fist and cried, "Why, by my own powers! Of course. There was no error! He CAN be the bait of my trap, even now."

And then Lucifer strode over to the window of the south, where lay expanses both of desert and plenty. "Woe, my dear Raphael," he whispered, as his blue eyes wandered, making plans. "You have loved well, but not at all wisely."

The baked white earth threw the heat against the baked white wall, which threw it back again. Hidden cicadas produced a tranced droning which was the perfect aural equivalent of the heat shimmer: a sound which a person might ignore for hours at a time before his consciousness came up against it, and which then would become unbearable.

Above San Gabriele the dark hills gathered, looming over the village like large friends who stood too close for one's comfort. Their blackish evergreen slopes promised a relief from the August heat to anyone who had the energy to walk so far.

For the most part, the San Gabrieleans preferred the blackish relief to be found within the wineshop. There, stretched out on the bosom of Mother Earth (the shop boasted no other floor), a handful of men with nothing to do let the sun fry the world outside.

Not that they were all drinking wine. Signor Tedesco, proprietor of the little store, would have been very happy had that been the case. But in all the village of San Gabriele there was not a man who had the money to spend his weekdays in a haze of vinous glory.

One man had a bottle which had been passed around a bit, and another had a half-bottle, which had not. The same fellow possessed a loaf of bread longer than his arm, which he guarded, waiting for the cool of the afternoon to give him the energy with which to eat. Another refugee from the sun had brought his lute, a very fine instrument, bright, sonorous, covered with a paper-thin inlay of mother-of-pearl, upon which he was trading songs with a chitarre player. A second lute, also belonging to the chitarrist, lay on the table unused because it would not stay in tune with the other instruments.

Signor Tedesco regarded his patrons with a jaundiced eye. He had had no intention of creating an atmosphere conducive to the promulgation of the arts. He hadn't even intended for the wine that he sold to be consumed in the confines of his shop.

He knew what an inn was: enough to know his wineshop didn't qualify. He wouldn't mind being an innkeeper, mind you, for he rather thought a man of that occupation might be a little wealthier than a villager who bought twenty casks of cheap red per season and filled bottles with the stuff. But if he were an innkeeper, Signor Tedesco would have tried to keep riffraff like this off his floor.

Especially the redhead in the corner making strange noises on the lute. He was the kind of musician Tedesco liked to refer to as having his ears on upside down. No more than seventeen years old, surely, the young pup bounced his hands up and down the neck of his pretty instrument with great concentration and produced a variety of sounds that Tedesco found quite unpleasant.

(But then, to be fair to the redheaded lutenist, Signor Tedesco had about twenty songs he liked, having known them from childhood, and he liked them played only in certain ways and on certain instruments, and thought the rest of the musical world might just as well go hang.)

The gangling youth pinched a smart octave on the sixth of the scale, then added to it a tenth above, then an eleventh and even a twelfth. Instead of resolving the progression, the musician then damped out the final sound on the beat and called the song complete.

Tedesco didn't know what an eleventh interval was, but he knew how to shudder.

"That's . . . very original," murmured the chitarrist, for although his ears, too, were a bit shocked, he was willing to try to understand. "Why does it end like that? Bomp!"

The redhead had an aggressive chin and eyes of a peculiar pale sage green, in a face which had not yet settled into its adult proportions (if indeed it had any intention of settling). His Adam's apple rehearsed his answer before he opened his mouth.

"That's so you don't fall asleep." Then he shrugged enormously and cast the question behind him. "What can I say? What do you expect me to say? That's how the song came to me."

"Came to you?" echoed the chitarrist, who was a round-faced fellow with a bristling mustache and three fat little babies at home. "You made it up?"

Gaspare drummed his fingers on the soundboard a trifle self-consciously and let his oversized eyes wander out the door as he replied. "Of course I made it up. Everything I play is my own.

"To play another man's music," he added righteously, "is akin to theft."

One who knew Gaspare well—one like his sister Evienne, for example—might have fallen face first upon the dirt, hearing this statement uttered in this tone by Gaspare of San Gabriele. But Evienne was not in San Gabriele but in Avignon, tending her own fat babies, and the villagers Gaspare had left behind some years ago found it easy to forget the scrawny, light-fingered street dancer when looking at this insolent youth with his foreign manners and his exquisite lute.

The chitarrist took this opportunity to run a fingernail down his strings. Signor Tedesco, behind his counter, perked up. But Gaspare had so cowed the round-faced man that he dared not go simply from the root to the fifth and then back again, as he had intended, so his endeavor led to nothing. The chitarrist stared glumly at his fingernails.

"But what about the master musician of whom you are always speaking, whom you followed from Lombardy to

France? I was under the impression it was his tunes with which you educate the village."

Gaspare's eyes did not exactly mist over, for he had not the sort of eye for that, but they expressed a certain feeling. He slumped back, letting his lute lie in his lap like an empty bowl.

"Ah, yes. Delstrego. You know—while I was with him I never touched the lute. Never dared, I guess. And then afterward, though I have had my training at the hands of his own teacher, and it was my idea to sound as much like him as possible . . ."

The redhead sighed. "It didn't work that way.

"And now I see that it could not, and I no longer desire to imitate him, for Delstrego was in a way a soft man. Whereas I . . ."

The bristling mustache stood out like a hedgehog's quills, as the chitarrist reflected on Gaspare's lack of softness. Gaspare himself ignored the smile.

"And when I tried to play Delstrego's songs with my own hands and my own spirit, then they sounded like little birds that had been put in a cage of iron." His long nose twitched and he sat up again.

"So I let them go." The redhead gestured theatrically toward the rough stone doorway.

"Still, if Damiano Delstrego himself were to come stepping in that door out of the summer heat, with his little lute under his arm—then you would hear some music," vouched Gaspare, whose self-importance, though considerable, had never been permitted to come between himself and his admiration for his first friend. "You would hear music more original than mine, and yet music even Signor Tedesco could appreciate."

The proprietor raised his head, frowning, uncertain whether he had just been praised or insulted.

Gaspare, still with his hand raised, stared out the pale shimmer of the open door. Cold water seemed to trickle up and down his spine, unpleasant despite the heat, and he wondered if perhaps he had said something he should not have said.

* * *

Behind the wineshop, and behind every other shop and
dwelling in their nudging row along this street in San
Gabriele, was a straight and narrow alley, which (since the
battle of the same name as the town, four years before) led
to nothing but a pile of rubble. Without a steady stream of
feet to keep the clay packed, this alley had been conquered
by grass, which had in turn suffered from a lack of sun.
Summer had killed this unfortunate growth and dipped it in
bronze, but still it held some value for a gelding who had
discovered it in the process of avoiding the sun.

This animal was black and lean. Its long neck was sinuous. Its long legs were . . . well, very long. One of its ears
rested malevolently back against its head, but the horse
gave the impression that its ill-temper was a chronic condition, not about to manifest itself into action on this stifling
afternoon. The horse's other ear made circles of uneasiness.
He chewed half a jawful of yellow grass and let the re-
mainder drop.

Under the thatch of the wineshop roof sat a brown wood
dove, colored such a pale and desiccated brown that she
might have been molded of clay and left to dry in the sun.
She was keeping a sort of uncommunicative company with
the gelding. She was also listening to the music within.

Doves are for the most part very conservative singers,
and do not appreciate any music but their own. This dove,
however, was only a dove part-time. She was a witch, and
what is more, a singing witch. She listened to Gaspare's lute
playing with a quick and educated mind.

It tended to give her a headache.

Bird eyes regarded the stripe of uncompromising blue
sky which was visible under the ragged thatch. She didn't
know what it was about the heavens which seemed so false,
or at least dubious, today. She rather suspected that Gaspare was about to do something he shouldn't. The boy was
much wiser than he used to be—the Eagle Chief's influence, if not her own—but still he had a long trial to sled
before he could be safely left to his own devices.

Saara could easily imagine Gaspare accepting a challenge
to a duel: he who had never held a sword in his life. She

uld even imagine him challenging some other to a duel.
ver some picayune point of music, of course.

Some hot-tempered village maiden could run him
rough with a pitchfork. Or her father could. At least,
ing simple (not a witch born), Gaspare could not lose
mself in the myriad dangers and seductions that came to a
ungster with Sight.

Saara felt a certain responsibility for Gaspare, born out of
th friends and adventure shared. She shifted from foot to
ot. Because she was a dove, this looked much like a round
t rolling from side to side on the table. She heard the
itarrist in the wineshop make his tentative dribble of
und and, like Signor Tedesco himself, she had hopes. But
seemed fated the man would not continue his plain, con-
ent melody.

The day would not permit.

Festilligambe, the horse standing below, felt the same
ease, for he wiggled an ear in the direction of Saara
hom he knew quite well, both as bird and as human) and
 stepped out into the unfriendly sun.

That white disk of light bleached the color of the soul,
d it stole the will away. Even Gaspare (bright of hue and
ightily determined) ceased playing. The two beasts heard
e murmur of his voice seeping through the metallic-hot
. Then that sound, too, dried away.

Someone was coming up the hill of San Gabriele, striding
g-legged past the ruin of the village wall. The rhythm of
 steps, and the regular thumping of his wooden stick,
oke the cicada's drone.

He was dressed in black, and his hair, was black, and as
 lifted his eyes toward the yawning door of the wineshop,
ey, too, were black. His face was comely, though the nose
s a trifle broad, and in those quick black eyes shone intel-
ence. From his staff flashed red and yellow, which shim-
ered, along with the entire figure, in the glare of the sun.

Cold shock crept from Saara's scaled feet up to her bare
ak as she watched the form of her dead love approach.
er dun feathers fluffed into ridges. The horse below
itched his tail and snorted.

That Damiano, so wise beyond his years, and so hungr
for understanding, should walk the scenes of his past lik
some miser riven from his horde . . . it was unthinkabl
And unspeakably sad.

"When I am dead," he had said, "you must let go an
thing of mine which you hold. The dead should be dead

But Saara's sadness was reflective and momentary, for sh
knew that this apparition was not Damiano. For one thin
Damiano did not wear black. For another, Saara herself ha
taught Damiano to do without his staff, and she did not be
lieve that, once dead, he would go back to using crutches h
had left behind in life.

And more importantly, this Damiano shape stood no
beneath her, in the wineshop doorway, and was unaware
her very presence. Even in his simple days, Damia
would have known Saara was near.

The horse, who saw something different from that whic
Saara saw, and from that which Gaspare saw from within th
wineshop (with all the hair on the back of his neck rising
protest), made no more sound, but turned his elegant t
and disappeared down the grassy alley.

The apparition carried a lute, Saara saw now, leaning h
sleek dove head over the ledge of stone where she sat.
was a marvelously ornate lute: Gaspare's own lute, in fac
That made quite a paradox, as even now Saara heard th
original of this spectral lute thumped clumsily upon the te
of the trestle table within.

"Delstrego!" gasped the youth, in tones of mixed joy an
terror.

This is how Gaspare is going to get himself into troubl
said Saara to herself, as she launched out from the eaves
the building.

2

e Devil had his plans. He would work upon the unfortu-
te Gaspare with his twin needles of guilt and pride. The
uth would provide no challenge, certainly, for his
ughty and sullen tempers stood out like so many hooks
 which the Devil could latch. Raise that hauteur, ruffle
at temper, and there Gaspare would be, trussed like Sun-
y's goose. Lucifer's greatest worry so far had been that he
uld be required to play the lute as Delstrego had, which
s a thing he could not do, having abjured music along
th the heavenly choir.

It was not that the prize in this game was Gaspare's little
ul; such as Gaspare was merely coarse bread and dry. But
 peril was sure to bring Raphael fluttering in, for the
gel watched his protégés like a hawk.

So Lucifer was understandably surprised to find himself
der the assault of not a hawklike angel, but a small dove,
ind of keel—at the moment of his subtle plan's unfolding.
th not the least peep of warning, this avian flew at his
n-shape and pecked it smartingly under the eye. Lucifer
iched away from it, displaying very natural confusion and
noyance.

The greatest of angels had no interest in the animal king-
m. The world's furred, feathered, or finny creatures were
much beneath his peculiar temptations as the denizens of
 Na nOg were beyond them. He was not even very know-
 about animal behavior. Did this miserable atom think
at Lucifer, wingless as he appeared in his present form,
s yet a sort of greater bird and therefore a competitor?
d it have a nest nearby? He cast a glance around him, as
e dove swooped to the ground at his feet.

Even as Lucifer perceived the obvious truth, that the
ature was not a bird at all but a human shape-changer, it

had swollen to its full status: that of a woman almost as tall
he stood in his Delstrego form.

"Liar!" she shrilled in his ear. "Filthy liar!" Curious
enough, she spoke a barbaric tongue of the far north.

Lucifer had no idea what a Lapp would be doing in
Piedmont village by the Lombardy border. He was furth
piqued to discover he didn't recognize this woman at a
Perhaps, he considered momentarily, he hadn't given t
tribal primitives of the earth their share of his attention.

In certain ways they were so much like the beasts.

And he reacted to this unknown creature in the way
which he usually reacted to anything which frustrated hi
or set back his plans. He turned color and hissed at her, a
prepared to strike her to cinders where she stood.

But, worse luck, this was not merely a shape-changer, b
one of those unspeakable Lappish singing witches.

He felt her puerile sing-song cutting through his disgui
like a razor through hide. As shape fell away, he was oblig
to grope for wyvern form to cover his nakedness. He shot
the woman a blast of pure, shriveling hate, only to see
deflected by a thread of melody. The malice shudder
sideways and scraped lime off the wineshop wall.

She dared smile through her teeth as she said, speaki
in heavily accented Italian, "You made another of your gre
mistakes when you took the face of Damiano, you gree
old man. I will crush you for it." Then the bitch's song act
ally did try to squeeze him. Though Lucifer himself was
beyond being hurt by the spell, the wyvern he wore cou
not breathe.

With the vision of his spirit, the Devil was very aware
the round eyes and dropped jaws in the wineshop so ne
Cursing, he gave up his present ambitions toward Gaspa
and rose into the air, determined to escape this constrai
and blast the beast-woman from the face of the earth.

Certainly Lucifer had the power to destroy one sil
witch, once he'd recovered from his surprise and from t
unbearable feeling of having been cheated by this bea
woman's popping from nowhere. Simple physical destr
tion was both Lucifer's pleasure (albeit not his highe
pleasure), and his right.

The wyvern circled in the air, persecuted by the witch who was once more in dove shape. Lucifer snarled at the bird with the contempt he felt for all simple or straightforward creatures. Once lured out of human shape, the witch's ability to sing (and therefore her power) was sadly curtailed. The wyvern drew a deep breath, gathering fire.

But the bird's anger was so insane as to approach the maternal, and she seemed unaware of her danger as she fluttered about the two-legged dragon-thing, pecking at its eyes.

Lucifer, once collected to himself, was a very clever spirit, and excellent at drawing together odd threads of information and making tangles of them. It occurred to him that there was some connection between this creature and the matter at hand; after all, it was the shape of Delstrego that seemed to set her off.

And then he remembered a small interchange with Damiano on the streets of Avignon in the mortal's last days: an interchange not comfortably called to mind.

He had dropped a gentle hint that the fellow had carried the plague with him into Avignon. (Not true, as it happens, but it very well **might** have been true, given the dreadful medical ignorance of the populace.) The man had dared to bray back at him a denial. "We were all clean. Saara said so."

And when asked who this Saara was, Delstrego had replied, "Someone you don't know."

Now Lucifer laughed, and ashes sullied the hot air around him. So even that septic little trading of insults could be turned to good use.

Someone he didn't know. Perhaps. But such an oversight was quite easily rectifiable. He beat off the drab-colored dove (quite gently) with a wing as hard and as supple as chain mail, and he peered at her with new curiosity.

A mascot of some sort? She could have meant little more, farouche as she was. Pretty enough, in human shape, but he knew quite well that Italians liked their women both clinging and coy. Probably a pet. Whatever, she was doubtless of some value to his sentimental brother, and Lucifer was not one to turn his face from fortune. He cringed from the bird and fled upward.

Saara's anger was like a wind which blew through every room of her soul, cleaning it of years of suffering.

Not since she left the fens had she had an enemy she could fight with whole heart: an enemy she had no compunction about hurting. And she had no fear for herself, for after losing two children and three lovers to death, it was a very familiar presence to her. In fact, there was nothing more appropriate which could happen in her life now, after all she had been through, than to be given the Liar himself as target and a clear field of attack. Especially when she remembered the miserable confusion this breath of wickedness had caused in Damiano, both to the man's head and his heart, before cutting short his life.

Along with Saara's slow-blooming happiness. Saara had never thought to ask herself why the Liar had oppressed Damiano so; she knew that too much interest in that demon's mentations only invited him into one's life. But still she could hate him for it.

For she had loved Damiano and loved him still, not with the wise passion Saara had felt for other men in her time, but with the sweet and choking emotion always before reserved for her children.

Saara had neither hope nor plan for survival as she spun about the loathsome, heavy reptilian shape, buffeted by the wind of its wings and suffocated by fumes; survival was meaningless next to the chance to do harm to the Father of Lies. This wild and selfless fury with which a bird weighing all of three ounces flung herself at the Devil he mistook (as he always must) for lack of brain.

Up they went in a flurry of wings, until the air about them grew cooler and lost the flavor of earth, and the sun spun about the sky as a dizzying white disk. Without warning, Saara traded her bird shape for that of an owl, and her talons raked the wyvern in its great yellow eyes. But the owl was half-blind in the light and the wyvern, disdaining battle, escaped it with a bob and dart to the right.

Saara followed, her muffled white wings straining, and for a moment she hung above the wyvern, untouching. Then suddenly the witch flickered and changed shape again, not this time to any sort of bird but to an enormous white bear of the north, which dropped like stone onto the reptile's back.

The wyvern's wings collapsed like sails of paper, and both beasts plummeted toward the earth.

After his first shock at this attack, Lucifer decided to let the bear fall—he could escape the wyvern form before impact: let the witch do the same, if she could. But then he shrieked, for the bear had its massive jaws around the snake neck of the wyvern and those jaws were closing. He suffered a certain amount of pain before he could dissolve his physical form, fleeing Saara now with no more substance than a passing thought, nor any more ability to do harm.

In an instant the bear, too, had vanished, and though it took Saara precious time to pull out of the tailspin caused by this last transformation, the pale dove skimmed the Lombard forest unharmed and returned to her pursuit, chasing nothing more than a nasty glitter in the sky.

There was no hope she could catch a disembodied spirit, however, and furious though she was (with the taste of the Devil's blood in her memory, if not in her mouth), she had half a mind to give up and return to San Gabriele.

Gaspare deserved some explanation, after all.

But against all expectation, she saw the Liar resume his damaged wyvern form in the sky high above her. She flapped harder to catch up, wishing she had studied the shape of the chimney swift instead of that of the dove.

She could not gain on the creature, but neither did she fall behind. Now they were so high above the earth that she was giddy, and her small lungs worked like bellows in the thin air. The wyvern, too, seemed affected, for its wings beat more slowly and blood sprayed in sunlit droplets from its wounded neck. It looked behind it and hissed.

Then Saara's giddiness grew very serious, for down seemed suddenly to become sideways, and the dove lost its purchase in the air and fell sickeningly before righting itself in a different attitude.

Saara looked around her and cursed, for her perceptions had been quite correct; down **had** become sideways, and below her naked tucked feet she beheld a broken regiment of peaks, touched here and there with snow. What it was that had happened to bring her here she was not quite sure, and how to return, if there was any question of return, she had no idea.

But the wyvern was still ahead of her, and that was what counted. She chased the scaly thing down among the mountain peaks; it seemed so weary now and weak from loss of blood that she slowly gained on it.

A spirit could not be destroyed utterly: not even the spirits of little things like mice and frogs, let alone a strong spirit older than mankind. But if she could get over the wyvern again and crash it into the rocks below, then she could do harm to the Liar—oh yes, real, satisfying harm.

With the prize so near, Saara's own weariness dropped away. She saw the wyvern disappear behind the shoulder of a gaunt gray peak, but she found it again in moments. Once more she lost the creature and once more found it.

Now purplish blood spattered the bare stone shelves below as the wyvern snaked its way deeper into the cracks of the mountains. It was heading for one high, solitary cone shape on the horizon. Perhaps there to make a stand.

Saara pressed still harder, for she did not want to encounter this thing on the ground, where even a bear of the north would be no match for the half-dragon. She wanted to drop it from the sky—to smash it to jelly. She was almost upon it.

But the wyvern, with all the appearance of terror, put on a burst of speed and together they approached the face of the mountain, tiny beak to writhing great tail. Saara cried in fury, and the wyvern bellowed back its wrath.

There was a window in the sheer cliff of the mountain: a perfect, tall, arched window, larger than the doors of men. The dove gave one astounded blink and cry, watching the wyvern disappear into it. She beat her wings wildly to the front, but it was far too late to stop her own progress, and Saara fluttered rolling into Satan's watchtower.

Lucifer, seated in his tall chair, caught the bird easily as it

kidded across the table. He prisoned her within the com-
pass of his fingers and lifted her, feet upward, into the light
or better viewing.

In neither his appearance nor demeanor was there any
race of the wyvern he had been: no no scales, no blood. He
vas in his most usual and comfortable form, that of a king in
ed (red showed off his golden hair to good advantage), and
he family features rested agreeably on his face. He regarded the rumpled dove with a certain curiosity.

But none of this is to say he was in a good mood, or that
he had forgotten the jaws of the white bear on the wyvern's
neck. Pink flesh showed between the rutched feathers and
down of the dove's breast and belly. The little legs kicked,
and the head which protruded from between his finger and
humb squirmed right and left. Lucifer felt the tremor of
her heart, quick and nervous as a tree of leaves in the wind.

He discovered that when he squeezed the creature, her
tiny twiglike beak opened, and when he released the pres-
sure of his hand, it closed again. He amused himself in this
fashion for a minute or so, and then he said calmly, "You
have a sadly inflated idea of your own abilities, little hen."

Suddenly the dove writhed in his hand, and at the expense of a few feathers, twisted around enough to deliver a
sound peck on the skin between his thumb and forefinger.

Lucifer cursed and shifted his grip. He called Kadjebeen,
and before many seconds had passed, the small raspberry-
shaped demon had erupted through the door in the floor.

"Bring me string," said Satan very quietly. Kadjebeen
disappeared once more through the door.

After the demon's disappearance, Lucifer's complacent
smile returned. Kadjebeen was his current favorite among
the palace staff, being quite handy and even more afraid of
him than most. Very soon he returned with a spool of red
twine, which he carefully tied around one of the dove's legs.

The other end of the length of twine was attached to one
of the barbed turrents of the image of the palace on the
table. Kadjebeen bit his lips anxiously as this was done, for
he feared damage to his handiwork.

Lucifer was aware of his servant's trepidation, and it gave
him a good deal of satisfaction. Throwing the spool of red

twine at Kadjebeen's head, he pointed to a far corner of th
room, to which the demon retired.

Saara was dumped onto the tabletop, where she lay pant
ing and blinking. After a moment or two Lucifer found th
sight of the tied dove less than interesting. He gesture
vaguely toward her and her bird shape melted into Saar
shape, complete with bare feet and embroidered blu
dress, but no bigger than the dove had been.

Saara plucked at the red band around her ankle, but i
was so much rusty iron. "Filthy liar," she spat once more
somewhat wearily. "You cannot touch me."

Lucifer giggled. "But my dear little pullet! Obviously
have touched you.

"And you made it inevitable that I should," he added, i
the tone of exaggerated seriousness which adults reserve fc
talking intelligently with children.

And which drives all intelligent children wild.

"If a man gives me the slightest encouragement, I ar
able to help him hither to my fastness. But you—how lovel
it was—came here under your own power, almost agains
my very will."

"I am not a man," said Saara, sitting with one leg folde
and the other knee propped. "And I still say you canne
touch me."

Lucifer smiled wider than was his wont, until Saara coul
see the serrated edges of his teeth. "It doesn't matter tha
you are not a man, for 'the male,' (he quoted) 'embrace
the female.'" He laughed at his own rather stale wit an
poked her belly with his little finger.

Saara had never been to a school in her life and he
knowledge of grammar was embryonic. "What on earth ar
you talking about, you dirty thing? Nobody would embrac
you!"

Then the whimsical light went out of his eyes. "Scrawn
pullet," he barked, and he ground his teeth at her. "I wi
derive a great deal of pleasure out of pulling you apart."

Saara looked directly at him, and then through him, an
finally turned her back on him and sat staring at the win
dowless wall of the model to which she was tied.

Lucifer's high color rose higher, from carnelian to the hue of fresh-butchered meat. Hissing, he plucked up the red thread and dangled the woman by her ankle. Her brown braids swung below her head, and her dress crawled up to her armpits. Sniggering, he pulled it off, leaving her to dangle naked. Bestowing this additional humiliation upon Saara did a lot toward restoring the Devil's temper.

Her body was lithe, and blushed like the skin of a peach. "You know, little insignificant peeper, that you weren't even the sparrow I was out to snare? Not even THAT important."

Saara climbed up her own leg and then up the length of red string until she hung upright by her two hands. She didn't seem to care or notice that she was naked.

"I know," she replied. "It was pretty obvious you were after Gaspare. Well, you won't be able to use that trick on him again, dressing up like Damiano. Gaspare must have seen an eyeful."

The red cord trembled with Lucifer's annoyance. "Have you no sense but to hang there and throw offense at me, savage? Don't you know how I'm going to make you suffer?"

"I know how you made Damiano suffer," was her undisturbed retort. "Yet it didn't get you anywhere, did it?"

The tiny woman's body was spinning around with the natural movement of the twine, and the chamber of four windows passed under her review. She noted it as carefully as she could, especially the vista outside the window by which she had entered.

Obviously they were not really in the Alpine mountains. They were probably in no definite place at all; Saara had enough experience in the realms of magic to know that its geography was unpredictable. When her spinning brought her around to Kadjebeen, squatting in his dim corner, she actually laughed.

"What an unfortunate creature!" she cried aloud. "I wonder how it can manage, looking like that!"

The raspberry-shaped and raspberry-colored demon did not particularly like being laughed at, but he found some comfort in the knowledge that this stranger had immediate sympathy with his biggest problem in life. His Magnifi-

cence (who had had a clear hand in the molding of Kadje
been) had never deigned to express any interest in hi
servant's consequent plight.

Still Saara spun, coming back around to face the Devil'
perfect features and exposed fangs.

"So you noticed little Kadjebeen, did you?" Lucifer
snickered, enjoying his captive's dizzying movement. "How
would you like to be turned into another like him?"

But Saara had spent too much time as a bird to be made
motion sick. "You can't," she replied casually. "I am no
afraid of hunger, so you have no power over my belly o
mouth, and I am not afraid of YOU, so you cannot make me
shrink like that against the ground. And as for his eyes—
well, they must bug out from fear, as well, for he can have
no great desire to be able to look back at that face of his!'

"Enough elementary lessons in transmigration," Lucifer
growled. He blew Saara into a faster spin.

"There is, after all, a reason I have brought you here."

"YOU brought ME?" The spin added a peculiar tremolo
to Saara's words. "A moment ago you said I came in spite o
you."

"Some of each," replied the Devil equably, and losing
interest, he dropped the whirling woman to the tabletop
"It is of no account by which way you came. Nor does i
really matter that you're not Gaspare of San Gabriele. Wha
matters is that you are a good enough bait to draw my
brother Raphael to me."

Saara had landed on her feet, still holding the length o
red twine in her hands. She stared blankly at the huge car
mine face above her. "Raphael? You mean the Chief of Ea
gles? You mean the music teacher?"

Lucifer's amusement spread all over his face. "We cer
tainly have the same party in mind, little witch. Raphae
the many-feathered warbler, who happens to be my disgust
ing lesser brother."

The naked woman rolled a coil of twine and sat hersel
down upon it. She examined Lucifer appraisingly. "They
say the eagle is kin to the bald-headed vulture—who also
has a very red face, like yours."

In an instant's ungovernable fury Lucifer spat at Saara:
pat an incendiary spittle which exploded around her like
Greek fire. She barely had time to roll herself into a ball
efore the flash was around her. To the stuffiness of the air
as added the stench of burnt hair.

Saara uncoiled, slightly pinker than she had been and
missing most of her braids. Her heart was pounding and she
ould feel the blood rushing into her face and even through
er ears.

But none of this was fear. Instead she felt a mad exhalta-
on, as it seemed her long life had at last come to some
oint.

"You picked a bad bait to use, if you want to attract the
Chief of Eagles," she said casually, examining a slightly
charred fingernail. "We haven't gotten along very well."

"I wonder who you HAVE gotten along with, you tusked
ow!" growled the Devil, but he was unable to hide the fact
nat this information displeased him. He drummed enor-
ous fingers on the tabletop (his rhythm was off).

"That hardly matters," he said at last. "Raphael is the sort
ho would not let a small thing like justly despising you
and in the way of self-sacrifice. He is quite perverse that
ay, my brother. In fact, a mortal he dislikes may be the
etter for my purpose." Then Lucifer yawned.

"Likely ANY mortal would have done."

Boredom recalled Lucifer to his own intention. "Why do
sit here communing with this bit of insignificant spleen?"
e murmured. "I need only raise my voice now, and . . ."

Suddenly the witch on the table seemed infected by
nadness. She rose from her stringy chair and began to
mp up and down, her round breasts jouncing in opposi-
on to her movement. "He'll blast you, windbag! The Eagle
ill tear you limb from limb. He'll turn you into a bright-
ed leather handbag. He'll . . ." and then Saara stopped
ouncing long enough to perform an extremely complex
d obscene gesture which she had learned in the Italies.
Vhen she felt she once more had Lucifer's attention, she
egan to curse him in earnest.

Forbearance was not the Devil's strongest attribute. Yet
is only visible reaction to this torrent of abuse was a mo-

mentary tightening of the jaw. "If you didn't believe I coul
damage this spirit you claim to hate," (Saara actually ha
claimed no such thing) "you would not be so eager now
have me kill you.

"You will just have to be patient," he adjured the tin
woman, and turned from the table.

Lucifer looked out each of his windows in turn, wastin
not a glance on Kadjebeen, who was still squatting obe
diently in his corner, feeling his mouth with his spidery fin
gers and staring ruefully at his stumpy short legs.

In the Prince of Earth a fierce emotion was rising: a sati
faction which thought itself joy but bore more resemblanc
to pride. Like a player of some intricate, slow-moving boar
game, he had plotted out a hundred future moves in th
bitter duel with Raphael (more bitter because he suspecte
that Raphael was not even aware of it as a duel) and ha
decided that he could not lose.

Meanwhile the Lappish curses continued from the litt
witch tied to the model on the table. Only Kadjebeen li
tened.

"Raphael," called Lucifer composedly, in a voice r
louder than that he had used to call his servant. "Raphae
my dear brother, why don't you drop by and see me?"

There was a minute's silence. Lucifer knew this didn
indicate that Raphael hadn't heard him, or that the roa
were bad. Sharpening his very flexible voice, the Dev
added, "I advise you very strongly to make the visi
brother. You will find you are not my only guest."

Suddenly a wind swirled through the windows of th
chamber, as though whatever barrier had kept the airs
the world from entering had been breached. It was a co
fused wind, as the mint dryness of the Alps met the brea
of orchids, while sand and sandalwood clashed with pin
But it was very fresh. It made Saara lift her head and sni
and little Kadjebeen, in his corner, began to burble wi
worry.

The air flickered with a light like sun filtered through
net of pearls: a soft radiance which rippled and danced.
was the gleam given off by the white wings of Raphael.

The face was the same as Lucifer's, though perhaps there was a greater virility in the high, sharp set of Lucifer's cheekbones. Lucifer's hair, too, was a richer color, to match the more-than-ruddyness of his skin.

But Lucifer's eyes were a pale and watchful blue, while those of Raphael were summer evening itself, with stars shining through darkness.

He was dressed very simply, almost sketchily, in a white garment which Lucifer called (under his breath) "the same old undershirt." He was shorter and slighter than Lucifer. But the thing which distinguished Raphael from his brother was, of course, that frame of enormous, opalescent, galleon-sail wings: wings which seemed to be nothing more than the radiance of his nature taking on form.

So although Lucifer was striking, Raphael was beautiful, and no creature who had ever had the luck to see him had denied his beauty, or had come away unaffected by the sight.

Raphael had never seen himself, nor had he ever had any desire to see himself.

Kadjebeen saw Raphael and his blue eyes yearned forward on their stalks. He regarded the face of light and the brilliant wings—yes, especially the wings—and he thought in his artisanly way that he'd like to build something that looked like that.

Saara gazed at Raphael with an expression akin to pain. She was not considering his face or form, however, but his danger. And as she remembered that Damiano had loved the angel, she also remembered that she had not always been understanding about that. She turned her head away.

Lucifer looked at his brother and flinched; the Devil himself flinched and uttered a strangled cry, for he was as sensitive to beauty as any creature born. It hurt him.

Raphael saw his brother's wincing without surprise. Lucifer always reacted to the sight of him like that. He regarded Lucifer with his own, quite different feelings. "What is it, Satan? What wicked deed is in your hands now?"

Lucifer's great eyes rounded and he lifted his hands in protest, if not to heaven, then at least to the sky. "And they dare to call me cruel! He convicts me of crime without

knowing there has been a crime, and though he is kin to
me, refuses me my proper name!

"Raphael, you are nothing but a bigot—a narrow-minded
and conventional burgher among a similar rabble, fearing to
be anything more or less than your neighbor." Lucifer
sighed with sad disapproval, but he found his eyes sliding
away from that visage of light.

"But no matter, brother. I brought you here only to help
me identify a creature. You have always been so interested
in . . . animal husbandry.

"See," he proclaimed, gesturing openhanded toward
Saara on the table. "It attacked me in Lombardy and hung
around my neck halfway home."

As he approached the table; Lucifer waved his hand once
more and a buff-colored dove appeared, wings spread and
beak open in threat. At another motion of Lucifer's the dove
became a snowy owl which blinked, hissing, in the light of
day.

At a third command the bird swelled into a white bear,
which, though miniature, was still large enough to yank Kadjebeen's model after it as it lunged wildly at the Devil's
throat. The demon squeaked in apprehension.

"What do you suppose it is?" inquired Lucifer of his
brother.

Raphael stood beside the table. His wings spread out
sideways, almost dividing the chamber in two. His face was
gentle.

"She is the greatest witch in the Italies," he replied to
Lucifer. "Perhaps the greatest in all Europe.

"God be with you, Saara of the Saami," said Raphael to
her.

As though she were throwing off a great weight, Saara
divested herself of the shapes the Devil forced upon her.

"Get out of here, Chief of Eagles. It's a trap."

Raphael met her eyes, but made no reply. Instead his
wings rose slowly to the vaulted ceiling, and he asked,
"Why did you do this, Satan? This woman was never any
business of yours."

Lucifer's sculpted eyebrows echoed the movement of the
angel's wings. "Satan you call me, as though you were some

rubbing mortal yourself! And you tell me what is my business . . ."

He strode across the room, his hands locked behind his back and his gaze wandering mildly out the windows. "That miserable manners even when the busybody is right, but this case, Raphael, you are quite mistaken. There is in his little female a streak of bitterness and jealousy I can quite appreciate—jealousy of whom, I wonder, brother? but even if there were not . . . even if she were that rare, malformed, or brainless sort of mortal content with everything that befell him . . .

"All mortals are my business and have been so since the plague of them were spawned. They are far more MY business, Raphael, than yours. In fact, one might almost say that I stand in the place of their shepherd.

"On earth, that is."

Then Lucifer turned in place and regarded Raphael with bored disdain. "But we have had this discussion before."

The angel nodded. "I remember the last time. It was with Damiano. He won the argument."

The delicate, carmine nostrils flared. "He died."

"He won the argument," repeated Raphael evenly.

All the while he sparred with Lucifer, Raphael's wings twitched, keeping time like a steady heartbeat, or like the rhythm of a song. His face was very quiet, but not with a stiffness which suggested he was concealing his feelings. Rather it seemed the angel's feelings were so consonant with his form that they did not disarray his features. He glanced over to Saara on the table, and his head was hidden from Lucifer by a momentary upcurl of his right wing.

He winked at her.

At this little message of reassurance, Saara's fine rage bid fair to desert her, and she felt her throat close in panic.

To perish in combat with evil was one thing, but to die dragging with you one who was greater and older than you: one you had been asked to protect, as well . . .

"Go away!" she hissed at Raphael again, and made ineffectual shooing gestures with her hands. "This is MY fight, spirit. You can only get hurt!"

But Raphael was speaking to his brother. "What do you think to do with her, aside from burning off her braids?"

"Think?" snorted Lucifer, returning to the table. He stared down at Saara and the air around her once again began to grow very warm. "I THINK, dear brother, that I will keep her a while for observation. That is the accepted course when one studies nature, isn't it? In a jar, perhaps, with straw over the bottom. Of course it might get smelly and I have no great enthusiasm for catching her natural food . . ."

The Devil scratched his chin reflectively. "But then, after a suitable length of time—say a year, I will make a close study. Of the inner organs. It will be interesting to see whether they really resemble more those of a bird or those of a bear."

As Lucifer spoke, Raphael's wings expanded up and out sideways, as stiff and smooth-feathered as if they had been carved of stone.

So would an angry hawk have displayed, protecting the fledglings in its nest. And, in fact, one of those stainless wings did block Saara from Lucifer's sight or touch, while the other pushed Kadjebeen bodily out of his corner. The demon stopped to finger a white pinion appreciatively.

It was a figure of Byzantine splendor that confronted the Devil. Pale glory circled Raphael's head and his gown gleamed like the noonday sun. The four winds rose together and swirled about the chamber, lifting ancient dead ashes from the cracks between the flagstones and blowing them away.

Lucifer seemed to have memories of what it meant when an archangel spread out his wings like that, and when his mild face went as hard as justice. For he stepped back, once and then again. His heel touched the low sill of the window ledge and Lucifer put a steadying hand out. A sneer covered his embarrassment.

This was not the vanguard of the Almighty, sent to cast him once more from his heights. This was a single spirit and one that had undergone change in the streams of earth Lucifer had planned carefully, and he was in the house of his own power. He was not about to be intimidated by

mpty show. He was now bigger than Raphael in all but
rings, and wings were not weapons of war. He advanced
gain and stood beside his brother, looking down. He
laughed.

Raphael spoke, and his voice cut through the forced and
raucous laughter. "I am supposed to beg you to release her,
atan. That is obviously your plan. You, in turn, will refuse
o do so."

Lucifer did not demur.

"There are two reasons," said Raphael, "why you might
have called me here to participate in this charade. Either
you want me to know you are engaged in this cruelty, or you
want something from me in exchange for foregoing your
pleasure.

"If you only wanted an audience, then I tell you that you
have failed. Now that you have brought me here, I will not
ermit you to harm Saara of the Saami. I will oppose you in
ny way I can.

"If, on the other hand, you want to bargain—then explain
our terms."

Lucifer stifled a laugh. "Well spoken, Raphael. You have
ondensed what might have been a half hour's stimulating
onversation into a scrap of dull prose.

"And I will answer in the same terms.

"Dear brother, you cannot prevent me from harming this
mortal. Perhaps once you might have, though I doubt it.
ut when you might have had the power, you certainly
ouldn't have had the interest to do so. Now you can't.

"Let me list for you the reasons why: First, you answered
he summons of a mortal and, not content with that indel-
acy, you stayed to talk to him. And you returned to him,
gain and again. You taught him a style of music and of mor-
s he had no right to know, and in the end he was unfit for
he place and time in which he had been born. And if he
as not what he had been . . ." The Devil paused and
lanced at his brother from under an exquisite eyebrow.

". . . neither were you."

Lucifer took another step forward, as though to prove to
imself that his retreat had been an accident. "Secondly, in
he wretched village of Sous Pont Saint Martin, you stood

for some seconds on a dimple in the snow. Below that dimple was an uncovered well, and a mortal man was forced walk around you and miss the drop. It was a quick an smoothly handled bit of prestidigitation on your part, an I'm sure you thought that since the mortal never notice you had saved his skin, perhaps no one else would. Yo were wrong.

"Thirdly, in the almost equally wretched village of Sa Gabriele, and at the instigation of an unaesthetic and incon sequential little dog shade, you opened a locked door an cheated the hangman of his employment."

Another small step. He was almost in touching distance of Raphael now. Saara shouted a warning.

"Fourthly, you cut a man's hair and tied his horse's har ness in neat little bows. Very decorative, but not your des tined work, I think.

"Fifthly—if there is such a word as fifthly—you com mitted what even among mortals is a crime. You hid a dyin man from sight for an entire day, preventing anyone wh might have saved his life from discovering him.

"And last of all, the decisive moment came here not thre minutes ago, Raphael, as you announced quite baldly th you intended to squabble with me over my little prize.

"Could you not feel yourself shrivel as you spoke brother? And each time you dirtied your hands in this mo tal muck, weren't you aware of your light dimming? Yo have diminished till you are little more than a length black wick lying in a puddle of wax."

Lucifer's tone was soft, sorrowful, almost caressing, an as he finished speaking he reached out into that clea brightness which surrounded Raphael. He put his hand to ward his brother's face.

It stopped, or was stopped by something: some quality the light or of the shining smooth cheek itself, and the han clenched empty air as Raphael answered.

"My size and form are whatever they are. I have don nothing to cause our Father pain."

"HE IS NOT MY . . ." The Devil's skin went from red purple. Both of his hands leaped out at Raphael's throat, bu it was as though a wall of glass came between them.

Lucifer swung angrily toward the table. Though Raphael's wing concealed the witch from his sight, the intricate dollhouse sat there, vulnerable. He raised his fist above it.

From the far corner came a squeal of dispair, and Kadjebeen hid his face in his hands.

In the middle of his rage Lucifer smiled, hearing the music he loved best. He allowed his fist to unclose and once more turned to Raphael. "You are quite right, Raphael. I do want something of you—something very easily in your power to give, and a generous act besides. And if you give it to me, I promise I will put the creature back where I found it. Unharmed. I further promise to leave it alone in the future: as long as it leaves ME alone!" Lucifer spared a haughty and scandalized glance in the direction of his captive.

"It's a lie!" shrilled Saara from behind her white screen. "He won't release me, no matter what you do for him. He hates me; I bit his neck.

"And he hates you, Chief of Eagles, worse than he does me!"

Lucifer smiled sidelong. "Just listen to the little shrew. And what a name she gives you, brother. 'Chief of Eagles.' Don't you find it embarrassing?"

"Not at all. I prefer it to being called the Liar," replied Raphael shortly. "Now enough of this tuneless twist. Tell me what it is your want of me."

Lucifer's shrug and smile were a bit coy. "My desire is small and well-meaning. I want to break down the old and unfortunate barrier which has stood so long between you and me, dear brother."

Then his pale gaze sharpened. "I ask nothing of you, Raphael, neither service nor friendship nor understanding (for I know I will get none of these), but only that you take my hand in yours once more."

Raphael stood unmoving, but the feathers on the backs of his wings where they joined the body rutched out, as the hair on a man's head may seem to crawl. And the wings themselves started a barely perceptible tremor.

"No!" cried Saara. "Whatever he says, it is still treach-ery!"

But the angel was not listening, or at least not to her. He stood motionless, his head tilted slightly to one side, and his dark eyes unfocused. Then Raphael answered his brother. "I want to see Saara sent back first."

"NO!" screamed the witch.

Lucifer smiled and his eyes grew white-pale. "Afterward, dear brother. I don't trust your decision will remain the same once the motivation is gone."

"Yes, you do," replied the angel, as he shook his feathers into place. "You DO trust my word, Satan, or you would never have called me. The only reason you would refrain from returning Saara now that I have agreed to your terms is that you have no intention of returning her. Therefore it must be done now."

Lucifer, who had admitted to Saara already that he did not intend to free her, sulked for a moment. "If neither of us trust the other, Raphael, then I guess there can be no bar-gain, and the woman is sacrificed to your stiff-neckedness."

"It is your bargain, Satan. You offered it, and you must perform your promise first. If this entire scene was set with me in mind, then you should have no objections to letting your bait go free."

Now it was Raphael's turn to close the space between them. "Otherwise it is war between us, and though you are stronger than I and I cannot prevail, you will still not escape that battle unharmed."

Lucifer growled in his throat, but he reached a negligent hand toward Saara, in her concealment behind the wing.

"One moment," called the angel, and the pearly screen lifted like a fan. He leaned toward the woman and spoke. "Saara, when you are home you must forget this and not try to involve yourself with the Liar, neither out of anger nor revenge. Or once again he will have the power to take you captive."

The minature naked woman ran toward him until the cord tightened against her leg. "Listen to me, Spirit! I don't want my life from your hands. I can't take another sacrifice on my behalf. You and I love the same person and by his own request I was to watch over you. I cannot live with the shame of this failure!"

"There is no shame, Saara," whispered Raphael. "And no failure. Not for you nor for me."

Lucifer found this conversation immensely distasteful. He completed the gesture which caused the tiny shape to vanish.

"She is now back where I found her," he announced.

Raphael's eyes grew a bit vague as he made sure the Devil spoke the truth. Then he glanced once more at the table. "You forgot her dress."

"We didn't bargain for the dress," snapped Lucifer. Then he strode away from the table and let the irritation of this minor defeat disappear in the satisfaction with the great victory it had bought him. He stared at Raphael with an expression of rapt wonder for some moments, knowing he had won. Knowing, despite his own acccusation, that Raphael was true to his word and would make no effort to avoid what he had promised.

His. HIS. The beautiful and hated brother, symbol of all that feathered crew who had dared to conspire against him and to stand against him at the gates of eternity with their inane swords aflame! The Devil was trembling as Raphael had trembled, hearing Satan's terms. But it was neither fear nor disgust that caused him to shake, but a lust that was nearly love: a lust to touch once more, in the person of his brother, the very substance of heaven. A broad smile split Lucifer's face, exposing all his unangelic teeth.

Raphael also stood silent. Once again he did not seem fully aware of Lucifer before him. His eyes were almost closed. The angel's lips moved and he nodded, though no sound was audible in the chamber. Finally he came toward his brother. He held out his hand.

But now that the moment had come, Lucifer felt a desire to delay it. "A moment more, Raphael," he whispered. "Let me realize my success." His face was tight, and white patches stood out against his mottled cheeks. His jaw worked. His cloak of urbanity fell away from his face and form, revealing the demon tyrant that he was.

"You would have done better to go with me from the first, brother!" he hissed, and adderlike he struck out with both his blood-red hands, clasping Raphael's hand of ivory.

A shock passed through the room, sending stinging pain through Kadjebeen's ears, and causing the little round demon to go rolling over the floor. It vibrated the dollhouse palace until its tiny turrets rattled.

Raphael gasped. He fell to his knees. But for the grip upon his hand he would have fallen flat on the floor. His face was blank, like that of a man struck by lightning, and his mouth hung open. Wings beat spasmodically.

Lucifer's face was a mask of lust as he gazed down at Raphael. His nostrils were distended like those of a pig, and like a pig his tushes overlapped his thin lips. His eyes became slits and he whined a bestial delight.

Two outstretched wings beat the floor stiffly, showering the walls and ceiling of the chamber with glimmers of pearl. The silvery pinions were twisted in disarray. Then, ceasing their convulsive movement, they fell twitching on the stones.

Lucifer grasped Raphael's hand harder, brutally squeezing it, and he panted with the effort of his satisfaction; his ashy breath fell gray and dismal onto Raphael.

Where the ashes fell the great wings smoked. Their luster faded to the color of snow, and like snow they melted away into the wind which scoured the room.

Under that dusty fall of ash the gleam of Raphael's gown, too, faded, till it was nothing but shabby linen cloth, and the radiance of his face went out.

With an audible pop the chamber asserted its rights. The wind trapped within the four windows threw itself against the barriers and died.

There was nothing on the flagstones of the chamber but a yellow-haired man lying motionless: his eyes closed and his lips parted. Already a bruise was forming where his face had struck the floor.

Kadjebeen emitted a small grunt of unhappiness. He had really been very interested in those wings. But it was a small grunt meant for his own ears only. He watched his master drop the pale hand, which slapped the flagstones limply.

Lucifer raised his eyes. He found he was still trembling. He paced over to the single chair and sat in it, waiting for the tremor to pass. Unaccountably he was tired—tired and somewhat shaken—somewhat at a loss. As though it had been he himself reduced to a thing of clay and blood, and not his enemy.

But he had his victory, and he stared down at it. Things could hardly be better. Of course Raphael's new shape was still beautiful, as measured by the standards of man. Lucifer briefly considered making alterations.

He could cut off the fellow's nose and ears, or put out his left eye. A hole in the cheek, perhaps, by which the food would dribble out. That would be amusing.

But frowning reflectively, he put away that further pleasure. Anything which changed that face would make him seem less like Raphael to Lucifer, and therefore damage rather than enhance his revenge. It was sufficient that his brother was reduced to the scum over whose interests he had dared oppose Lucifer. That was the main thing. And besides, there would be plenty of time later to add artistic touches.

Let him sing his songs of praise now, and boast of his close relatives in high places. As the Almighty hadn't lifted a finger in defense of his seraph up until now, Lucifer was confident that He wouldn't be quick to reach out a hand to an archangel of human clay.

Now—what to do with the fellow. Lucifer's first idea, when he had solidified his strategy, had been to keep his brother as he had discussed keeping Saara: caged in squalor, under his eye.

But he had had to toss that idea away, for even in the wretched form into which he had been locked, Lucifer didn't trust Raphael's influence upon the palace staff.

Not one of them was loyal, he reflected bitterly. Not a damned one of them, no matter how much he burned and beat them.

Least of all did he trust Kadjebeen, who had trundled out into the middle of the room and stood regarding the man on

the floor. Kadjebeen was TOO handy, and inclined to ha
ideas.

But he was useful.

"Have this thing scourged," Lucifer growled to his se
vant. "I want him half-killed. Then find . . . find Perfecto
Granada wherever he is and sell the brute to him. If th
slaver has no money, give Raphael to him anyway and te
him I'll collect later.

"He is not to refuse."

As Kadjebeen scuttled (albeit unwillingly) off to set th
wheels of torture in motion, Lucifer regarded the fruit of h
labor.

The fall of flaxen hair half hid Raphael's features—whic
were as always, except for the light which had gone out
them. But there was a pale dust of hair on the arm whic
poked out of the simple white sleeve, and a network of fir
lines creased the flesh between the thumb and forefinge
The robe had fallen crumpled to one side, exposing or
quite ordinary leg up to the knee. The man's breath can
raggedly, and a trickle of blood ran out of his nose.

Lucifer chuckled to himself. "As perfectly imperfect
any on the earth!

"Behold! I have made a man," he whispered aloud, an
then he shook his head at his own cleverness. "If that isn
creation," he added, "then I don't know what is."

3

Dull anguish rolled over him like waves of an untirin
ocean, pierced by bolts of lancing pain. But worse than th
pain was a nagging conviction which lay beneath it tha
something was missing; something was terribly wron
Confusion thwarted all of Raphael's efforts to think; he ha
no weapon with which to fight it, for he had never befor
known what it was to be confused.

"I am screaming at myself," he thought wonderingly. He heard the parts of his body—his wounded back, his bruised cheek, and savagely twisted hand—howling their protest against the rest of him. "I know," he replied to the pain. "I know what you are saying, but I can't help it. I can't."

Not for comfort exactly, but for understanding, he threw himself upon mercy.

"Tell me what it is, Father," he begged within himself. "Tell me how to hear this pain rightly. I'm frightened; tell me what it is that is so wrong, which I've forgotten and I know I must remember."

But this message only echoed in his ravaged head. No answer came.

No music, no words. No vision, comfort, chiding, or instruction. No touch of awareness at all. The Other within him was gone as though it had never existed. And suddenly Raphael knew that THAT was what had been wrong—wrong beyond pain and beyond confusion. A dreadful closed emptiness within him.

He flailed his arms, not knowing what the motions were. He made noises.

Lombardy in August could not hold a candle to the heat of the Moorish State of Granada during the same month. In Lombardy the grass was dry, but at least it was grass.

On the brown hills forty miles south of the Andalusian city the ground was crazed like pottery glazing. The midday heat drove even the birds from the sky. Beasts of all sorts sheltered in the shadows of the rocks.

Beside a sheer walled table of stone (a divot laid carefully on the dry dirt) a single iron chain looped in swags through seven iron collars. Seven slaves had spaced themselves out evenly like birds on a fence, seeking their own space in the sliver of shadow left by the table's overhang.

Three of the women were Saqalibah: the pale, broad-faced people who had been slaves to the Moors for so many hundreds of years that they fell in the same class with the Arab horse and other animals of pedigree. Two others had spoken Spanish as children, and one spoke Spanish, Arabic, and Langue d'Ouil, all of them badly, and was uncertain in her muddled memory which language had come first. The last woman, at the end of the chain, was a black, dressed in heavy desert indigo, complete with tassels and coins. She had been put at the end of the chain because she picked fights.

All the slaves were women. The merchants Perfecto and Hakiim specialized in women—women and eunuchs.

Hakiim gazed sourly at an eighth slave, who writhed over the sandy ground at the end of a separate chain. His partner, Perfecto, had brought him in about an hour ago, slung over the back of a pack horse, and dumped him there on the ground. Neither Perfecto nor Hakiim could bring himself to touch him.

"The currency of that one's understanding has been devalued, I think," Hakiim drawled to Perfecto. "If it is not entirely counterfeit."

Perfecto could do little but shrug. "I had reasons to buy him."

Hakiim didn't want to start an argument, for Perfecto was a man of chancy temper. And he was underhanded (like most Christians), and unpredictable. Hakiim was not a Spaniard, and he had no desire to gain enemies in a country where he had so few friends.

Still, that the fellow should wander off into the dry hills and return with THIS—this piece of damaged property, probably crazy to boot. Perfecto usually had good business sense, at least.

"Saqalibah?" mused the Moor, turning the blond head gently with a boot toe. "Either that or Northman, I imagine. We might as well claim he is Saqalibah; with a eunuch, purity of line cannot matter.

"Were it not for the scars, he would make a good harem boy. Or . . . plaything. Fine face, to be sure, and the coloring is uncommon."

Perfecto regarded his prize with a jaundiced eye. Truth to tell, he liked his prize less than Hakiim did, having been forced to pay good money for him and to act grateful into the bargain.

And he shuddered, remembering the interview during which he had acquired the slave. Perfecto hated doing business with the Devil's crew. His fears ate through him like acid, worse and worse with every summons, and he longed for a graceful way to close the account which stood between the Devil and himself. But it had been almost twenty years now since Perfecto opened this account with a bit of casual homicide, and pay out as he might, the Spaniard always seemed to be in the red.

Perfecto wasn't at all sure what he had been forced to purchase. Was this pretty-faced imbecile a straight bit of goods—some court eunuch who had incurred hellish displeasure, or the slave of some high official who had perhaps made contract with Satan and then tried to recant? He had a splendidly noble face, after all, or would have had, had any intelligence remained behind it.

Or was this but the Devil's bad joke on Perfecto himself, ready to change into a lion or a monstrous adder when least expected? Perfecto had certain nightmares . . .

He answered Hakiim grimly. "He must have been some man's little toy once. But he's a bit large for such cuddles now.

"And of course there will be scars on the back, especially with the way he's grinding the dirt in."

For the blond slave had stopped thrashing and lay quietly now in his much stained linen, directly on the wounds of his back.

Hakiim glanced covertly at his partner's disgusted face. The Moor could no longer restrain himself. "I quite agree! My friend, tell me; why did you accept the creature? Even or free he would have cost too much . . ."

Perfecto's fingers pierced holes in the arid Andalusian earth. Sand dribbled out of his balled fists and his eyes were like little beads of brass.

Hakiim relapsed into silence.

At the far end of the line the black woman began to chant Berber chant, in the tight-throated, ornate, ululating fashion of the desert. Every time the little company stopped, the black had to do something strange: throwing pebbles at tree, or covering herself with sand, or swinging her chain

back and forth. Otherwise she ignored everyone in the
party, slave and slave merchant alike, except when they go
in her way.

Perfecto's lips drew back. Now all he needed was troubl
from that bitch, who was unfortunately too valuable to
bruise.

Hakiim, too, lifted his head. He had more tolerance fo
the chanting than Perfecto had, for it was familiar music t
him. But because it was in the Berber tradition, it unsettle
him. The Berber tribes had swept the length and breadth o
Islamic Spain a handful of times. They out-Arabed the Bed
ouin tribes with their narrow-minded asceticism an
xenophobia. Even now, under the more urbane rule o
Muhammad V of the Nasrid dynasty, Berber warriors mad
up a goodly number of the forces of the Alhambra. Berber
were not to be found on the end of a chain.

Perhaps it was not only on account of her temperamen
that Djoura had sold so cheap . . .

Hakiim forced this worry out of his mind. After all—wh
in the State of Granada knew or cared with what accents
black slave sang her songs? "There's our lovely she-as
again," he sighed instead. "Making her presence known."
Then he shrugged.

In Granada they would sell the black. None of the upstar
Muwalladun would care what she called herself; to them, a
blacks were Nubian, just as all blonds were Saqalibah
Being young, sound, and well-proportioned, she'd bring
good price. In Granada they'd get rid of the entire chain o
slaves

Except, perhaps . . .

But as his glance fell on the eunuch, who lay within tw
yards of the rug the merchants had spread for themselves t
sit on, Hakiim started and did a clear double take.

For the imbecile had lifted himself up by his hands, an
he sat bolt upright, his ludicrously fine face filled with won
der as his deep blue eyes sought along the length of chair
until they rested on the ebony face of the singer. He stare
intently, swaying side to side with the beat of the chant.

Hakiim almost choked with amusement. Perfecto fol
lowed his partner's eye and a grin stretched his features
The imbecile's parody of emotion was just too perfect.

"Look," giggled the Spaniard. "Our eunuch is in love. With Djoura the Nubian, no less.

"At least he can sit up," Perfecto continued. "Maybe by tomorrow he'll be able to walk, and then we can move again."

"He'll walk," retorted Hakiim. "Just let the Nubian lead him, like a goat leads the sheep."

And that quip called forth an idea. "The fellow is a bloody mess and must eventually be cleaned up. Let's give him a real treat in the process. We can bring Djoura to take care of him."

Perfecto looked less than satisfied by this idea. "What if she kills him? What if he kills her? The investment!"

"If she kills him," answered Hakiim, rising to his feet, "then I'll cover whatever he cost you out of my own pocket, and I'll buy her a box of sweets as well. If he kills her—well, I'll crawl to Mecca on my knees."

Then the swarthy Moor turned and grimaced pleasantly down at his partner. "Or do you want the privilege of washing the half-wit yourself?"

Perfecto waved his acquiescence to Hakiim's plan.

Since the black was at one end of the long chain and the only place where the eunuch's collar could be attached was on the other, bringing them together occasioned much shifting, curses, and complaints. None of the women wanted to squat in the sun, so the displaced slaves bickered and poked at one another over a few square inches of shadow, until the chain was folded in the middle, and the unhappy slaves were crowded together with exactly half the elbowroom they'd had before.

Hakiim sat the woman down with a rag and a pot of water. Beside the pot he placed a small lump of lard soap.

"You see that big baby there," he said to her in Arabic, pointing at Raphael. "You pretend he's your baby. Wash him all over. And don't waste soap."

She glared not at Raphael (who had greeted her arrival like the coming of springtime) but at the sky. The Moor stood above them both with arms folded. He scowled, but he was rather more curious than annoyed.

Raphael smiled at Djoura, and he sighed. He put his hand out toward her neck, awkwardly, and when she flinched away he touched his own throat.

"He likes your singing," explained the patient Hakiim.

"Does he?" replied the black doubiously, for no one else in the slave chain had expressed similar feelings. (She addressed her master without respect, indeed without civility, but Hakiim had expected no different.) But then Djoura, like Hakiim, had to laugh at Raphael's eloquent expression. "Well, then, he must be a person of very good taste."

She soaked the rag, wrung it out, and soaped it. "Close your eyes," she barked at Raphael and she touched the rag to his cheek.

He started with surprise at the cold contact and Djoura laughed again. She proceeded to lather his puzzled face.

"Hah! You poor sieve-head! How pink you are, underneath the dirt!" she chortled. "We'll see just how pink we can make you. We'll get that hair too. Maybe it's pink as well, when all the sand is out of it."

But when she dribbled water onto the blond head, he sputtered and shook like a dog. Perfecto cursed from his spot on the square of carpet, and Hakiim backed off. Both the merchants retreated some yards away.

"Good," growled the black. "Being stupid has it uses. You got rid of them, and if I'd done it, they'd beat me. Or they'd try!"

"I don't like them," she whispered, pouting furiously. "And I most especially don't like the Spaniard. They can crawl in with any of the girls they like, they think—it's their natural right, they think.

"Until they meet ME! I showed them, you can tell the world."

Raphael's head and face ran with thin lather. He squinted his eyes against the sting of soap. Djoura gave him a careful rinse, using as little water as possible. "Sand is better for washing," she instructed him. "It doesn't crack the skin like soap, and doesn't waste good water. We had sand yesterday and I gave myself a good scrub. Hah! You should have seen these ignorant ones look at me, like baby owls along branch, blinking. They know nothing, being content to stink.

"But here there is not sand, but only dirt. Who can wash herself in dirt, I ask?"

Looking slyly around first, she dabbed the soapy rag at her own face and hands, and then thrust her arm with the rag down the front of her many-layered clothing. As the cool rag swabbed her skin, she sighed in ecstasy. Raphael watched every move with interest.

Having washed down to the fellow's neck and up each arm, Djoura sat back and announced, "Now you have to get up off your hams, eunuch, so we can pull that shirt off you."

But she had no real hope of being understood. She scuttled around behind the fellow and yanked on the garment, but there was too much of it, and his legs were tangled in its folds. "Curse you!" she growled, but without real rancor, for washing the eunuch was the first interesting thing for her since being sold to Hakiim in Tunis. "How you stare at me with those big blue eyes of yours—just like a white cat! I wonder you can even see through them. Well, the shirt's all stuck to your back with blood. We'll have to soak it off."

When the water hit Raphael's back, he stiffened and gasped. Djoura put a hand on his shoulder. "It's all right. It won't hurt forever," she whispered, adding soap. She examined the length and number of the scourge marks with a kind of respect. "Pinkie, you must have done something pretty terrible to deserve THIS!

"I, too, cannot be broken," she hissed into his ear, "though maybe they will make me a sieve-head in the end, like you."

She smiled grimly at the thought. "Or maybe I'll only pretend to be one, and amuse myself laughing at them all."

There were long openings in the back of the eunuch's gown—not whip slices, for they were parallel and neatly hemmed. She wondered at them while she reached her hand through and worried the cloth from the wounds. Perhaps some kind of iron chain or body-collar had passed through these. If so, this eunuch must have been a handful when he still had his senses. Her approval of him grew by leaps and bounds.

"You may not know it," she whispered (as though the hills were full of spies), "but I am a Berber! People think I am not, because I am black, but Berbers are really of all colors." Then she giggled. "Maybe even pink!

"To be a Berber, it is only necessary that you live like a Berber and follow the ways of the Prophet," she added with hauteur, and she crawled back in front of him to glare deep into his eyes. "To be a Berber is to be free!" she hissed, with no thought of the irony of her words.

She threw back her head and all the coins and tassels on her headdress bobbed together.

Raphael listened carefully to the sounds Djoura made. His eyes devoured her color and shape and his skin rejoiced at her touch, even when it hurt him. For her song had broken his terrible isolation, and her chatter kept him from despair. So now, as she at last fell silent, with her brown eyes looking full at him, he tried to give her something of the same sort back.

He repeated the chant she had sung at the other end of the line, word for word, note for note, with perfect inflection and time.

Djoura clapped her hands in front of her mouth. "Oh, aren't you a clever one!"

It was not actually cleverness, or not cleverness in the sense the black Berber meant. Raphael's repertoire of music was immense, and neither pain nor transformation could steal it from him.

He knew that piece. He repeated it for her an octave down, where he found this new instrument (his throat) was more comfortable, and then to the Berber's amazement, he followed the solo chant with the traditional choral response.

The woman sat stock-still in front of him. The rag she had been wringing fell from her hands. "You are a Berber too? My kinsman? And I have been making mock of you!" She bit down on her lip until the pain of it brought her feelings under control.

Could this pink fellow be a Berber? She had just said there might be pink Berbers.

Well, if he were not, then he OUGHT to have been a Berber, between the lashes on his back and the knowledge of the chant.

But how could he have ever lived in the high desert with
that silly coloring? Why, he was already sunburned; she
could tell because her fingers left white marks on the skin as
she touched him.

Perhaps he had not always been this color. Perhaps he
had lain in a dungeon some long time. She had heard that
years in the darkness could bleach the finest dark skin to
white.

She harked to the querulous complaint of the women in
the shadows behind her. She reminded herself that they
were not alone, Pinkie and she. She listened. Hakiim's reply to the complaint could not be made out, but the Moor
was laughing. He laughed a lot, swine that he was. She
could not hear the Spaniard. She imagined his hard little
eyes watching her.

It was necessary to keep busy, or they would take her
back to the far end of the wall and she would never get near
this fellow again. "Lie down," she whispered. "Lie down,
Pinkie, on your side."

He seemed to understand her Arabic, which was heart-
ening, and further convinced her that her ideas of his ances-
try were correct, but he was so clumsy in his movements
that she had to push him gently onto his left side. "There.
Now we'll get your long legs and your bottom.

"I've never seen a eunuch close up," she added con-
versationally, "not what he lacks, anyway." But as that
thought led to another, she scowled. "The man who makes a
eunuch out of a Berber ought to have his own balls torn off
and his belly ripped open and both holes stuffed with red
ants! He should lose his eyes and his tongue first, and then
his feet and then his left hand, and then his right hand . . .
and . . ."

As she spoke, searching her imagination for greater and
greater punishments to inflict on this nameless castrater,
her hand with the rag continued to soap and scrub, until by
the time she arrived at the words "his right hand," her own
had climbed up the tube of the white linen gown, where it
made an astounding discovery.

She popped her head under the hem of the gown to ver-
ify what her fingers told her, and then very quickly with-

drew it. Out of ingrained habits of concealment, he
features adopted an expression of heavy boredom as she
dipped the rag once more into the pot of water. She
hummed a little tune as she rinsed it out.

The blond man stared at her with bright interest and
scratched at the spot she had left wet. The Berber could
barely hide her grin. "Don't do that, Pinkie. If they see you
playing with that, you'll lose it for sure."

Casually humming, she scrubbed his other leg. And his
sickness-fouled buttocks. It must have been the fellow's
very foulness, she reflected, that spared him. Hakiim had
been too delicate souled to examine him, and Perfecto . .

Djoura had never granted the Spaniard an ounce of sen
sibility, but it was he who had dumped the blond among
them and called him a eunuch. Maybe he had just been too
lazy to look. The black woman leaned forward and put her
finger under his chin. She was smiling no longer.

"Listen to me, Pink Berber, if there's a grain of sense left
in that poor head. Don't lift your skirt around anyone here
except me. Not even to make water. Do you understand
me?"

The blond stared back at her.

"Do you understand me?" she hissed in her urgency.

Raphael's clean face sweated with effort. His mouth
opened. "I want," he said, slurring like a man drunk on kif
"I want to understand."

She ran her hand over his sleek wet hair.

"Here's your soap," she said flatly to Hakiim. The Moor
drew back his hands in distaste. "Wrap it in the rag."

While she did so he took a glance over at the blond eu
nuch, who sat gazing vacantly at them, his hands in his lap
as neat and sleek as some mother's favorite child. "Was he
filthy?"

The Berber rolled her eyes and desposited the wet rag in
Hakiim's hand. "Of course he was. And sick, I think. He
cannot be left to himself. You had better put me next to
him."

The Moor's jaw dropped. "You WANT to be next to him?
"My sweet lily of the mountains: the fellow is yours!"

* * *

Night fell: Raphael's first night in captivity. He lay on his stomach, trying to look up at the stars.

It was getting bad again. As soon as Djoura had gone away from him—ten feet away, which was as far as the chain would allow—the confusion rose like a mist from the ground, enfolding him.

And the desolation.

His Father had abandoned him. In all the length and breadth of Raphael's existence that had never happened. He would have said with confidence that that couldn't happen. Without His presence an angel should go out like a light.

And perhaps that was what had happened.

He lay with his cheek on bare earth, all his muscles tightened as though to ward off a blow. His eyes closed against a vision of hatred, borne on a face which might have been his own. Why he was so hated he could not recall, nor did he remember how that hate had led to . . . to this. He shivered, despite the sultriness of the night, for he didn't want to remember.

He wanted to remember something good: something which would provide a comfort to him in his misery. He searched in his memory for His Father.

And found to his horror that without His Father's presence in his heart, he could not begin to imagine Him. He couldn't even call up a picture of His face, for all that came to him, unbidden and insistent, was the image of a sparrow on a bare branch, its drab feathers fluffed and its black eyes closed against the wind.

Whenever he moved the iron collar chafed his neck. He also found his eyes were leaking. That was uncomfortable, for it made the ground muddy. He laced his hands under his cheekbone, to keep his face out of the mud.

But the damp earth released a dark, consoling sort of smell, and he was glad for it. He turned his attention to the little noises of the camp, where the women were whispering lazily before falling asleep.

The rule of midday had been reversed now; the chain which had spaced the slaves out at maximum distance to one another now tinkled in little heaps as six bodies huddled companionably under five blankets.

Raphael and his nursemaid had been removed from the communal length of chain and put onto a special little chain of their own. He didn't have a blanket, and didn't know he ought to have had one. The Berber had a blanket, but she also had a lot of clothing on her body, so she threw the blanket to Raphael.

It was a magnanimous gesture, but as he didn't know what to do with the blanket he let it lie in a heap, till she crawled back and reclaimed it.

He heard one of the slaves stagger out of the cluster to make water, squatting on the dirt with her skirts lifted. That was also how Djoura had taught him to do it, that evening. It seemed to him, even in his newborn clumsiness, that there might be easier ways to go about it.

But all his memories had been turned upside down. It seemed this human head could not contain them properly—not the important or meaningful memories. He could recall scattered images of his visits upon the earth: a black horse, a white dog. A young man with black hair and a white face.

He remembered singing.

Always Raphael had been fond of mortals. He thought them beautiful, even when only in the way a baby bird is beautiful—through its awesome ugliness. Some mortals, of course, were more beautiful than others.

Finally he had something to cling to. To build on. Raphael made a song about the baby-bird beauty of mortals. Turning on his side he began to sing into the night.

This was better—much better. Here there was consonance and harmony, and even the beginnings of understanding, though he had to work his mouth and lungs to get it. When singing, it was impossible for Raphael to be confused or alone, or to be anything else but singing.

Behind him came a rustling. Djoura rose from her place, stepped across the ten feet dividing her from Raphael, and stood above him, listening. He raised his eyes gladly to her.

Then she kicked him. "Don't make noise," she hissed, and shuffled away the length of the chain.

In all his existence, no one had ever, EVER disapproved of Raphael's music. He had no experience with this sort of criticism at all. He curled into a ball of hurt and his eyes leaked harder.

He thought about all the music he had ever made and he found himself doubting it was any good. That foot had been so decisive. He wondered, despairing, if his owm creation had been some sort of divine mistake: a piece badly con-ceived and played.

But if Raphael lost faith in his own music, he did not lose faith in music in general. He had never been too proud to sing the music created by others, so he sought in his mem-ory for a song that might make him feel better: one that had warm edges to it, and that was somehow connected with . . . he couldn't remember.

He sang this song so quietly no sound left the shelter of his huddled knees. It was a very simple song (compared to his own) but it reached out to the things he no longer under-stood and it gave him strength.

He remembered one little word. "Dami," he whispered, liking the sound. "Damiano."

There was a brush of cloudy warmth over him, lighter than a fall of leaves. Raphael squeezed his eyes to clear the water out and looked up.

Wings as soft as woolen blankets: dark but with a light within like a lamp under smoked glass. A shadow of rough hair framing dark eyes which also had a smolder of light behind them. The face of a friend.

Raphael closed his eyes in rapture and he could still see that face. He crawled onto his friend's lap.

"You should have called me before you started to feel this bad," chided Damiano. "I'm no angel, to be shuttling at will between earth and heaven, and I had no idea where you were."

"I don't know where I am, either," replied Raphael, grateful to be able to talk again without using the slow, awk-ward body. "And I didn't know you would hear if I called.

"Damiano!" cried Raphael, stricken. "God is gone!"

The dusky spirit started, and its immaterial wings gathered round Raphael's damaged form. "Hush, hush,

Raphael, my friend, my teacher . . . Can you hear yourself saying that?

"How could He be gone and I be here, holding you, eh? For what am I, outside of Him?" Damiano took Raphael's head between his hands and forced the frightened eyes into quiet. "Now do, you feel better?"

Raphael felt something. He felt the presence of his friend, and for the moment he could imagine nothing finer. But his scourged back picked that moment to communicate a huge throb of pain.

"He's gone," he repeated childishly. "I can't find my Father anywhere."

The sad, sweet face above him (a mere suggestion of a face really, dark on darkness) filled with compassion, and he embraced Raphael gently, as though the poor pale body would break at a touch. "That's what it's like," he whispered. "Yes, that's exactly what it's like."

He brushed the long hair out of Raphael's face. "Don't worry, Master. He is there, and so am I."

"What did you call me?"

The ghost laughed. "Master. You never liked that word. But it's what you are to me. My music master. You must remember you are the Archangel Raphael, and a great person all around!"

Raphael took one cloudy hand between his clumsy ones. "My memory . . . isn't working properly. I think of people and I see baby birds. I think of the Father and I see another bird—hungry—in the middle of winter.

"What does this mean, Damiano?"

"Birds?" The ghostly voice was quizzical. "Well, don't birds sing?" Damiano shrugged heavy wings and gazed intently at nothing.

"It means, Seraph, that God is not missing at all, believe me."

"I will believe you," answered Raphael. "But I have no other reason to believe except that it is you who say it." His shivering had stopped, and without knowing it, he was sinking into sleep. But as the gray shape about him began to fade, he woke with a start.

"Don't go!" he cried out, and even his body's mouth made a liltle noise. "Don't you leave me too!"

Damiano patted his hand. "But you are a living man now, and must not spend your time talking with ghosts. It isn't good for you, and besides—they will think you are mad as a hare. But I will be with you, you know, anytime you think of me.

"Here—if you think you might forget." The spectral arm reached out and plucked a nondescript pebble from the ground. "I give this to you. If you begin to doubt I am there, take it out of your pocket and look at it."

"I don't have a pocket," whined Raphael, as that fact loomed into an insuperable problem.

The ghost's smile broadened, showing white teeth. "Then knot it into the hem of your gown. Or in your hair. Or keep it in your mouth. Just remember."

Raphael took it into a sweating palm. "But you'll come back like this again, won't you? So I can talk with you. So I can see you?"

"Raphael," Damiano whispered, grinning. "My dear teacher. I am always at your command."

Gaspare was still standing by the door of the wineshop, mumbling and scratching his head, when Saara fell out of the sky.

He knew it was Saara, though he had never seen her naked before, and her hair was hanging in tatters. He winced at the thump she made, hitting the ground.

With his lute in one hand, he slid to his knees at her side. "Lady Saara," he gasped. "Was it really YOU who pecked Damiano in the eye a few minutes ago?"

She lay on her back, but her eyes were closed. Still, she was breathing: breathing rather hard, and her chest rose up and down. He gazed down at it, fascinated.

Gaspare shot a furtive glance around him, to see whether anyone on the street had noticed. But of course there wasn't anyone on the sun-whitened street, and by fortune Saara's return had happened out of the line of sight from within the wineshop.

"Oh, what am I to do?" he mumbled to himself, shifting his lute from hand to hand as though that would help. Finally he stuffed the neck of the instrument down the front of his shirt, bent down, and picked up the limp woman in his arms.

Thus burdened he shuffled through the dry grass down the windowless abandoned lane. There he encountered Festilligambe, the horse, chewing furiously at the grass in an effort to recover from his earlier panic.

"Uh. There you are," grunted Gaspare. "You can carry her easier than I."

Groaning with effort, he lifted the woman high. The gelding stepped neatly away. Gaspare almost dropped Saara onto the grass.

"Dammit, you bag of bones. This is the Lady Saara. She is supposed to be a friend of yours!"

Festilligambe cocked an ear and his large nostrils twitched. While not disputing Saara's character as a friend, he seemed to deny that it implied such a heavy responsibility. But after a moment's reflection, the horse allowed her to be laid gently across him like a sack of meal.

"Now," muttered the redhead, "let's avoid prying eyes, shall we, horse? I know I have a reputation for being a rake, but the picture we present here is not charming." On sudden thought he removed his shirt and lay it over the naked woman. It didn't cover much.

At the end of the alley was a pile of rubble. Gaspare, leading the horse by the mane, turned left and walked through a gap in a wall and found himself abruptly out of the village of San Gabriele.

Down the grassy hill and into an open pine wood. Not five hundred feet along there was a stream and a clearing beside it where a crude thatch of branches was upheld by rough wooden poles.

This was Gaspare's retreat, where he had lived since the spring made it possible: a mansion perfectly suited to one who liked his privacy and also hadn't two pieces of copper to rub together.

He lay Saara down upon his crackling, piney mattress and regarded her long. When he was done regarding her he dropped the shirt once more over her middle.

Festilligambe, too, peered at Saara, whom he had never before thought of as the sort of creature that rides on a horse. He whuffed her singed hair.

The horse sneezed and Saara woke up.

Her eyes snapped open like shutters caught in a wind. She woke up with jaw clenched and nostrils flaring. Color splashed her cheeks as she sat bolt upright on the bed of branches. Gaspare's shirt fell. She said one word.

"No."

She said it quietly, almost absently, and she said nothing else. But the horse, who had been leaning with herbivorous curiosity over her vegetative couch, leaped stiff-legged into the air and came down running. Gaspare heard his receding hoofbeats but paid them scant attention, for he was lying flat on his back where the blow had knocked him, both hands wrapped protectively around his own throat.

As she sat there rigidly, amid no sound except that of Gaspare gasping and choking on the ground, the red in her cheeks faded to white. The rage which burned behind her tilted eyes faded, so once more they shone like the gold-green of a river in sunlight. She sighed and rubbed her face with both hands.

Gaspare took a long, shuddering, welcome breath. "Sweet Gesu, woman: what did you do to me?" he cried shakily, struggling up from the earth.

Saara became aware of the youth. "There you are, Gaspare." Her regard became awkwardly intense. "What a terrible trouble you have gotten me into!"

His long jaw opened and closed rhythmically. He made fish mouths. "I? Got YOU into trouble? My lady, you nearly killed me just now; I couldn't breathe!"

She waved aside this discursion.

"Do you know who that spirit was, who came up the path in the shape of Damiano?"

He frowned heavily and shrugged. "I guessed myself that it wasn't—wasn't Damiano, I mean. When it turned into a dragon . . ."

"A wyvern. It had only two legs."

". . . when it turned into a scaly monster. Damiano, in all the time I knew him, never showed any signs of doing such a thing. Who was it, then?"

"It was the Liar," and she hid her eyes behind her hands once more.

"Ah!" Gaspare nodded sapiently. "That's better. I had half a notion it might have been Satan himself. After me for my sins."

Hazel eyes popped open again. "But it was. It was the one you call Satan, and he had come for you. For your sins."

Gaspare collapsed again to the earth, and he stuck all eight of his fingers into his terrified mouth. He gave one high, thin wail.

Saara glowered at this lack of discipline. "Don't worry. You're safe. I went instead of you."

"You did what?" He pulled himself toward the cot of branches, a look of dazed gratitude illuminating his ill-assorted features. "You took my sins upon yourself? You went to hell? Suffered for me?"

Saara flung herself to her feet and peered vaguely around for her dress. "I went to his hall, yes, and it was no joke. But if you want to know who is suffering, it is your teacher. Your Raphael."

"The angel?" Gaspare squatted at Saara's feet, growing numb from too many surprises. "Raphael is suffering for my sins?"

Finding nothing around except Gaspare's shirt, she put that on. It did not quite reach her knees. "Sin I know nothing about," she stated. "Just suffering."

She ran her hands through her hair; they snarled among the blackened burned ends of her braids. She looked into the woods about her, as though marshaling unseen forces.

"Let me cut the damage out of your hair, Lady Saara," offered Gaspare, in order to put the conversation on a more manageable level. And he added, half-regretfully, "And then we will try to find you more suitable clothing. After that we will be more in a position to talk about sin and suffering."

She shot him a glance of such coldness he might have been Satan himself, with a voice of treacherous temptation. "I don't have such time! I was asked by Dami to protect your Raphael, and I have failed! I must find what the Liar has done with him—for a spirit cannot be destroyed, you

know. The Eagle is somewhere, in a dungeon. Or a jar, perhaps."

"A jar?" echoed Gaspare, uncertainly.

She ignored him. "I will find him and I will bring him
away, unless death comes first. This I vow, who have made
no vows since leaving the Saami." She raised both her arms
into the air.

"Wait!" Gaspare made an expert dive and caught the
woman about the waist. "Don't turn into anything, Lady!
Tell me where we're going?"

She peered down at the redhead clinging to her, with
irritation mixed with surprise. "I am going," she corrected
him. "Home, to Lombardy, first.

"And then to Satan's Hall, or Hell, or whatever you call
it." Without further discussion, Saara grew feathers and
flew.

After she had gone Gaspare sat back into his bed of
branches and stared at the scurf of dead needles that coated
the ground. Gaspare was thinking about his sins, which he
knew to be many. He was thinking about his sins of commis-
sion rather than those of omission, and especially thinking
about his sins of the body.

Gaspare's sins of this nature had actually been few and
exploratory in nature, but whenever he thought of sins,
they were the ones to come immediately to mind.

And he was feeling very badly, for though it might be the
act of a bravo to follow a giggling girl into the dark, as Gaspare had done more than once (but less than four times), it
was the act of a worm to let a pure angel take the blame for
it.

He was very fond of his lute teacher, with a hesitant and
wary sort of affection which sprang from his knowledge that
they were very different sorts of people, Raphael and himself. Without the fortuitous chance that Damiano had been
the friend of both, they would have had no reason to meet.

And Gaspare felt, too, that Raphael in his sinlessness
never had been able to recognize just how wicked Gaspare
himself could be.

And now, unfortunately, Raphael had caught the brunt of
that wickedness and was suffering. In a jar, of all things,
Gaspare cringed queasily and tried to feel repentance.

What he felt, he found, was resentment. Gesu the Christ
had been enough, he considered. What other load of guilt
did a man have to bear? And even the Lady Saara . . .
(Thinking of Saara as he had just seen her, his thoughts di-
gressed immediately. It was a number of minutes before he
could get them back on the subject of guilt.) Even Saara had
tried to purloin his sins from him. Surely a woman who
looked like that might have some of her own . . .

It seemed the earth was inhabited by posturing heroes,
with Gaspare of San Gabriele as the only poor dolt among
them. Fit for nothing but to be saved from himself. It
couldn't be borne!

Well, he WOULDN'T bear it, he decided with a few redheaded curses. He rose to his full height (in three years he
had grown prodigiously) and strode off toward the sunlight,
seeking his wayward horse.

Lombardy in high summer was a green cathedral, with
its constant murmur of clean waters and its odor of shadowy
frankincense. On a round hill between spires of rock flour-
ished the wild garden of Saara: a meadow of heavy grass, cut
by interlacing streams, dotted with the early blue aster, and
wound about with the sprawling late red rose. Not far from
the lawn, in the shade of the pines below, she had a little
house of sod, built after the manner of her northern people,
to which she withdrew only to sleep.

Here also grew rosemary and comfrey, eyebright, and
mullein, the vervain which makes the wild cats drunk in the
springtime, and orris, for sweetening clothes and hair.
Above the meadow, among the feathered birches which
crested the dome of the hill, was a stand of hazel also: all
plants with uses for the leech, witch, or wise woman.

Saara was all three of these, and on her garden no frost
came, though through the winter the high peaks on either
side of her hill were painted white.

Under the last full moon of summer she sat, on the round
dome of the hill, where the scattered birch striped the

darkness with silver, and the fingers of the trees twisted moonlight into chains. She sat tailor fashion, wearing nothing but Gaspare's linen shirt, her brown hair cropped halfway down her neck. Her face, splashed with light and shadow, was not that of a girl.

There is a spell almost all witches know, though some chant it and some read it from books and still others play it through the length of a staff, or scratch it out with the blood of a cock. It is not a complicated spell, only very dangerous, and for that reason it is often learned and rarely used.

Saara, in her long life, had never sung this spell before. When she had lost her lovers, she had refrained. When her children died, even then she had been wise, for she knew the gate of death had its purpose.

But now she, too, had her purpose—a purpose beyond loss or loneliness. Her purpose was rescue.

Through no other means had she been able to find Raphael. He was neither in the wind nor in the voice of the water, and he didn't hear her call—or he could not answer. She hadn't really expected to find him so easily, for she remembered that spinning disorientation in the air and the strange bare peak with a window. That was the place she must find again. For that she needed help.

So the greatest witch in the Italies sat with her hands folded in her lap and her legs bare to the wind as she sang up the dead.

It began with a wail and rose into a chant of four ascending notes, the last of which she held clear and unshaken until her breath failed her. She sang the line again. And again.

There was no expression to be seen on Saara's face, had there been any to see on that dome of trembling birch. She had no feeling in her once the song had begun. And the moon put a severe light upon her features, emphasizing their odd Asiatic cast and draining all color. She appeared neither girl nor young woman under that stained white globe. In fact, there was nothing particularly feminine about the figure on the dry earth. Nothing particularly human. She might have been a peak of rock among those of the Alps nearby, eternally white, cloaked with loud, grieving winds.

The same four notes, building like stairs upon one another. Carving a black path into blackness. They droned on while the soiled moon rolled from the slopes of the eastern hills to its zenith. Untiring, unchanging, they rang over the sparse dome of birch trees and down into the pine-woolly coverts below. At the foot of the hills, beyond the little lakes fed by the streams of Saara's garden, people in the village of Ludica shut their doors and windows, shivering despite August's heat.

And not least of all, Saara's song echoed through the spaces of her own head, until she was mad with her own singing, and her mind and soul became the pure instruments of her purpose.

And when the moon balanced directly over the earth—directly over the round moonlike dome of the hill—Saara let the stair she had built open, and she spoke one name.

"Damiano," she whispered. She closed her eyes and let the new silence hang in the air.

There was a whispering around Saara, and a rustle like the soft feathers of many birds. "Speak!" she commanded without opening her eyes.

The rustling grew nearer. It grew warm. "Saara," came the sweet, caressing answer. "My beautiful one. My princess. My queen."

Saara's stern face slackened with sorrow, but only for a moment. "Ruggerio," she whispered. "Forgive me. I did not mean to wake you." Her eyes screwed themselves more firmly shut.

"I know, bellissima," the thin, distant voice replied, chuckling, and ghostly lips kissed the very tips of her fingers. "And I do not mean to prove a distraction. May all the saints go with you."

Then the air went thick with vague calls and whispers. Saara repeated the one name "Damiano" and sat as still and unyielding as a rock.

One sound rose among the others: that of a man's laughter. But this was not Ruggerio, though it was a voice she recognized. "The greatest witch in the Italies," it pro-

unced, and then laughed again. "For a while perhaps.
erhaps stronger than I. But my son was another matter,
asn't he, Saara? My poor, half-blind, mozzarella boy!
'ho'd have thought it?"

Saara sat as rigid as wood, as stone, and chided her heart
r pounding like a hammer. No response she gave to this
irit, and soon it sighed. "Ah. Well, no matter, Saara. God
 with you."

And it was gone. Surprise alone nearly made Saara's eyes
ack open, but she restrained herself. To think that thirty
ars of bitterness and fear toward Guillermo Delstrego
uld lead to this. "God go with you?"

Had the proud, predatory soul of Delstrego bent to that?
e had grown to think the man almost the equivalent of
e Liar himself in his wickedness.

Her strength trembled and came near to breaking at this
uch to an ancient wound.

But now the hilltop was filled with a confusion of spirits
d sounds and the witch's guards came up by instinct.

Presences surrounded her like a roomful of smoke rings,
lf erased by the moving air. These were perhaps spirits
ho knew her or had touched somehow her long life, or
re by some unknown sympathy attracted to the stern,
iseeing woman in white linen, who held the gate open
d yet spoke to no one.

For though the spell is called a summoning spell, its
fect and its danger is that it brings the user very close to
at world which is not a world (being placeless and in-
ite), wherein a living mortal has no business to wander.

And though there was no malice in the vague fingers that
uched Saara, or in the soft whispers that questioned her,
ere was also not one of them without the power to do
ara great harm (should she let them), or to cause her great
in (whether she let them or not).

She took a deep, shuddering breath and her nostrils
itched, as though the air were too thick to breathe. "Da-
iano!" she called again, this time with a touch of urgency.

There was a moment's silence, and then came a small
ice, a sweet child's piping voice, speaking the language of

her northern people. "Mama?" it cried wonderingly. "Is
Mama?"

She gave a despairing gasp. "Go to sleep, baby," s
whispered into the blackness, while tears escaped the co
fines of her closed eyes. "Go back to bed. I will come to y
soon."

Now it was late and she had almost no strength left
hold the gate and fight the river of innocent, deadly voice
She had a sudden, desperate idea. "Little white dog," s
called out. "Little white dog of Damiano's. Spot, or wha
ever your name was . . . come to me."

"Macchiata," was the matter-of-fact answer, which can
from very close in front. Saara held to this spirit and let t
rest go. She opened her eyes.

Sitting before her, legs splayed, was a very pretty plun
girl with hair that shone silver in the moonlight. Her gar
also, was a simple white shift that gleamed without star
with a red kerchief which tied about the neck and sprea
out across her back, sailor fashion. She had little wings li
those of a pigeon.

She smiled at Saara with bright interest. Her eyes we
brown.

"Some mistake," murmured the witch. "I summone
only a dog. A little white dog which belonged to . . ."

"To Master—Damiano. Yes, that's me." She started
scratch her spectral left ear with her spectral left hand
short, choppy forward motions. She seemed to get grea
satisfaction out of doing this. "Damiano likes me in th
form."

"He does?" Saara exclaimed with somewhat affronte
surprise. Then she remembered Damiano's peculiar preju
dice toward the human form above that of all animal
however splendid. "Well, I thought the dog looked pe
fectly fine."

Macchiata was still for a moment, and then resume
scratching. She metamorphosed between one stroke an
the next, going from girl to dog, and continued her scratc
quite contentedly with her hind leg. "Like that?"

"Lovely," stated Saara.

The deep brown eyes regarded Saara, asking no questions. The white dog smiled with all her formidable teeth exposed and her red tongue lolling to the right. Her fluffy pigeon wings scratched one another's backs behind her.

Saara had not forgotten how last she had seen this animal, frozen like a starved deer in the snow, with her dark master above her, equally frozen with grief. She said, "You died by my hand, dog. But it was not by my intent."

Macchiata pulled her tongue in. Under the spell she had attained an almost lifelike solidity, but still she glowed with milk-glass light. "I remember—I think. You were upset."

"I was," admitted the greatest witch of the Italies. "Upset and afraid, and I struck thinking only of defending myself. Do you forgive me, spirit?"

The dog, in reply, flopped over on her back. "Sure. Why not? Scratch under my left elbow; I can't reach."

Saara obeyed and was surprised to feel warm fur beneath her hand. "Have you fleas, then?"

"No." As the human's hand rubbed in expanding circles, the dog's left foot began a spastic, regular pawing of the air. Macchiata grunted like a pig. "No. No fleas in heaven. Only scratching."

Saara settled back on her heels and looked about her. The moon was descending the western sky; the night was getting old. "Spirit, I haven't much time. Will you help me find your master? I called and he could not hear me."

"He heard you," said Macchiata, flipping onto her legs. She gave a great shake. "Everyone heard you. You called very loud. He just wouldn't come."

Saara felt a cold needle of misery pierce through her. She was some time in answering. "He . . . wouldn't come?"

"No." The dog's nostril's twitched, smelling the salt in Saara's tears. "Don't get upset! He stayed away so you wouldn't get upset. He wanted to come."

Saara swallowed, beyond words for a moment. Finally she said, "I have to see him about Raphael. If I can't help Raphael, I will be very upset."

Macchiata's sticklike tail thumped appreciatively. "I like Raphael. He has never been upset. Never."

"That could change," replied Saara ominously, "unless we help him."

"I'll get Master," announced the dog, and she faded like an afterimage on the eye.

Once Macchiata was gone, Saara wiped her eyes on the sleeve of her shirt and blew her nose into a handful of birch leaves. She had been shaken by every pull on her living memory, and the spirit that had refused to come had shaken her hardest. Had there been some malice in the little creature, to say so brutally "He wouldn't come"? Indeed, the summoning spell was the most dangerous of all spells, to soul and to body, for now that she had done it, she felt hardly the strength or the desire to go on living.

Her children: Could it be they were no more than infant spirits, grown neither in heart nor mind since the day they bled to death with their father on the floor of the hut? Something in Saara, instinct or sense of justice, rebelled at this idea. Was there illusion at the base of the summoning spell? Had Ruggerio not really kissed her fingertips?

Had Guillermo Delstrego not come after thirty years of her hate to say to her, "God go with you"? Something had happened nonetheless, and someone had come to her behind the darkness of her closed eyes. It remained to be seen whether her task had succeeded or failed.

She stared at the disk of the descending moon, and so deep in thought was she that she did not notice the silent approach of one behind her.

"Saara," he whispered. "Pikku Saara."

Saara turned slowly, effortfully, as though a great weight sat on her shoulders. She was suddenly afraid.

Behind her, illuminated by the moon, stood the shape of a man. It was dark, from its rough hair to its booted feet, and a cloud surrounded it like great, soft folded wings. As Saara looked up at the apparition's face the wings opened wide.

Smoky he was, and immaterial: not like the dog nor yet like the spirit who had kissed her fingers. For it was not her spell but his own wish that had brought him this very long way to a hill in Lombardy, in August, and he had little magic with which to clothe himself in flesh. Only the eyes of the ghost were clear to see, and full of tenderness.

"Damiano," she began, and her voice left her as she uttered the name. "I'm sorry to call you. I don't want to cause you pain, when you have the right to peace."

He knelt by her, and she sensed in her witch's soul a hand upon her face. "The only pain which can touch me," he whispered, gently and from far away, "is to see this pain in YOUR eyes, Saara. And I will gladly endure it if I can help you. But I didn't think that I could."

"You thought I called you out of loneliness," she stated, and her words held a hint of accusation. "No. I have more love in me than that, Dami, and more sense too. I called you because of Raphael. He has fallen into the power of the Liar . . .

"And I . . . I was the bait used to draw him. It was my fault."

Damiano sank down beside her and the round moon shone unobscured through his spreading wings. Slowly he grew more solid to look upon, as he gazed rapt into her green, tilted eyes. He put his weightless hands upon hers. "How could it be your fault, love, that Satan hates his brother?" He stroked her weathered hands gently. "If it is a matter of fault, then it is my fault that I wrapped my friend so tightly in the bonds of earth he could no longer stand against the Devil's malice."

But the dark unghostly brown eyes reflected no sense of guilt. "There is no fault here at all, Saara, except that of Satan's jealousy. And even that may be borne."

Saara gripped Damiano's large hands. They had become solid and warm. She brought them together and laid them against her cheek.

In another moment he was kissing her and curtains of wing shrouded them both.

"I love you," whispered Damiano, with his head against her neck. "Oh Lady, how I love you!" And then he sighed. "Forgive me, Saara; this does no good, I know!"

So it can be done, she thought to herself. The dead may touch the living in the very manner of life. Her heart raced, burning with the conviction that all vows would be well broken, and the future profitably traded—in exchange for this.

Saara hissed between her teeth and turned her head from him. "By the four winds! How wise I am—how wretchedly wise. Wise enough to put you aside, dark boy, even if you were fool enough to want to stay with me."

When she looked back again her face had hardened. "You see what a woman can be made of, after seventy years of living? I am so strong even you cannot break me, my dear.

"And as for being hurt—what does it matter if I am hurt, Dami? Why should my friends want to hedge me from my greatest desire lest I be hurt? Is it not to be hurt, to have one's desire thwarted? Is it not to be hurt, to be left always behind?"

She turned on the ghost with a sudden, deep-felt anger. "You thought it were better to hide from me and die, rather than risk being saved at the expense of my life. How noble it was of you!

"But would it not have been greater to have given me the chance to prove myself as noble as you? Do you think my own love would have made it less than a joy to die in your place?"

He shook his head, and now the black curls moved with the fingers of the wind. The setting moon haloed his face: large-eyed, ram-nosed, smiling gently. "It would have been a great act, love. I was not capable of it."

Saara was crying, but her voice came firmly. "And Raphael too . . . Walking into the Liar's snare, knowing it was a snare, and I the bait. I told him not to. I told him the truth: that I am old and my life is full-lived. There is nothing which now could please me more than a good death in battle . . ."

"Which you would not get from Satan," replied the ghost simply, shrugging. "But rather pain, confusion, and the shame of weakness slowly overcoming you, like that of an old man who cannot hold his bladder. The Devil has no sympathy with anything quick and clean, and it isn't human death which pleases him, but human misery." He searched her stern face for understanding.

"But in the end it did not matter, Saara, that you were ready to endure the Devil's torment. I believe you have the strength, beloved, if anyone born has ever had it. But Raphael also knew that if he left you in his brother's power, Satan would merely find another mortal tool, and then another, until Raphael could no longer resist him."

Damiano's voice was slow and gentle, and he caressed her hair as he spoke, and when he was finished all she said was, "I love you, Dami Delstrego. We had only a few days together as man and woman, but when flesh is laid aside I will still love you, then and always."

His sad smile widened, lighting all his face. "You are so beautiful, beloved. Like a great song . . . As for me, Saara of Saami, there is nothing left but love. That is why I feared to see you, lest it seem to you another abandonment, when the moon sets and I am there no longer."

She whispered, "I have heard your father tonight. And I have heard the voice of my child. I have heard and seen a great deal in my life and I do not call up the dead to ease my heart, but for help."

"Help?" he echoed, and his wings rose expectantly.

"Help in rescuing Raphael."

Those shadowy wings beat the air in complex, unheeded rhythm, as a man may drum his fingers while thinking. "Of course," he murmured at last. "Knowing you, how could I expect less? But I have no magic with which to help you," he replied at last. "Nor force of arms. I am not a spirit of power."

"You think not?" Saara looked away from his brown, human, dangerous eyes. "But, I don't seek power but knowledge. Once you summoned the Liar—Satan, as you call him."

"Twice," he replied gravely. "I was a fool."

"But I am not," she stated. "And I do not want to meet Satan again. But I must get to his hall, where he has bound Raphael."

Damiano shook his head. "No, beloved. There is no need. Raphael has passed back onto the earth from there."

Her head snapped up. "Where?"

Damiano was slow in replying. "I don't know."

"Have you seen him?"

Once again the spirit smiled slowly, and then he turned his head as though to listen to the rising wind. At last he replied. "I have been to see him. He is in a dry, hot place. He is on a chain. It is a land to which I never traveled. More than that I can't tell you, for even as I look at you now, Saara, beautiful love, I am not here but far away, and there is little besides you yourself that is clear to my eyes . . ." And then it seemed he turned and peered down the hill again.

"For I am neither angel nor devil nor God Himself, to be prowling up and down the living world. Dead or alive, I am only Damiano, and my eyes have their limits."

She snorted, bending to his humor unwillingly. "Then I shall have to steal into Satan's window, as I first thought."

The smile died from his face as the belly of the round moon touched the hills behind him. "Don't try that, Saara."

"I will. I must," she replied. "Look at me, Damiano. Even simple eyes can see now that I am no more a child. This misadventure has aged me. But I am Saara of the Saami; I know what I must do, and I do it.

"Besides, I have sworn that I will find Raphael, so all choice in the matter is over."

Damiano looked into her green Asiatic eyes and nodded his head in submission to the inevitable. "So you will find him. But not this way. Instead comb all the hot lands of the earth first, and all the places where men are kept on chains."

She laughed a trifle scornfully. "No one can live so long! Most of the world is hot, to me, and most everywhere but among the Saami are men kept on chains! No, Damiano. You must tell me how to find Satan's Hall, where someone of greater information may be made to talk."

"That would not be the act of a friend," he said, staring away from her down the wooded hill.

There was a crashing among the trees below, like a deer leaping among the hazel, but Saara was too roused to attend to noises. She pointed a chiding finger at the ghost as she cried, "Was it the act of a friend to help a man die in his own

ay, when there was another who might have saved his life?
aphael said it was the act of a friend. Do you agree?"

Damiano's eyes were pulled to hers, and breathless spirit
hough he was, he sighed. "Will you throw me by my own
vords, Saara? Yes, that was the act of a friend.

"And it is your decision how you will live or die, and your
ows are your own to keep. But the pure truth is that I no
onger know the way to the Chamber of Four Windows, if I
ver did.

"For Damiano is dead, you know." The shadows of his
and touched his own breast. "This is only memory, lent
hape by love." As he spoke, his face was growing paler and
ss defined with the setting of the moon, but the look he
ave Saara was an obvious mixture of sweetness and amuse-
ent. He raised his hand and pointed beyond her.

"But THERE is one I think might know the way to
atan's palace," Damiano said.

Saara spun in place as the hulking black shadow barged
mong the birch trees. Above it was a thinner shadow that
as cursing continually in a very familiar voice.

"Gaspare!" the witch cried out in recognition.

The horse shied at the sound and Gaspare came nearly
ff, hanging over the gelding's back by one crooked knee
nd a handful of black mane. He cursed fluently, sliding
own to his feet.

The gangling youth strode closer, staggering and flailing
is arms as though blind. He encountered a few birch boles
efore coming close enough to spy Saara, sitting solid as a
oint of stone at the crest of the hill.

"Lady Saara!" he began. "I have had the Devil's own
rouble finding you. And it's dark here as the inside of a
ritch's . . ."

Gaspare had a pack on his back and the neck of the lute
tuck out of it sideways like an insect's leg. His lank hair
ung around his shoulders. Somewhere he had found an-
ther shirt.

Saara watched his approach in wonder and consternation.
t had been scarcely a week since she had flapped home—a
ery weary dove—and in that time she had forgotten about
e clownish Gaspare. She was not too happy to have him

interrupting her ghostly tryst, painful though the meetin
had to be. "As the inside of a witch's what, Gaspare?"

The only answer was a mumble and a clearing of th
throat, as the youth realized what he had said. Saara turne
her attention back to the waiting spirit, who glimmered lik
ice in the last rays of the moon.

Gaspare, too, noticed Damiano. The young man hisse
drawing himself back, and he made the peculiar Italia
magical sign of protection which has been used from tim
immemorial by men who don't understand the least abou
magic.

"Again!" he cried in wrath made slightly hysterical by th
touch of fear. He scooped a birch branch, complete wit
withering leaves, from the soil. "Again you try your trick
Satan! Villainous wibbert, or wyvart . . . wyrven . . ." Giv
ing up on the ungainly word heard only once, he lashed th
branch at the apparition, which sat and watched him, wing
pulsing slightly.

"Worm!" bellowed Gaspare, slashing his weapon left an
right through the translucent form. The colors of Damian
trickled over the thrashing branches like dappled sunligh
while he ghost himself sat placidly waiting.

As soon as Gaspare stopped, panting, to survey his de
struction, Damiano spoke again. "Hello, old friend, an
God keep you."

Gaspare, leaning on his branch, stared uncertainly. Afte
a few moments, he whined.

"I see you have that pretty lute on your back," continue
the spirit, grinning at Gaspare's discomfiture. "I remembe
it somewhat, though I owned it less than a week. I hav
heard you play with great enjoyment, Gaspare."

"You? Have heard me play? With . . ." The redhea
struggled with the idea that the Devil might like his musi
It was almost as difficult for him to believe the alternat
explanation. At last he let his leafy weapon fall. "Could it b
you are really Delstrego?"

"Damiano Delstrego. Or I was. And I have no one any
more to call me 'sheep-face,' Gaspare. What a shame."

Gaspare blinked away a sudden brightness in his eyes
He turned to Saara, to find that the witch, like the ghost

vas grinning. "Lady Saara," he said decisively, "I think you
have made a mistake. I don't think this is Satan at all. I
think this is really Damiano."

"Of course it is Damiano," stated Saara.

Gaspare sank to his knees. He yanked the pack from his
back and began to pull it apart, until the pearl inlay of the
lute belly shone under the moon like the spirit's wings.

"Play for me," he demanded, thrusting the beautiful instrument at the ghost. "Play for me this minute, before you
turn to moonlight or I wake up and it will be too late. For
my worst fear, old partner, is that I will forget what you
sounded like, who were—who are—the finest musician
in . . ."

Damiano shook his head, and the gray wings gathered
closer. "There is no time left for that, Gaspare. I AM moonlight; I came with the moon and will fade with it. Besides—
the lute and the playing of it is yours. But I will tell you one
very important thing—old partner . . ."

Gaspare leaned close to the dimly shining spirit, trying to
quiet his ragged breath. Damiano's serious face grew clear,
and more intent, even as the rest of him darkened.

"Gaspare. In music, as in everything else, 'best' is an
empty word. Don't strive to be best, or you will wake up
one day and know yourself no good at all."

Saara's voice rapped out. "Enough! The moon is almost
gone! What did you mean, Dami? That he might know the
way to Satan's Hall?"

The ghost's smile returned again, ruefully. A ghostly hand
laid itself very lightly on Gaspare's bosom. "There." The
words came faintly. "He knows it there, for pride calls to
pride." Gaspare gasped and shrank away, but the spirit consoled him.

"I am not saying you are wicked, Gaspare, nor that you
belong to the Devil's own. Don't be a fool like I was, to let
him make you believe that! But you . . . like me . . . may
have an understanding of Satan. Raphael wonders if that is
what men are for, did you know? To understand the misery
of wickedness, as angels cannot. To feel pity for it."

The hand, almost invisible now, rose to touch Gaspare's
still unbristly chin. "I'll help you as I can, old friend. I

haven't forgotten that you were a very good manager to
me."

Gaspare swallowed hard. He wanted to believe he felt the
touch of that hand. "And I, sheep- . . . Damiano. I pray for
your peace each night—when I think to pray, of course."

"I know," whispered Damiano, and then Gaspare's eyes
could no longer see anything.

Saara rose to her feet, her trembling hand raised before
her. "Farewell, love," she called to the air.

"Love," came back the reply, or else an echo.

The moon was gone.

"What did he mean?" demanded Gaspare, as the whites
of his eyes glinted at Saara.

The Lapp woman subjected Gaspare to an uncomfortable
scrutiny. "He meant," she said at last, "that you can tell me
how to find and enter Satan's stronghold."

"He meant that?" Both Gaspare's hands clapped to the
sides of his head. "I know Satan's stronghold?" His stiff fin
gers stood up like antlers. "If he knows I know that, then he
knows a lot more about me than I do about myself!"

Saara yawned, glancing up at the starlit sky. "That is the
first wise thing I have ever heard from your mouth, Gas
pare." She walked over to him, somewhat stiff from her
hours on the chill earth. She laid her hand on his rather
pointed red head and rumpled his hair. "Come now: It's
time to sleep. In the morning we can worry at the spirit
puzzles."

4

The night was more confusing than the daytime. During
some hours Raphael slept, forgetting pain, abandonment
and the unpleasant feeling of being cold. But these inter
ludes were interrupted by wakefulness, which, like a prod

ding finger, reminded him he was lost. And toward morning he was visited by an experience as miserable as wakefulness but different: his first nightmare.

It was the sparrow again, gripping a bare twig with claws more brittle than the wood, its dusty feathers rutched against a light fall of snow.

It had no song. This vision brought with it a sense of desolation unalloyed by hope.

There was something here he was supposed to understand—he knew that much, at least—and with undemanding patience Raphael was prepared to let the dream unfold until he did understand. But with the first light the slave women began to stir in their chains, and very soon Perfecto (who had also spent a very bad night) was awake and kicking everybody else except Hakiim into rising. His kick to Raphael was perfunctory, for, truth to tell, Perfecto felt an inexplicable distrust of this gift almost amounting to terror.

The new slave did not respond to the urging, because he was not yet finished with his dream. But with the increasing noise and bustle of the camp, the dream finished with him; it flew off, offended.

Still Raphael did not move. He had an idea that if he kept his eyes closed long enough—if he denied the activity around him long enough—they would all pack up and go away. And that seemed very desirable this morning.

He listened to the chatter of the women and the bray of the mules. His throat tightened with unconscious imitation of the noises both made. Stop it, he told himself. Rest again. Make it go away.

Perfecto came back, and the kick he delivered was harder. "Get up, idiot!" the Spaniard snarled. "We're traveling today if we have to drag you by a mule's tail."

The blow hurt, but it certainly didn't induce Raphael to obey. Instead he screwed his eyes tighter.

Make it go away.

And Perfecto did go away.

Raphael was immensely heartened. He curled into a more comfortable ball and waited for sleep to take him again. Hakiim, the Moor, was whispering to someone close by. It was easy to ignore the sound.

The pointy little foot caught him between the ribs and its big toe jabbed and wiggled. "Get up, Pinkie! You get up right now or I'll stuff dirt up your nose!"

It was not the threat but Djoura's tone of voice that smote him. Guilt and remorse splashed through Raphael, all the worse for the fact that he'd no experience with either feeling. He clambered up, tripped in his voluminous gown, rose again, and stood tottering beside her, looking down at the top of her jingling headdress.

The Berber possessed no veil to her headdress. Her excellent teeth shone whiter against a skin as opaque and lampblack as she gave Raphael a wolfish smile. "I knew you just needed encouragement," she said.

Then she walked around him. He gave a yelp of pain as his dress was pulled free of the scabbing wounds on his back. Djoura patted him as one would a horse. "There there. It's over now. Better quick, I always think."

Again the Berber stood before him. "Well, sieve-head, how are we this cold morning?"

"We are unhappy," he replied carefully in her own tongue. Djoura's eyes opened wide.

"Don't!" she hissed at him, peering left and right from uner the folds of cloth. "If you want to keep your . . . don't seem too able, you see? Don't let them know!"

Raphael did not see. He had difficulty following elliptical statements. In fact, his confusion at this point was so great it did not allow him to ask questions.

Djoura, after ascertaining that no one in the little caravan was paying attention to them, continued. "You must hide two things, Pinkie, if you wish to come to a better situation. Your brain is the first, and your bollucks are the second. No one must see evidence of either one but your friend Djoura—do you understand?"

"No," he answered readily, glad to have a question within his ability.

The Berber snorted and shifted from foot to foot. In this manner she resembled a tall, thin tent swaying in the breeze. "I will say it in different words.

"I say to you, Pinkie: Do not show anyone your manhood! And do not speak to anyone but Djoura, and then only

when no one else can hear. She alone is your friend. Will
you do that?"

"I will do that."

Djoura heaved a great sigh and rolled her eyes to heaven,
which she could not see for the row of copper coins which
shaded her forehead. "Excellent." Then she brushed her
hands together, removing invisible dust.

Hakiim was passing near. Out of habit he put out a hand
to slap the Berber woman on her hip. Habit germinated the
gesture, but prudence and Djoura's warning stare aborted
it. "Now, Pinkie." She spoke in a loud voice. "Last night we
practiced pissing. This morning I think we should do some
work on eating, don't you think?"

Raphael considered this with furrowed brow. He remembered to wait until Hakiim had passed down the line (to
another woman with a more approachable anatomy) before
he replied, "I think I would like to practice pissing again."

Watching the eunuch eat was a good joke; it almost
served to quell Hakiim's new mistrust of his partner. First
there was a problem getting the poor stick to open his
mouth. After harsh words and some manual probing on the
part of his nurse, Djoura, it was discovered that he had
been sucking on a stone. When the black attempted to
throw the pebble away, he clawed it from her and locked it
in his right hand, from whence none of the woman's
strength could release it.

After this he got his face stuffed with cereal.

The slave merchants sat beside their chain of human
wares, eating their own breakfast. They had only bulgur in
oil and vinegar, the same as everyone else; their condition
elevated them by no more than the two squares of silk car-
peting on which they rested. Except, of course, that one
tended to feel much more elevated without chains upon the
neck or wrist.

"Look at him!" cried the Moor in glee. "Such emotion—
pathos and ecstasy! Our new boy wears his heart upon his
sleeve!"

Hakiim hardly exaggerated, for Raphael's first taste of
food brought tears to his large blue eyes. One taste and it

was to him as though all the world's jangle and whine were being brought into harmony. Once Djoura put the cool, oily mass on his tongue his mouth took over and transferred custody to his throat, which effortlessly took it down, and after that he was not aware of the bulgur at all, except as a spreading contentment.

He took some in his own hand. (His left hand. Disgusting.) And he repeated the process.

Perfecto watched with an eye which was physically as well as morally jaundiced. "Hugghh! Perhaps the idiot will work out after all."

Djoura's own eyes, very black and very white, flickered from the Spaniard to her charge. She leaned unobtrusively forward. The next time Raphael scooped from the red clay pot and filled his mouth, the little toe of his left foot was violently wrenched.

He choked. Cereal spattered from his mouth and nose. The Berber came forward with her bit of rag. "Hah! See what happens when you play the pig?" she said loudly. Then, in a whisper, she added, "Don't be so cursed independent."

"I wouldn't get my hopes up," replied Hakiim to Perfecto.

The mules of Andalusia were justly famous, being bred from the giant asses found in that country. Hakiim and Perfecto rode two sleek gray animals the size of large horses. Four other mules ambled behind, laden with gear. Beside the mule train, like an attendant serpent, paced the line of female slaves. As the morning was still cool, they were chattering among themselves.

For it had been found impossible to keep seven women (most of whom must not be disfigured in any way) from talking, and the quietest, most orderly solution had been to attach them in linguistic groups. The Saqalibah spoke in a patois of their own Central European language and Arabic. The two Andalusians behind them spoke Spanish and ignored the poor mongrel creature at the tail of the line. They were young, these two Spanish women, and therefore valu-

ble. They hissed slyly to one another without end and
naded their faces with tattered shawls.

On the other side of the mules, proudly isolated, strode
Djoura the black Berber, with Raphael stumbling after.

She went fast: as fast as any mule desired to walk. Hakiim
atched her without moving his head.

Now there was a valuable property. Perfecto didn't un-
erstand how valuable Djoura was, being blinded by the
paniard's distaste for black skin. But the woman was
oung, straight, immensely strong, and had all her teeth.
nd pretty, too, if one could look past her scowl.

Still, she talked like a Berber.

Hakiim was not a Moor of Granada, but a Moor of Tunis,
nd he knew that in the far south there WERE blacks ac-
epted as Berbers. A few.

I worry too much, he thought to himself. And imme-
iately the eunuch bobbed into view, presenting himself to
Iakiim's attention.

Djoura had been very industrious, and now the gangling
reature wore not a shapeless gown but a pair of baggy
omen's pants. Where did she get them? His gaze darted
ack to the moving tent that was the black woman.

She must have been wearing them, all this time. Hakiim
ched to know what Djoura WAS wearing. He had seen her
aked, of course, in Tunis. He was too downy a fellow to
urchase a woman on the strength of flashing black eyes and
white smile. (No. Snarl.) But he hadn't then paid atten-
on to the dusky pile of cloth on the pavement beside her.

Hakiim itched to know Djoura in other ways, too, but his
nstincts told him not to scratch. The world was full of
omen, with most of whom one did not require a club.

That eunuch too. Had he been raised for pleasure? Filthy
egeneracy. Hakiim spat sideways, causing his mule's
ars—long as the leaf spears of a palm—to rotate toward
im.

But that sort of thing was done, and it was none of a mer-
hant's business to lecture the world. And the tall boy, with
is pink, hairless skin and his head as yellow as a buttercup:
Ie might still serve for any man who cared for idiots.

Analytically the Moor regarded the eunuch's scourge back. Not bad, really. Not as bad as it had seemed at first all covered with dried blood and with the gown stuck to it. Pale skin showed scars least. He would have it covered with grease tonight.

If only they had a month instead of two days to reach Granada. Then the welts would have a chance to fade. Perhaps they should farm the creature out to sell later, or cheaper, keep him in a stable until the others were sold and he was ready to leave Granada.

But as Hakiim pondered and watched, the fair slave took a tumble, tripping over nothing at all. Without sense to grab onto his chain, he let it tighten around his neck. Djoura's wrist was whipped back by the force of Raphael's fall, and she rushed back to him, where he lay flat out on the earth, making little gagging sounds and clawing at his throat with his left hand. The right still clutched his pebble firmly.

No, whispered the Moor to himself. Nothing could be worth keeping him another month. Nothing.

Perfecto pulled his steed up beside Hakiim. The serpent of women jingled to a stop. The Spaniard's yellow eye swept over the creature he had purchased, growing more glazed as they stared.

Raphael tottered again to his feet. Djoura examined his knees for bruises and brushed him off. Once more the mule train ambled forward, with the serpent shuffling beside.

"Do you think," Hakiim casually asked his partner, "that maybe our black lily has had children before? She certainly knows how to mother."

Perfecto had an odd complexion, which the sun tended to darken toward orange. He turned his yellow eye upon the Moor. "If she had, she wouldn't be acting this way. She'd have got it out of her system."

Dust deadened the color of what greenery grew beside the road; the berries of the juniper had lost their gloss. To the right of the road the land swept downward, and through the gaps in the stones glimpses of small, summer-blasted pools were visible. Those which were more water

ɪan mud scattered a sunflash so bright it hurt the ob-
ɛrver's eye.

Dust clogged Hakiim's nostrils and stung his cracked lips.
ᴇrfecto must be suffering worse, the Moor thought, in his
ᴘanish singlet and shirt which left the back of his neck and
ɪs few square inches of forehead exposed to the sun.
Ɩakiim regarded his partner's squat form analytically.

The fellow actually LOOKED the part of an ill-tempered
ɪan: rolls of fat under his neck burned the color of a village
ɔt, little hands darkening the mule's leather reins with
ᴠeat, eyes like those of a pig. Had Perfecto always looked
ᴋe that? (Had August always been so hot?) Three years the
ᴀrtners had plied their trade together, buying domestics
ɪd selling them. Eight times had Hakiim made the voyage
ᴐ the markets of Africa and returned to Granada with ex-
tics. Eight times had Perfecto disappeared into the wilds
f Spain and reappeared with oddly assorted women. It was
ᴐssible he crossed into Christian lands to gather his mer-
ʜandise. If so, the Spaniard was ready to risk a lot for
ɪoney.

More than Hakiim was, at any rate.

Eight times was enough, the Moor decided. Dealing
ᴠith slaves had given him a certain sense about people, or
ɛveloped a sense that all are born with. Hakiim could
ɪell when a slave was mad, and when she was dangerous.
ɪd he could usually estimate the amount of danger in-
ɔlved.

So with Djoura, Hakiim felt no fear, but neither did he
ɛt too close. With the idiot eunuch (not mad, only con-
ɪsed) there was no danger except that of soiling one's
ɔthes.

But Hakiim dropped his mule back behind Perfecto and
ᴇ watched his partner. Eight times was enough.

Why don't you die, Perfecto silently asked his new ac-
ʊisition as the eunuch followed Djoura, alternately stum-
ᴅing and scampering at the end of his iron chain. After a
ᴡ hours the fellow had learned to hold the links in his
ᴀnds so that he was not choked every time the black caught
ɪm unawares.

If only the creature had curled up and died last night: of cold or of injuries or merely of Satan's malignity. He certainly looked ready to be carried off, with his breath panting and his blue eyes rolling and all the flies on his back. If he had died, then Perfecto would have had the perfect excuse for Satan, and he would not be sitting there now in such a sick funk of worry that his bowels were churning and his collar seemed too tight.

What sort of creature was it? One of Satan's human servants who had failed his task? (Perfecto had never YET failed, he reminded himself.) A recreant priest, perhaps. The robe he had been sold in had a clerical cut. The Spaniard shuddered, and his mule replied in sympathy.

He could be anything—even a eunuch. Perfecto had announced him a eunuch, certainly, but that had been only to smooth over the inconvenience of this arrival in the pack train. He had expected Hakiim would discover the untruth of this claim within minutes, upon which Perfecto would proclaim himself ill-used by the seller and would promise to have this mistake rectified in Granada.

But Hakiim had trusted his word. How odd. And Djoura had said nothing. He glanced mistrustfully at the black woman.

Well, maybe Perfecto had told the truth by accident. The demon had not said the man was entire, after all, and Perfecto hadn't bothered to pull off the gore-soaked dress. Why shouldn't Satan be served by eunuchs?

But what if he were neither a gelded man nor entire? It was still possible the noble fair head would blossom into a thing of horror and teeth.

Tonight Perfecto would sleep under a crucifix, if any of the women possessed such a device. If not, he would piece together a cross of some sort, even if only two sticks. Let the cursed paynim laugh! Perfecto was sick to death of Hakiim's sneers and slurs and Moorish pretense. If he had his way . . .

Come to think of it, it might be figured that Satan owed him something for disposing of the blond. (If it was not a trick. If it was not a trick.) Once the lot of them were sold in

Granada. Once the money was in his hands . . . It would
not be difficult to find another partner.

Perfecto embarked on a reverie which imparted a much
sweeter expression to his face. Hakiim was emboldened to
speak.

"You know how I call it, Perfecto? You want to hear the
order in which they will sell, for how much and to whom?"

Perfecto returned to the breathless, stifling present. "Oh,
not that again."

"Why not?" the Moor replied. "Am I not always correct?
About both the money and the buyer? I have a knack for
these things . . .

"First," Hakiim continued, urging his mount up to his
partner's, "the larger of the two locals will go, because her
age will make her cheap and yet she is sound. To a miller or
a weaver perhaps: some small businessman who doesn't
want any fight in his bondswomen.

"The Saqalibah will go next, but not together. As domestics, is my guess: all of them. The little local will sell after
that, for a good price and to a peasant.

"The old woman? I don't know, but I think we'll keep her
longest. Depends how many households are looking for
goosegirls or goatherds this summer."

Perfecto listened to this involved prophecy without a
murmur. He didn't give a damn, himself, as long as the sale
produced enough gold to take one man (one man) from Granada to some place far away. But it occurred to him that
Hakiim had made a large omission.

"What about the black? Don't you think we can sell her at
all?"

Hakiim's eyebrows rose and he gestured one finger in the
air. "Perfecto, my old friend, you still do not believe in our
dark lily's worth! I have no intention of standing her under
the sun in the common market."

"Why not?" growled the other. "Can't tan her any
worse."

The Moor's eyes shifted under his immaculate headdress.
This was better: more like the crude but predictable Perfecto of past years. If only he could rid himself of that prick-
ling down his back when he looked at the Spaniard . . .

"Djoura is a beautiful girl, Perfecto. Strong and young."

"Who'd as soon kill you as look at you."

Hakiim shrugged. "She comes from the desert (Although it would be better, maybe, if we didn't mention that in Granada. At least not around any sons of Islam.) and she has gone from hand to hand, not knowing a steady master. With expert taming, she could be made loyal, and even affectionate. I will advertise her by private treaty only."

Some streak of pugnacity prodded Perfecto to remark, "So why haven't you mentioned the eunuch?"

The answer was inevitable. "I don't believe we can sell him." But the silence which followed this answer had a character which terrified Hakiim. He found himself babbling, "I want no trouble about this, Perfecto. How much did you pay for him? If the price was not exorbitant then I will pay you its equivalent out of my own pocket."

The Spaniard turned in his high wooden saddle. His eyes were set so deep in the seamed and folded flesh that Hakiim could see but one tiny spark out of each. "And then what," he growled. "And then do what with the eunuch himself?"

"Loosen the chain," Hakiim replied.

Despite the jouncing weight of Perfecto's face, it contrived to set in hard lines. "Leave the idiot in the desert? He would die before nightfall."

(How he would love to. If only he dared.)

Hakiim's confusion slid into pure mystification. He had always been the one of the pair whose natural bent had been toward liberality, as long as it didn't cost too much. What was there between the idiot eunuch and Perfecto? A relationship of blood, perhaps? He glanced again at the slave's features.

The eunuch was walking more competently now, and his face bore a very convincing look of deep concentration. His newly washed hair, like silk fabric, fell in waves and folds about his face.

No relationship. Impossible.

"Not in the desert," Hakiim replied to Perfecto. "In a village, secretly. Or at the walls of Granada itself. He will have as good a chance of charity as any beggar—and he can be nothing else but a beggar."

Perfecto turned his body back to the front. He looked neither at the eunuch nor at his partner. "Moor," he announced. "I swear I will sell this boy in Granada. I HAVE sworn it. I will shed blood before denying my oath."

Hakiim stared at the back of Perfecto's head. Whose, he wondered. Whose blood?

In the middle of the day Raphael was fed once more of the same cereal and vinegar, and he was allowed a few minutes' rest in the shade of a wall.

This was in a small village, where the houses crowded together as though they had been built in the middle of a city and the city then taken away from around them. The slaves in their bird-flock fashion lined the cool stone wall, ignoring the villagers with the same intensity the villagers ignored them. Indeed, in everyones' eyes, the difference of caste between these tattered Spaniards and the slave women was insuperable. Yet each group felt itself the more respectable, for the slaves took their status (in their own eyes, at least) from their masters, and no one in this congeries of huts would ever own a domestic.

Djoura alone bothered to look at the scene around her, with its naked babies and almost hairless yellow dogs. And her gaze was as removed and disinterested as that of an observer at a menagerie.

Her Pinkie looked, too, of course. Raphael gazed about himself with friendly curiosity, unbroken even when an infant of four years scuttled up and threw a wad of dried cow dung into his lap. The blond closed his eyes and listened to the chatter as though it were music.

Once again life erased its miseries for Raphael and he was free to think about his condition.

It had been terrible, and now was only bothersome. The difference between the two conditions seemed to be connected with what he had eaten and drunk, and when. The time of day mattered too. Cold and dark were unpleasant.

But so was hot sun. And hard stone. And flies that bit. And being kicked or glared at.

It seemed to him he was suspended between a thousand little-understood needs of the flesh and another thousand outside sources of pain. These established his course, as the course of a pebble was established once it was dislodged from the top of a hill.

But that reminded him of his own pebble. Raphael's hand felt sweet relief as he opened his fist and looked at Damiano's gift.

It was such a pretty pebble, all brown and rough with faint white stripes, and it looked as much like a piece of a corkscrew as anything.

Damiano had been a man—he had been born a man. Yet HE had not seemed to let himself be knocked back and forth between pain and desire, like Raphael was. Damiano had called, "If you have the time, Seraph . . ." very considerately, and had smiled to greet him. Had he been in such misery, then, hiding it all from his friend? Surely Raphael would have seen.

No, it must have been that living as a man was an art which might be mastered. And Damiano, who had done so, was still with Raphael—somewhere, somehow. In a pebble. Flexing his cramped fingers, Raphael stuffed the pebble into the corner of his mouth, beside his back molar.

"I am Raphael," he said aloud, in Damiano's language. "I am not just kicks and heat and hunger. I was before these things, and will be after. I am my Father's musician." He raised his eyes to the southern distance, where sand and dust fell away toward the sea he could not see, the sea they were leaving further behind each day.

Djoura heard these foreign words in Pinkie's voice. Surreptitiously she glanced over, and the blond's face startled her.

He looks as stern as a king, she thought. Praise be to Allah, could it be my sieve-head's mind is coming back to him?

But if it were so, why didn't he talk sense? She gouged his hip with her muscular toe.

"Hiss, Pinkie! Who are you talking to?"

He shifted the pebble in his mouth before answering. "I am talking to my Father," he replied.

She giggled. "I see. Did he answer you?"

"No," Raphael answered simply. "He doesn't anymore."

* * *

Perfecto was thinking, I will accompany him out of the city this time; he will not suspect anything in that. And with all the money I will buy a hundred Masses for protection.

It was an act of grace to kill a paynim. It was holy.

"My uncle will take me in easily, and with this last profit I can buy a small date-palm planting and a couple of boys to keep it. I will not say a word to him, just get on my ship and disappear."

Hakiim's mule swiveled its ears, seeming to reproach him for the plan. "A promise to the infidel is no promise at all," he whispered to the beast.

Djoura observed Raphael narrowly. No longer did he move like a lout, nor roll his eyes like a simpleton. Too much longer and the swine on muleback would realize what they had here, and her new-budded plans would go for nothing. The woman sidled up to Raphael and did her best to trip him.

"The birds in the air," Raphael sand silently, despite his sore feet and scourged back. "The fish in the water, washing their backs in light."

Joy came from somewhere to him: a gift as solid as stone.

5

The bees were already awake, but then the bees had retired earlier than Saara. She stepped from her hut into the light to find Gaspare stretched on the ground, waiting for her. His orange hair and red face shone like two clashing flames against he green of the bee balm. The young man leaped to his feet.

"I can do it for you, my lady," he stated, biting off his words with force. "Give me two silver florins and seven days and I can do it." His frosty green eyes bore into hers, while his long mouth fairly trembled with intensity.

Saara, who had not slept well, was beset with a desire to turn around and go back indoors, pulling the door behind her. Instead she yawned, combed her hair with her fingers and replied, "Do what, Gaspare?"

"Go to the Devil," he replied.

Saara lowered herself onto the gray rock which stood beside her door. This rock had a shape rather like that of some quadripedal animal with very round sides and stubby legs. She called this rock her housedog, although the rock had come first, with the house being built behind it.

She considered the possibility that Gaspare were joking with her. He did not appear to be joking, and certainly the boy had had enough stupid ideas in the past, but one could have stupid ideas and still make jokes. Finally Saara said, "I have known men to go to the Devil before without needing two silver florins."

His lips pulled away from his teeth as he answered, "Ah, but without money it takes longer."

Now Saara was certain he was joking. Almost certain. She sighed, wondering once again why Italians had to be like that. "The problem is, young one, that we want to find the Liar, not be found by him."

Gaspare smiled and sat himself down at her feet. His face pulled into a taut smile as he looked across at her.

Not up at her, but across. And there was something in his thoughtful expression that prefigured the man that was to be, once all of Gaspare's tempers and gangling limbs had come to terms at last.

Saara felt something like a blow over the heart as she remembered the starved boy Gaspare in ragged clothes who grabbed her about the knees, spouting gallant rubbish, on the road to Avignon, and the same fourteen-year-old who stood white-faced and silent beside the body of his friend.

So she had seen one more boy grow out of childhood, and once again she hadn't noticed it happening.

This cannot go on forever, she said to herself. Everyone growing and growing old and dying except Saara. I do not want it to go on forever.

Gaspare was watching her face attentively. "Don't despair, my lady," he comforted her. "If Delstrego believes I can find old Scratch for you, then it must be that I can."

She shook her head. "It is too great a risk for you, Gaspare. Not only a risk of the body, but . . ."

He flushed to deep burgundy. "What? That again? By San Gabriele, woman, haven't you learned by now that I am Gaspare the lutenist, not some postulant of a cloistered order, to be saved from the contagion of the world!

"Why, Delstrego himself told you you needed my help. Would you throw away the word of the greatest musician of all Italy and Provence—and a blessed spirit besides?" His narrow form swelled with passion and he waved fingers all through the air.

"Delstrego himself," repeated Saara silently. Had Dami become history already, or a legend? What kind of legend died of the plague at the age of twenty-three?

A legend with one believer.

Or two.

But she understood the anger behind Gaspare's words. "No, Gaspare. You are right, and I of all people know better than to protect a person against his own will. If you want to help me find the way to Satan's Hall, I will accept your help thankfully."

Gaspare, who had been building up his emotions in case tantrums were necessary, felt his fury leak away. "Hah? Good, then, my lady."

But his voice still held an edge as he added, "You must remember that Raphael is my teacher. And my friend."

Saara stared at him coolly. "He makes a lot of friends, that one," she stated, and began braiding her damaged hair.

At the crown of the hill stood Gaspare, turning left and right in place. The sun of early morning sent shadows of birch over the ground like tangled lace, while the looming shadow of the larger sister peak to the northeast lapped up through the pines. The morning was impossibly sweet and beautiful, predicting a scorching day.

"Once," the young man pronounced, drawing his brow and scowling fiercely, "when Delstrego wanted to locate a man he didn't particularly like, he walked back and forth through a city, noting when he felt most bothered and irritated. In that manner he drew nearer and nearer, until he could feel the fellow's presence directly."

"It sounds like a good method," replied Saara, who sat with her back against the bole of the tree, chewing a stem of sourgrass. "Of course, HE was a witch."

Gaspare's overlarge pale eyes pulled away from the horizon to focus on Saara's small face. "Could it be that I am too, my lady, and never have known it? Perhaps that was what he meant when . . ."

"No," Saara cut in evenly. "But I wouldn't let that worry you. Being a witch has its drawbacks.

"Do you feel more bothered and irritated—or perhaps more proud, since it was supposed to be your pride which connected you to Satan—in one direction more than another?"

Once again Gaspare revolved, this time with his eyes closed and hands out, while his cheeks brightened to a cheery red. "I just feel immensely ridiculous," he replied.

The northerner nibbled her tattered leaf thoughtfully. She stared at her bare toes. "Is there any direction in which you feel more ridiculous than another?" she asked reasonably.

"Yes. To the north, where I can feel you watching me spin like a top."

Saara shot Gaspare a quick glance. "But I'm not. Not until now. I haven't looked at you once." Very quietly she rose and stepped past him.

The redhead dropped his hands to his hips, but his eyes remained sealed. "Well, how am I to know if you are or not?" He had a habit of forgetting to call Saara "my lady" when the least bit excited. Saara never noticed.

"I still feel ridiculous when I am facing you."

"Facing me or facing north?" came her voice from behind him. Gaspare jumped and swiveled. He blinked at her confusedly.

"Facing . . . north." His words were almost a whisper.

Saara's smile was slow and drawn. It aged her face.
"Good, then. Tell me, Gaspare, if you had to guess, and
Damiano had never said a word about pride calling to pride,
in which direction would you expect to find the Li—the
Devil?"

Gaspare folded himself on the turf beside her, mindful of
his skintight hose. "As a child, of course, I believed the
Devil lived under the Alps, in the heart of winter. All the
babies in San Gabriele are taught that.

"Now, being a man of some experience," (he did not see
or chose to ignore the flicker behind his companion's eyes)
"I know he is more to be found in the cities of the south,
doing his work among men."

Saara lifted her eyes to the green-black southern slopes,
out of which the third sister peak rose like a rock from the
sea. In the distance the haze was golden.

Then she turned her head (and like an owl, Saara could
turn it very far) to inspect the looming, purple north.

"I think we should not be in too much hurry to grow up,"
she commented.

"What would we do with him?" Saara exclaimed, for the
third time. "He is no goat, to bounce over the raw
rock . . ."

Gaspare clutched his handful of black horse mane
obstinately. "This is the very animal that Delstrego rode
through the mountains in the month of November, from
Partestrada to San Gabriele and beyond."

Saara ground her teeth together and thought that she
would shortly have heard enough about "Delstrego." "That
was on a road, I think. If I am right, we will have little
enough to do with roads on this journey. And when we
reach the Devil's window in the rock (if we ever do), then
what is the horse to do: grow wings and fly in?"

Gaspare glared from the restive gelding to Saara. "Then
he will walk home alone. It is no new thing for Festilligambe. He's more than half savage as it is."

Saara, too, peered into the animal's aristocratic face.
"Why don't we let him decide. If he is to take the risk . . ."

Gaspare snorted sullenly. His rapprochement with the black gelding was too hard-won for him to want to walk when he could ride. And he wasn't sure he trusted the witch, who could pretend to ask and then tell him the horse had said whatever she wished it to say.

But the justice of her proposal could not be denied. "As then."

Saara put one little hand beneath the horse's round chin where spiky guard hairs grew untouched by knife or razor. "Festigi—Festilli—Festie—oh, horse! Tell me, do you want to accompany us north into the Alps, toward that presence we saw together by the wine-shop door in San Gabriele? And will you help us to fight him?"

The gelding's head snapped up into the air. He did an oversized double take, and then, rearing, he spun around and vanished down the hillside.

"Don't feel bad," said Saara gently to Gaspare. "Horses are not meant to be brave."

But Gaspare did feel bad. He felt utterly desolate, and unworthy besides, for he remembered this same cowardly gelding standing foursquare over his injured master, holding off eight men and four whips. In three years he—Gaspare of San Gabriele—had not won the animal's heart. Doubtless he never would.

"It's nothing," he told Saara, looking away. "He always knew I preferred dogs." And he paced heavily down the hill among the birch trees.

Gaspare's few possessions were tied in a square of linen, two ends of which went around his waist and two ends of which went around his shoulders. The lute in its sheepskin case he carried. Saara carried nothing.

The day was fulfilling its high-summer promise, but in the aromatic pine woods of the hill's lower slopes, it was still cool.

"There is a broad road not far north of Ludica," Gaspare was calling to the woman behind him. "It runs all the way from Franche-Comté. In the east it leads to . . . to the faraway east, I think. Once we strike that, we will have easy

ng, and our choice of trails going into the Alps them-
ves . . .

"Then we will have to take our bearings again, and I must
rch my heart for presence of the Devil, as Delstrego
d. In fact, I ought to do so constantly, lest we lose our
h and valuable time . . ."

Though she knew more about the roads of Lombardy
n Gaspare could hope to, Saara let him prattle on. She
s used to Italians by now, and besides, she wanted to
ep an eye on the shadow in the woods—bulky, black,
ry—that was following them.

As Gaspare detailed his plans for self-examination (they
olved certain mental imageries of food, drink, cards,
e, and other appealing objects to which he alluded ellip-
lly), this shadow rose onto the path behind, stepping
ntly on the carpet of needles. Saara faded off the path
l let it pass.

For twenty steps the black horse paced behind Gaspare
hout making his presence known. Then he nudged with
nose.

The gangling youth skittered forward, flailing for balance.
en he turned in outrage and confronted Festilligambe,
o stood motionless behind him with muzzle touching the
und and ears flat out to the sides.

Gaspare also stood frozen, though he blinked repeatedly.
last he put his hand on the gelding's bony withers and he
hed.

Since Delstrego had been known to play his lute while
ing, nothing could stop Gaspare from doing the same.
: did not do so happily, however, for he was never com-
tely relaxed on horseback, and his knees gripped Fes-
igambe's sides like iron tongs.

But the horse picked its way along the rough ground with
g-cherishing care, for the dove which perched on its
inted head had told him just what would happen if he
lled the lutenist. Slowly the gelding climbed into the
sh air of the mountains, wondering all the while why any-
e would want to go to a place with so little grass.

Saara's bird body was breathing heavily. She had shru
to dove size so as to keep up with the horse without burde
ing him further, but by the give-and-take of magic, it co
her just as much effort to ride thus as it would have to clir
at the gelding's side.

Listening to Gaspare's lute playing was another payme
of sorts, for Saara. That the boy had control of his instr
ment was obvious. His sense of time was good, and I
rhythms were highly original. But Saara had been born in
a culture where chant was the most respected form of m
sic, and Gaspare's carefully cultivated dissonances ups
both her nerves and her digestion.

Yet she said nothing, for among the Lapps (who were
song wizards), to tell a person to stop his music was to te
him to stop his being. She merely wondered if the twigs
the alpine willow would be effective against headache.

Gaspare, who had been raised (or who had raised hir
self) in the shadow of the mountains, drank deep lungfuls
air scented with evergreens, and he turned his eaglet's fa
to the stony north. He felt sparks of energy within him li
the sparks the horse's feet made hitting stone. Gaspare h
only the vaguest idea where they were going, but he h
confidence.

Saara did not, for she had no faith in their present cours

It was not that she doubted the words of the spirit, b
she knew that there is no translation as difficult as that b
tween the living and the dead, and what Damiano h
meant by saying Gaspare knew the way to the Liar's h
might be something completely different from having t
boy lead her there.

In fact, would Damiano—who had rather died than l
her risk herself—have sanctioned bringing this clum
young fellow into danger of body and of spirit? If he HA
meant for Gaspare to fling himself against Satan, then t
dead were indeed a different order than the living. A
though Damiano's suggestion was little more than Saara h
protested that same night on her own behalf—that o
must not keep a soul from its proper risks—still she found
difficult to extend that liberty to others whom she felt we
not fit to meet the challenge. Gaspare, for instance. Wl

could he do against pure wickedness, and how could he
survive?

Saara shuddered over the ruthless understanding of the
dead.

But perhaps it was all in error. Perhaps he had meant she
would find the path by looking in the boy's eyes, or in some
ceremony of their Christian church. She had never studied
these Italians' rites. Perhaps Gaspare was right in supposing
that the Devil (this time) lay in the south.

Perhaps, perhaps. Doubt, like black water, seeped into
her small feathered body and chilled her. She felt old.

She WAS old: old and past her prime. Off on a fool's errand, and caught in a battle of spirits which would have
been too great for her strength anytime. She would be trod-
den underfoot, and Gaspare—he would fly screaming, only
to be taken by the Liar and twisted beyond recognition. It
would have been better not to have come. It would be better now to turn back. To Lombardy or farther. All the way
back to the frozen fens of home.

The dove's heart tripped and pounded. Her vision swam
and her wings grew numb. She felt the cold, groping fingers
search toward her, impelling rout.

She felt rather than saw Gaspare raise his head from his
instrument. He made a noise in his throat.

"Play, Gaspare," the bird cried. "Don't lose the beat!"

Gaspare obeyed out of a musician's reflex, counting silently and coming down heavy on the bass, while Saara retreated into the simple, incorruptible thoughts of a bird.
After a moment or two the vile blind fingers passed over
and faded.

Saara sighed and fluttered to the stones of the road. In
another moment she was human again. She clutched her
head in both hands. "Gaspare," she began, her voice
quavering like that of an ancient. "Gaspare, young one. You
keep your lute handy; it is your greatest protection.

"Do you understand me?" she added, for Gaspare was
staring blankly down at her braided head.

He did not answer directly, but asked in turn, "What do
you mean, protection? Has something happened?"

Saara herself was shaking. She slid down against a rock and hid her head in her arms. "Yes, of course. Didn't you feel the attack? I can still smell it in the air!"

Gaspare shifted his scarecrow anatomy on the horse's black back. "I feel only that my butt is a little sore. And smell?" He took a deep snort. "I smell the air of the mountains. It's very good."

Saara's hazel eyes pitied his obtuseness. "Nonetheless, young one, there has been great danger here."

She bit her lip. "It is as I feared. All the while we are looking for the Devil, he is looking for us."

It was quite correct; Lucifer was attempting to repair his neglect of the primitives in this world, at least to the extent of locating Saara and dealing with her.

And though he had enjoyed Raphael's misery with good appetite, it was the angel's confusion and sense of abandonment which really pleased his palate. After a little while that confusion subsided, because even in the form of a human slave Raphael could not be kept wholly apart from grace. In fact, the most satisfying waves of desperation in the little drama were coming from the Spaniard Perfecto, and such anguish was a cheap drink and unsubtle.

So now Lucifer was taking the time to seek out ants, which is to say, he was looking for the bothersome Saara. He had not forgotten the teeth of the bear in his neck.

But Saara, though powerful, was not a terribly complex person. She was not prone to greed, and understood neither sin nor sanctity. She had no more shame than a bird on a branch.

Consequently, she was very difficult for Lucifer to find.

He stepped away from his window. "Kadjebeen," he whispered sweetly to the air. "Kadjebeen, I have a bone to pick with you."

The raspberry demon waddled unhappily out from under the table. His eye stalks were wilted as he regarded his infernal master. "I'm sorry, Your Magnificence," he squeaked nervously. "Whatever it was, I will not do it again."

Lucifer's blue eyes flickered. "You won't disarm me so easily, you mountebank. I thought I told you to beat that scum till he was half-dead."

"Yes, well, so I did, Lord."

Lucifer's elegant brow rose in feigned surprise. "You did? Then why, may I ask, can I perceive him from out this window, trotting quite competently down a road in Granada, only four and twenty hours later?"

Kadjebeen's eyes (also blue, like those of a scallop) stared at one another and blinked. They knotted together in thought, and at last the demon replied, "Your Magnificence, it is difficult to know exactly how much of life or death makes half. I thought that if I erred, it ought to be on the conservative side."

"You have always got an answer," drawled Lucifer, frozen faced, and he raised his carnelian hand. The raspberry demon ran (rolled, really) across the floor at great speed, but he was not fast enough.

"What use IS the stupid beast!" spat Gaspare with childish disdain as he and Saara together tried to haul a scrabbling Festilligambe up the slick bulge of a road-blocking boulder. On the other side of this obstacle lay miles of road, flat land and a choice of roads, but it seemed that near was no closer than far, for they had been struggling with the horse all afternoon. The gelding's frantic pants left little crystal clouds in the air.

"Do not blame him," chided Saara. "He cannot help that this is no road for horses." With what would have been suicidal confidence in a less stock-wise person, she got behind the horse, next to his dancing hind feet, and pushed. Festilligambe wedged one hoof securely into a crack in the stone and his sweating black quarters rippled with effort.

He was up.

Gaspare, who was still pulling, was knocked flat and overrun. Festilligambe's hooves slipped and skidded around Gaspare's head.

The redhead rose howling, both hands clapped to the back of his head. "Murder! Son of a sow! Bladder full of piss! You touch me once more and I'll knife your black belly!"

Saara put her hand against Festilligambe's shoulder, averting the horse's natural hysteria. She herself was scandalized. "Gaspare! What shame to threaten a fine, useful beast—who didn't even step on you!

"Control yourself, young one. It was you who wanted him to come."

Gaspare did not often remember his mother or her abortive efforts to discipline him. As a matter of fact, the woman was best forgotten, but Saara's maternal correction sent him into a rage.

"Wanted him? Yes, I wanted to ride, but the sow's son has dragged his feet for all of a week. He is spoiled meat, and overdue for the whip!"

"The whip!" he repeated, snapping his fingers by his right ear. The words had given rise to the idea. But Gaspare didn't have a whip, so frantically he grabbed for the end of the makeshift halter rope.

Saara had no intention of allowing Gaspare to beat the horse. To exercise one's passions on a beast of burden was one of the worst crimes of her nomadic society. She could stop Gaspare with three words sung in ascending melody, and she opened her mouth to do so.

But Gaspare needed no spell to freeze him, for he stood still with the rope end raised in one shaking hand, while the horse rolled his eyes at him. Silence was broken only by the sweet calls of the alpine birds. He shook his head, as though denying something which was being said to him.

And there was something in the heavy flush of Gaspare's face and the shallow glint of his mad eye which pulled a memory from Saara. That carnelian visage, and that cold light of hate . . .

Saara raised her head and sniffed the air. She felt no attack, no approaching hand of despair over her.

It was Gaspare's personal battle.

And it seemed the boy was at loggerheads with himself. His shoulders were hunched and his fists balled, as though he would throw himself at some invisible obstacle. His lip trembled and his hairless chin went slick with sweat. Saara watched with guarded pity, too wise to interfere. What was the Devil's weapon here: pride, as Damiano had warned im, and the anger that it nourished? Saara could not know. Nor did she want to know, for it was none of her business.

Without anything obvious happening—neither change in the light of afternoon nor in the interrogative calls of the birds—the battle was ended. Gaspare straightened. His large eyes softened from steel-white to green, and his hands relaxed. He gave a great exhausted sob.

"Gaspare," whispered Saara. He turned to her.

"Look about you now," she commanded. "And tell me which way."

The young man did not ask for an explanation. With a weary face he peered into the distance first right and then left. Finally he pointed directly north. "This way," he grunted. "There is no doubt."

Gaspare had not picked an easy path. After a few miles there was some doubt he had picked a path at all. The travelers found themselves in a cleft of round stones between jagged piled cliffs. There were few trees and little grass, though Festilligambe plunged his black muzzle into any damp-looking crevice he saw.

Coming to a crest in a trail which seemed to have been created only by the rain, they found themselves in the reverse of the position they had been in only an hour previously. The ground dropped suddenly by at least six feet, and the fall was almost sheer to bare stone below.

"We cannot take the horse down this," announced Saara. "We must retrace our steps and go around."

"Go around what?" asked her companion, with an ironical lift to his eyebrows. "The Alps?" He gestured from the slab of granite on their left to that of basalt upon their right. Evening light had turned the west to gold, while the black basalt loomed uncomfortably close.

Saara bit her lip. She was not feeling especially confident, and it was late in the day for decisions. "Back to the crossroad then. At least there is flat ground on which to sleep, and some grass."

Gaspare looked at the horse's ribs. "Yeah. He could use it," he grudgingly admitted. He took the animal's halter in his hand. "Although I'd rather be beat by fists than have to endure that upsy downsy one more time.

"Come on, boy," Gaspare said to Festilligambe. "You can't help being a dumb, clumsy horse who can't climb hills."

Festilligambe did not have a speaking tongue, and even after the association first with Damiano and now with Saara, he did not understand Italian.

But he did understand something, for with a twist of his sinuous neck he freed himself from Gaspare's grip. He gathered his quarters under him and threw himself off the little cliff and into space.

Festilligambe was an excellent jumper. He had once cleared an eight-foot wall burdened by two (very skinny) riders. But he had never before flown, so when Saara and Gaspare saw the gelding give a great kick with his hind feet, twist in the air, and disappear, they could do nothing but stare.

Gaspare flung himself face down at the edge. "He's . . . he's not there!" the redhead exclaimed. "Not running away, not broken on the stones. Where the hell DID he go?"

Saara, though she stood wide-eyed, was thinking. After a few silent moments she motioned to Gaspare. "Don't worry, young one."

"What do you mean, don't worry? The brute has my water bag on him. He has my LUTE!"

Saara only smiled. "Trust me, Gaspare. Trust me as I trust you. And I do trust you, for you are a true and faithful guide. Take my hand."

Gaspare glared dubiously at the witch, for after all her motherly proddings and botherations he could not believe she had suddenly perceived him as an object of romance.

She was forced to snag his hand by the knuckles. "Now, Gaspare. If you want to find your lute again.

"We go one, two, three, and . . .

"Jump!"

Gaspare had no choice. She dragged him to the edge and leaped off. He could either follow or be pulled head first.

A wrench. White granite blurred and twisted. Black

salt spread over the universe. Down went sideways and
hit on his hip and hands.

It was still evening. Festilligambe stood before him, with
spare's bag still safe, though it had slipped over the geld-
'g's neck and hung like a heavy pendant. The horse stood
three feet, resting one hooftip gingerly on the ground.
e nickered.

Saara was beside him, climbing slowly to her feet. Her
ess was dust-coated up the back and so was her hair. "I am
t a cat," the witch stated regretfully, rubbing the back of
r neck.

"What happened, my lady? What hit us?" Gaspare
hed his knees up under him. They were unwilling,
ming to belong to someone else.

Saara chuckled ruefully. "The edge of the world hit us,
spare. For me it was the second time, though it is easier
en one is a bird.

"But be glad. It means we are on the right path."

Gaspare ignored all this, for Saara was capable of talking
crazily as Delstrego in his prime. He stood up and stared
a welter of broken points of rock. "It doesn't look the
ne from down here," he said, and then he shivered.

"From up here," Saara corrected him. "And it shouldn't,
we've come a very long way, I think."

After a short cold night's sleep they were on their way
ain. Saara took bird form and made a sweep of the bare
ndy peaks, while Gaspare led Festilligambe along the
ly path they had.

It was a poor path and the beast was very hungry.

By the time the dove fluttered down again the horse had
used to move. Gaspare, weary of fighting and mistrusting
own temper, was seated on a bare stone. His back was
ned toward Festilligambe, while his gaze rested along a
re of the mountains, facing south. There the Alps tum-
d away to a low, mauve horizon. He started as Saara
ke.

"There is a tunnel ahead, boy: not natural, I think. The
th descends into it."

"Not natural!" Gaspare swiveled to find Saara seated on the horse's back, sidesaddle. "You mean it was made by . . . You mean we have found the doorway into hell?"

"I do not think so, for the hall I entered was high above ground in all its windows. Yet it is significant, I am sure."

Gaspare proceeded on tiptoe, though with Festilligambe's castanet hooves behind him he might have saved himself the trouble. Saara's little bare toes made no sound at all as they gripped rock and gravel.

"Odd," whispered the redhead, "that we've seen no one at all for days. We're not THAT far north, are we?"

His hissing voice echoed along the pass, amplified by some trick of sound. The noise continued long after he'd stopped talking.

"I have no idea where we are," answered the witch equably. "Not since we fell sideways off the rock. But I know it's where we want to go."

Now the sound in the air mimicked high wind, though no breath ruffled Festilligambe's mane. Then suddenly it was cut short, and the subsequent silence was even more ominous.

Saara slipped down from the horse, sniffing delicately. "What do you smell, Gaspare?"

The youth snorted obediently, and then again through curiosity. "I don't know, my lady. Sandalwood, perhaps?"

"Or, no: What's wrong with my nose to say that? I think it's a stable."

Saara did not laugh at these conjectures. Instead she wrinkled her brow. "More like fresh cut wood than horse dung, I think. But there's something animal in it, also."

They passed between a tower of granite and a sloping drop of some hundred feet, and there before them was white stone with a round black hole cut into it, and it was from this source that came both the odd wind noise and the smell.

Festilligambe balked. So did Gaspare. "We cannot go in there, Saara. It is altogether dark, and may pitch us down a cliff!"

The witch bit her lower lip and studied the entrance. It was regular and very smooth, but round as a foxhole. The rim of it was rounded and full of hardened bubbles, as though the rock were mere dried mud. "Not altogether dark. Unless it is very long, there will be some daylight in it. Give my eyes time and I will see what I need to see.

"You wait here," she said grandly, and she stepped under the arch.

Instantly Gaspare's refusal to continue warred with a contradictory anger at being left behind. He watched her glimmering slim figure fade into the depths. "Gaspare of San Gabriele," he growled aloud, "you ought to be ashamed. Really ashamed of yourself."

"And you too," he added spitefully to the trembling horse.

Dark, dark. Daylight faded much more quickly than Saara had expected. The witch had never studied bat form (not foreseeing that she would one day find herself in the velvet blackness at the heart of a mountain far above the plains of the earth), but she had studied the high art of making do, and she used every one of her human senses to test her progress.

The floor was smooth as a well-made roadbed and round as the sides of a barrel. The walls, scarcely fifteen feet apart, an smooth. Saara was tempted to give up a slow hands-and-feet approach, trusting the passage to remain level and intact. But Gaspare was right: there might be holes. If this tunnel had been built by the Liar (surely it was built by craft), there would likely be surprises of some nature.

Within, the smell was stronger: musky (like a stable, Gaspare had said) yet tinged with a dry perfume like that of no beast of her knowledge. The hissing wind came louder, and in regular gusts.

Surprises of some nature.

Saara resisted the temptation to change shape. What was the use in becoming a bear before one knew bear qualities were needed? It was hard to think, when one was a bear, and if she were forced to confront the Liar himself, it would be wiser (if anything about confronting the Liar could be wise) to do so in her true image.

On. It was unnaturally dark, though Saara could smell no sorcery around her. (No human sorcery, she qualified, for the deceits of the Liar were subtle.) There was only the musky sandalwood smell, and that grew no thicker, never approaching rankness.

Either her eyes adjusted between one moment and the next, or there was light ahead.

Air eddied roughly in the passage, like streams of water which smash against a stone wall. Saara turned to look over her shoulder at the still blackness she had crossed. Had she had the luck of passing through the tunnel without encountering its heavy-breathing occupant? How, when her witch sense hadn't hinted of any side passage?

Gray day shone on granite, sparking tiny lights like jewels. A dead end?

No, merely a right-angle turn. Saara crawled over something colder than stone. It was an enormous ring of iron, anchored into rock. A chain stretched from it, so heavy she could not budge one of the links which twisted down the tunnel, toward the light.

Sunlight and the smell of cinnamon, sandalwood, cedar: a dry, sharp smell.

The tunnel was not at an end, but here was a cleft in it, a break clean and cruel as though struck by a heavenly ax. One hundred feet away, on the far side of this splash of yellow, the foxhole continued, black and round. But in the middle of the sunlight sprawled the heavy-sighing wearer of the chain.

He was not coiled: not like withies are coiled to make a basket. His metallic length lay in a sort of G-clef pattern, and though in the sun he glinted in a rich array of red, green, and indigo, his color was black.

Black except his head, which was golden horned, his face framed by a whole series of scaly spiked collars, yellow, scarlet, and indigo, giving him the appearance of a chrysanthemum with a long, bare stem.

He had four legs, no sign of wings, and a crest like little burnished flames which ran from neck to tail tip, some ninety feet in all. His eyes were enormous, gold, slitted like a cat's, and staring down at Saara from great heights.

The greatest witch in the Italies had seen dragons and wyverns before, and would have recognized many fell beasts on sight, but she had never seen anything like this. She stood stock-still while she framed in her mind what might be the greatest power song of her life. Or the last one.

The creature pulled iron-black lips from teeth the blue-white of skimmed milk. Each of these was the size and shape of a scimitar, and his tongue between them was forked. The noise of forges increased. A movement began at the creature's tail and traveled up the serpentine length of him, like the flood crest of a river when the dam has gone.

Yards of gold crest vanished, to be replaced by flat, lustrous belly scales. Four long legs curled up, their etiolated, thumbed paws exposing claws the size and shape of cow's ribs. Last of all the ornate head flipped over and hit the stony ground, until it was gazing madly at Saara, upside down. The eyes were now at her level.

"*Bonjour, madame,*" he said very correctly. "*Comment allez-vous aujourd'hui?*"

She blinked. "I don't speak Langue d'Ouil," she answered in Italian, wondering if the beast's purpose was to distract her, and feeling he had certainly succeeded. "I don't speak any languages but Fennish and Italian."

"Fennish and Italian!" The dragon (if he could be called a dragon) chuckled. "Many people speak Italian. No one speaks Fennish but a native of the Fenland," he stated, speaking that tongue. "Therefore I presume you to be an émigrée of the Fens residing now in the Italies. The north Italies, if your accent is any indication."

Hearing the clear, comfortable sounds of home from this huge bizarrity struck Saara nearly dumb. But her wit returned to her in time to allow her to reply, "Then you, too, must be a native of Fenland. The south, however, I would say by your accent."

"Lappish is equally familiar to me," the creature replied, shifting his voice more into the nose. His five-fingered paw scratched belly scales reflectively.

"But it would be ludicrous to attempt to convince you that I come from the land of ice and snow. I am merely an exception to the rule I myself stated." Amber eyes hooded themselves complacently, and then the dragon rotated again, in the same direction, so that his jaw rested on the ground twenty feet from Saara's feet, while his body rested quite comfortably with a half twist in it.

"There ARE dragons in the north," stated Saara, taking the chance on his species.

Window-sized nostrils dilated and the creature emitted a huge snort. The dry, woody smell thickened. "Dragons, perhaps, but not such as I," he stated, pique shading his voice. Suddenly the beast flipped to his feet and his neck arced above her, coiling like black smoke in the air (which had grown very hot). "Do I have a barrel like an ox's, wings like a plucked chicken's, breath like rotten eggs, and incrustations both dorsal and ventral?

"Furthermore, have I attacked you with inhospitable fury on the suspicion that you come to rob me of some possession—not that I have any, mind you?"

With a song of seven words Saara created a forty-foot wall of blue ice between the dragon and herself. It was an arduous spell, though quickly done, and her heart was left pounding.

The dragon watched, then casually he leaned over the wall and laced his fingers together. "Really, now, madam. Can you claim that any of the graceless creatures who inhabit their charred holes on the steppes have more than the slightest resemblance . . . I do not mean to sound egotistical, but I am no more like your European dragons than you are like the Emperor's monkey!"

That glittering head full of glittering teeth was now only a few feet from Saara's. She refused to be intimidated by it, and felt some display on her part was called for. "Get back," she snapped, raising a very small hand beneath the dragon's nose. "Get back, animal, or I'll freeze you, crop and craw, into black ice." The sunlight which poured through the cleft rocks trembled and shivered, as hot air met the magic of the north.

The amber eyes grew impossibly wide, protruding like those of a lapdog. "Ugh! Magic," he snorted, turning his head away as though he smelled something foul. The dragon retreated five steps, and then the sight of Saara's set face set him into peals of echoing laughter. Rocks tumbled in the distance.

"Is it my breath, little lady? Or is it the length of my teeth that has swept your manners away like this? I assure you that had I any intention of doing you harm, I would not have waited to address you first."

As the creature backed, so did Saara, from sunlight into obscurity, until she stood at the turn in the passage wall. Suddenly she was around it and running in the darkness.

"Wait," came a bellow behind her. The walls vibrated. Then there was a sharper crashing, as forty feet of ice smashed like glass, followed by the sound of heavy chain being flung about.

"Wait, madam," the dragon called from behind her in the tunnel. "You take my witticism too much to heart!" Then the air rang and crashed as though an iron tower had fallen at Saara's feet. The dragon had reached the end of his chain.

But his voice rose once more. "I really WOULD like to speak with someone. I am a long way from home, and it has been years . . ." he said, before the echoes died away.

Ahead was a speck of light. Gaspare was waiting there for her with Festilligambe, if the racket hadn't spooked the horse. Or Gaspare.

But Saara's bare feet slowed, and then stopped. She was half-embarrassed to have run from a creature that had offered no direct threat.

And then the way the beast had spoken. ". . . it has been years . . ."

Saara was not without sensibilities.

But dragons were sly, and talking dragons slyest of all. And THIS beast was in the service of the Liar himself, wasn't it? It was chained there, at least.

Chained. The Lapps chained neither their deer nor their dogs. Saara thought all chains despicable. She turned her face around. "Dragon," she called.

The reply was immediate. "Yes! I'm here." Then he added, "Of course I'm here; what a silly thing for me to say."

Was there a touch of bitterness in his words, of self-pity perhaps? But the Liar dealt in bitterness and self-pity quite frequently.

"Who chained you, dragon?" Saara shouted down the passage.

She heard a gusty, whistling sigh. "It was a nasty fellow with the very inappropriate name of Morning Star." Once again the creature seemed to have regained his composure as well as his natural loquacity, for he added, "You see, madam, I was seeking after a book: a book which received high praise in certain circles. It is called *La Commedia Divina*, and it was written by an Italian. Perhaps you . . ."

"Never heard of it," replied Saara. "But then, I can't read."

"Ah. Well. I heard rumor of it as far away as Hunan Province, where news of events outside of Cathay hardly ever reaches. By report it contained great wisdom and excellent poetry, and . . . Well, I collect wisdom, you see . . ."

"You collect wisdom?" Saara murmured, but decided not to interrupt. The dragon continued.

"The book was divided into three sections, I believe. The first being Il Inferno; the second, Il Purgatorio; and the third, Il Paradisio." Another sigh-gale wrung through the darkness.

"I think I would have done better to seek after the third section first."

"No doubt." Saara had no idea what the creature was talking about. She wondered if dragons, too, grew senile.

"Why don't you break the chain?" she asked shortly.

There was a rustle. "My dear lady! I have been stuck in this inelegant place for a good number of years now. Don't you think I would have, if I could? It has some sort of disgusting . . ." the voice faded with embarrassment ". . . spell on it."

Saara lowered herself onto the smooth floor of the tunnel, facing toward the great voice and the smell of sandalwood. She sat, thought some, and picked her toenails. "It's not

ig a chain," she ventured. "And I have some ability with
ells. I think I could break it, if I spent a little time at it."

The rustling stopped. "Well, madam." She heard a self-
onscious rustling.

"I swear to you it will not damage my pride at all to have
ou succeed where I have failed. Please try."

"What will you do if I let you go free?"

This time the silence was longer. "What will I do? Almost
nything you should ask. Anything that does not conflict
ith any previous oath or commitment, of course."

The witch's feet were sore from too much stumbling
gainst rock. She squeezed them as she considered.

Time had taught Saara to have little trust in elementals,
t alone monsters. But she had to get by the creature.

And she was definitely not without sensibilities.

"How many years have you been here, again?"

He groaned. "Twenty-two."

"And what have you been eating or drinking in that
me?"

"There is a small stream in the passage beyond. As for
od—the last thing that passed my lips was a pig, roasted
unan-style."

"Twenty years without eating?" There was incredulity in
er voice. "How is it you are still alive?"

The beast gave a huge metallic shrug. "I am not a frantic
ammal, you must understand. And I sleep a lot.

"But I tell you, madam, that twenty years without con-
ersation has been a harder trial."

Saara rocked back and forth thoughtfully. "Well, I'm not
ne for long conversations at the best of times, dragon, and
don't know whether I believe a word you're saying."

A hollow thump through the darkness indicated it had
ropped its long chin on the ground. "Why should you?
he world is full of illusion," it agreed somberly.

Saara approached the creature, stepping from darkness
to half-light. It lay extended on its side and held one
aw—hand, really, with four spidery fingers and a thumb—
the other, flexing it gingerly. From a dull iron manacle on
s wrist stretched the heavy chain.

"One would think," it said to Saara waspishly, "tha
twenty years would teach me the limits of this thing."

"One would think," she agreed. The dragon massaged it
wrist.

Saara, standing beside a circlet of iron as large as a hi
bath, cleared her throat. "How do I know, dragon, that yo
won't turn around and eat me as soon as I release you?"

The gold eyes shone with more light than the reflecte
sun on the stone of the passage seemed to allow. They re
garded her with a shade of amusement. "You don't, c
course. Just as I have no security that you won't get it int
your head to freeze me into a lump of ice. But if words can
any weight with your people (and I seem to remember the
do), then it is enough that I say I will not. What is more,
tell you I have not eaten a human creature for approximatel
five hundred years."

Saara found this statement very interesting, as possibl
the dragon intended that she would. It implied that th
beast was more than five hundred, of course. (Unless it wa
a way of saying it had never eaten a human, but then wh
not just say so?) It also implied some sort of monument.
change in the dragon's habit. It positively invited question

But Saara refused to ask them. "But perhaps you haven
been this hungry for five hundred years."

The great beast yawned. "I was hungrier ten years ag
than I am now. But let's adopt a pleasanter subject, sha
we?

"Such as yourself, madam: What necessity brings you t
this dreadful, boring place, and how might I be of use t
you?"

Saara sat on a chain link. "You be of use to me? I though
it was the other way around."

The dragon's glorious face was turned to Saara, and be
tween the light of his eyes and the heat of his breath, it wa
like sitting under a desert sun. "Nothing runs in one direc
tion only except water, and that (I'm told) only in its lesse
beds.

"I am the Black Dragon," the creature announced, with
strange sort of dignity. "And though you see me at my disac
vantage, I assure you that there is little born of earth whic

s older, or which is my equal in strength." And with that
he dragon turned its head to the darkness and gave a short,
hollow laugh.

Saara raised one eyebrow. "Well, dragon, I am fairly old
and fairly strong and not tied up at all." And then, with a
sudden impulse of trust, she added, "And I'm on my way to
the Liar's Hall of Four Windows, to find and rescue the
Chief of Eagles, who has been imprisoned by the wicked
one."

The dragon started upright. Great writhing coils
slammed against the roof of the passage. Its jaw hung open.

The creature hissed like a boiler giving way. "You are
what?"

Saara repeated, condensing a long story as best she
could. As she spoke the light of the dragon's eyes flickered,
and amber rays moved like fish over the walls of stone. The
beast itself did not move a muscle.

But when she was finished, it spoke. "This Chief of Eagles, then, is the same the Hebrews call Rafayl, and the
Latins Raphael? He is a teacher?"

"Of music," stipulated Saara.

The dragon yawned. "There is only one Teaching.

"I have heard of this person, Raphael."

Then the dragon drummed his fingers against the stone
floor, making thunder. He looked neither at Saara nor at
anything else in the long gray tunnel, and the light of his
eyes faded. At last he said, very calmly, "To hoard or con-
ceal the teaching is a great crime. Perhaps the greatest."

"To keep a person's spirit imprisoned is greater," she said
boldly.

"One and the same."

"Then you will let us go by?"

The long head drew very close to Saara's and the yellow
eyes kindled again. "Free me."

Saara felt the beast's will beating down on hers, but there
was no magic in it, nor any compulsion she could not resist.
Her desire to break the dragon's chain was her own, sprung
of pity and nursed by her hatred for confinement of all sorts.
She spared one moment's thought to Gaspare, helpless and

unaware at the cavern's mouth, and then she put her hands
to the cold iron.

But Saara had underestimated the Piedmontese. Gaspare
was at that moment inching forward on his hands and knees
through what was to him unbroken blackness, cursing as he
went. He had heard voices, and he had heard hissing, and
he had felt shocks in the earth itself.

He was coming after Saara.

"Too late," muttered the youth as he went. "Too little and
too late, may San Gabriele boot me in the behind, but I am
coming. No man, woman, or devil may call Gaspare the
Lutenist a coward."

That no one save Gaspare the Lutenist had called Gaspare a coward did not occur to the redhead. He comforted
himself with the knowledge that he had shown greater bravery than that of the horse, which had bolted at the first
ominous crash from within. Carrying all belongings with it.
All save the lute, of course, which Gaspare now bore slung
under his belly. It banged his hipbone lightly with every jar.

No doubt it was the Devil himself ahead, ensconced amid
the quenchless coals. No doubt Saara was long since reduced to a cinder. No doubt Gaspare's own defiance would
last as long as it took for a moth to char itself in a candle.

Too little and too late.

Gaspare thought to himself of what it meant to live, and
to die. Slowly he stood. He unwrapped his instrument. He
walked forward, playing as he went. It was what Delstrego
would have done.

From time to time he bounced off the passage walls.

The dragon froze at the sound. He (Saara had ascertained
it was a he) lifted his ornamented head. "What IS that?"

"That is Gaspare," replied the witch calmly. "Playing the
lute."

He rumbled deep in his long throat. "I have never heard
the like."

Saara sighed. "He is very progressive."

Gaspare thought his eyes were acting up when the faint

mber swirls started to play over the passage walls. But he
ut one hand out and what appeared to be the wall WAS the
all, so he blinked and walked on.

In the center of the yellow light was a shadow, a shadow
at grew and came on, with a vague metallic rustling. The
adow grew to be that of the Lady Saara, surrounded by a
alo of gold light.

Lute strings faded to silence. "My lady," whispered Gas-
are. "Are you in heaven or hell?"

At that moment the halo lifted above the woman, and
aspare looked up into a shining, awful face.

"Christ!" he gasped, and then his tongue swelled to fill
is mouth. His right hand slipped over his open strings
ith gentle dissonance.

6

he street hawkers, heard faintly in the distance, called
eir wares in two languages, or three, if the patois of the
luwalladun was considered. All the flies of Granada
roned, and the Sierra Nevada made a jagged rip in the
orizon. Hakiim led his customer along a street baked hard
 tiles by the sun.

The latter fellow was a man of imposing size and girth,
ressed according to Moorish custom in white. Behind him
me another, a small person, heavily veiled, who tended to
ounce as she walked, after the manner of small dogs.

"Black?" asked the customer, not for the first time.
Black as ink?"

"Black as the abyss," replied Hakiim, and he said no
ore. It was his custom to maintain dignified silence before
ch customers as he thought might thereby be impressed.
nd there was something not altogether orthodox about
is potential customer: a shade of hazel about the eyes,
erhaps, or a slight fault in speech. Perhaps a converted

Christian, or a parvenu from Egypt come to Granada t
hide his origin.

Whatever, Hakiim's instincts led him to adopt a haught
attitude and Hakiim's instincts were rarely wrong.

"I've heard that the blacker a girl is, the sounder she i
and the better nurse she makes," remarked the man, as h
followed Hakiim with a heavy, rolling step.

"It could well be true," the Moor replied, still withou
great enthusiasm.

The small person who came behind tittered brightly.

"My little wife had a black nurse as a child. Now that sh
is . . . now that we are . . . we thought . . ."

Hakiim smiled to himself. Soon, if he kept his mout
shut, the fellow would reveal every fact and foible of hi
household. The Moor did not care, nor was he particular*
disturbed by the idea of the ferocious Djoura as a baby's dr
nurse.

The black's moods were various. Perhaps today she'
chosen to exhibit cold pride instead of homicidal fury. Le
the man look at her and decide; his family's safety was the
his business.

They turned into a door in the blank white wall of
house: a fine, expensive house, rented by Hakiim for th
express purpose of setting Djoura to the best advantage
They passed through to the garden courtyard, wher
among oranges and tiny cypress the black woman sat, wea
ing robes of white cotton, brand-new.

In the corner sat the idiot eunuch, who had been com
manded to sit still, and who obeyed like a dog. The Span
iard was there, too, crouched unobtrusively in a corne
where the welts on his face would not be visible. The welt
had come from Djoura, as a result of the merchants' abo
tive efforts to feed the woman a sedative dose of kif.

But no such drug seemed necessary, for the black Berbe
gave the approaching party only the most demure of glance
before lowering her shy head and lacing her hands togethe
on her lap.

Hakiim approached. He tentatively extended one han
which was neither bit, clawed, nor spat at. He lifted th
slave's chin for inspection. She smiled.

"This is Djoura," he said. A shade of question crept into his voice.

He had expected SOME trouble. He had been prepared with discipline, explanations of previous ill-treatment, promises of amendment, offers of help in training . . . He had set up this entire situation—house, clothing, sale by private treaty—as an attempt to gloss over Djoura's maniacal temper.

What was in the girl's head, to go suddenly all meek and winsome? (And didn't she look handsome, with her face not twisted into a snarl?) Hakiim had the sudden wish he'd stated a higher price.

The customer stepped forward. He gazed down at the woman from over his white-cased paunch. "Girl," he pronounced, "I am Rashiid ben Rashiid. I am looking for an attendant for my youngest wife and a dry nurse for the baby that is coming. Would you be a good one?"

Djoura batted her curly lashes and smiled at the ground. Then she smiled at the little veiled face that peeped around Rashiid ben Rashiid's bulk. She wiggled from one side of the seat to the other in an agony of shyness. "I think we would," she mumbled into her lap.

Rashiid liked the girl's attitude. He also liked her looks. And it occurred to him that the Prophet had ordained that a man might have four wives, while Rashiid (comfortably situated as he was) had only two.

No need to think further about that now, however. Now here was the baby to consider: perhaps his first son. It was enough that this woman be strong and biddable. Later, when he was ready to brave his present bride's pique, and that of her family, of course . . .

But by what strange custom did the Nubian refer to her owly self in the plural?

Rashiid ben Rashiid laughed tolerantly. "We, little one? Are you twins, perhaps?"

A giggle and a scuff of the ground with one sandaled foot. "No. My brother and I do not look alike."

Hakiim felt his ears prick up. In fact, it seemed those organs were moving to the top of his head through amazement. He opened his mouth to contradict the girl—to as-

sure Rashiid that there was no brother in the case—when
Djoura crooked her finger and the blond eunuch trotted
over.

Obedient, like a dog.

Rashiid stared a Raphael, who returned a blue gaze free
from either shyness or challenge. Then the large man
seemed to puff out larger. He gave out heavy brays of laughter.

"Merchant of women, what is this?" he gasped, when he
could. "There was no talk of a . . . a brother!"

Hakiim shook his head blankly. "I have no idea. The
yellow-head is of course no relation at all to her, and . . .

A voice in the corner spoke. "They go well together," said
Perfecto. "In contrast. Two for the price of one."

Hakiim shot a look of fury at his partner. It was not cus-
tomary for Perfecto to speak in the marketplace; he was not
a convincing salesman and his native accent was strong. In
dealing with customers of quality it was the Spaniard's business to keep his mouth shut.

And this . . . this bizarre attempt to get rid of the idiot by
making him part of a package with Hakiim's prize discovery . . .

But Djoura took Raphael by the hand, and seeming to
gather together slow reserves of courage, smiled into
Rashiid's glowering face.

"This is my brother Pinkie, master. He is not a man but—
you know—a boy. He is a good worker and does everything
I say."

Rashiid found his annoyance melting in this girl's black
velvet gaze. "I don't need a boy," he stated, masking confusion with gruffness.

Djoura seemed to wilt, and she gave a long sigh. "Without my brother," she said tremulously, "I must surely languish. Without Pinkie I think I will die."

Hearing no response, she continued in louder tones.
"Without Pinkie I will throw myself into the ocean, I guess.
Without Pinkie I will throw . . ."

Hakiim cut her off, feeling her threats were about to extend from suicide to murder. "Don't be silly, Djoura. You've
only just met the creature this week!"

Then he turned to Rashiid. "The eunuch, when we first got him, was sick, and Djoura nursed him back to health. I guess they developed some attachment, but it's surely nothing that cannot be forgotten in a few days . . ."

While Hakiim thus held his customer's attention and Djoura watched them with a gambler's blank-faced intensity, the small person stepped out from behind her husband to look at Raphael. Surreptitiously, she pulled aside her veil.

She had thick hair hennaed auburn, and eyes like a doe deer. She was no more than fifteen, and she stared at the blond as though he were something wrought in gold.

Her name was Ama, and as she met Raphael's eyes she gave out a little gasp. She herself wasn't sure what it was she found there, whether pity, understanding, or sheer stainless beauty, but from that moment she felt—like Djoura—that without Raphael she would surely die.

Rashiid was explaining very carefully to Hakiim that it was not that he could not afford either to buy or to keep a eunuch, but rather that his family was small enough that he had no need for a boy, when the small person tapped him on the elbow and stood on tiptoe to whisper something in his ear.

Rashiid accepted the interruption with the exaggerated patience of a man who is humoring a pregnant wife. He listened to Ama's excited whispering.

"That much? You want her how much?"

"Both of them," chirped Ama. "I don't want her to be unhappy."

Rashiid stole a glance toward Raphael, whose hand was in Djoura's, and who watched the interchange with disinterested attention. "Dearest swallow," the householder said, patting his wife on the head, "although your smallest word is law to me, here we must be reasonable. He will eat like a horse!"

"I will sell my jewelry," offered Ama, a little wildly. "My amber necklace, that my uncle gave me, and the gold chains. They are mine, and that will feed him—I mean them—for a long time. Oh, my husband, do buy them."

Hakiim knew enough to back away, lest his own persua
sion, added to the woman's, drive his customer to rebellion
Instead the Moor shot a glance at his partner, a glance im
bued with all the betrayed fury he felt toward Perfecto. Bu
the expression the Spaniard returned him turned Hakiim'
anger into something like fear.

In an effort to save face, Rashiid turned on Raphael
"Well, boy," he demanded. "Why should I buy you? Wha
are you good for?"

Hakiim began, "I'm sorry, sir, but the boy is unfor
tunately . . ."

But Djoura forestalled him. Squeezing Raphael's hand
with desperation, she hissed, "Tell him, Pinkie. Tell him
what a good boy you are!"

Raphael lifted his eyes to Rashiid "I can play the lute," he
said in faultless Arabic. "Either *al ud* or the lute of Europe
I can also make music with the Spanish chitarre, the harp
and most other stringed instruments. Winds I have no
played so often, nor drums, but I believe I could manage
them. I can teach others the mechanics of music. And I can
sing.

"There are other useful skills I could learn, probably, bu
as of yet I haven't had the opportunity." The perfect fair
brow lowered as Raphael considered the limitations of the
flesh.

Rashiid listened to this calmly stated catalogue of accom
plishments with some surprise, for he had assumed that any
creature which the slave merchants tried to lump into an
other sale was worthless. But the customer's feelings were
nothing compared to those of Hakiim. Had his mule stood
on its hind legs and begun the call to prayer, the Moor
could not have been more dumbfounded than at hearing the
eunuch talk.

Perfecto, too, was astonished, but his surprise was less
pure than that of the Moor, and Raphael's sudden display of
intelligence awoke all the Spaniard's nightmares.

"Well, then," Rashiid said equably. "I have not been suf
fering for lack of a musician any more than for a harem at
tendant, but if he comes free and has the brain to learn
what he is taught . . ."

He snapped his fingers in the air. "Bring the boy a lute."

Hakiim sat in red-faced silence as he listened to Raphael's playing. He reviewed in his mind all the stages of his acquaintance with the blond eunuch, and cursed himself for having at every moment mistaken illness and fear for idiocy.

Why had he never (after the first disgusting day) attempted to talk with the fellow, depending instead on Djoura's word that he was an untrainable idiot? It was always the Moor's wise habit to find the best and most salable skill a slave possessed and to emphasize it, and here he had been hearing the boy sing sweetly (Berber songs, among other unlikely musics) these two weeks and had assumed it was no more than parrot mime.

He shot a glance at Djoura, author of this deceit, but the black sat with her maidenly eyes on the ground, hands folded on her lap. Surely the woman had done it on purpose, but to what end? Had she fallen in love with the stinking creature, after washing the gore and dung from him, and determined that they be sold together?

Well, why not—women did become attached to eunuchs, and evidently there was much more to the blond than had appeared. Hakiim began to wonder how much more; he had never yet seen the fellow undressed. His face was hairless enough, having less mustache than many women, but with certain blonds that meant nothing.

What an error, if they had been traveling with a buck goat among all his does, instead of a wether! But remedial, of course. Granada was full of barber-surgeons. Hakiim determined to strip the fellow immediately after Djoura was sold off. His eyes roved from the black's to the Spaniard's.

Perfecto, too, refused to meet Hakiim's gaze, staring instead at the eunuch with such an odd combination of enmity and fear that once more Hakiim wondered how the Spaniard had come by him.

Most males in the slave markets were battle captives whose friends or relatives had denied ransom. These were chancy slaves, of course, since they might at any moment claim Islam, and all who took that yoke were supposedly

free of all others. A born slave, castrated in childhood, was
different story. The Saqalibah, for instance . . .

But this one hadn't the manner of the Saqalibah.

If the boy was not an idiot (and perhaps not a eunuch
then possibly he was not a slave either. Not legally, at leas
Hakiim thought furiously. He wanted no trouble, eithe
with the law of Granada, nor with a kidnapped man
friends.

Raphael, meanwhile, was so happy he had forgotten bot
where and what he was. He bounced back and forth be
tween the ancient, small-bowled *liuto* that had been bo
rowed for him, and the beautiful *ud* which belonged to th
dusky, somewhat unclean fellow from the bazaar who stoo
now shifting from foot to foot at the courtyard door. H
played a Spagnoletta on the European instrument, then le
the ud be jealous, he improvised upon it a long fantas
which shifted through three classical Arabic scales. The lu
spattered like rainfall. The fretless ud sang like a man.

The small wife of Rashiid ben Rashiid cried delighte
tears into her veil, while Djoura, equally transfixed by th
art of Raphael, was filled with an inchoate pride.

Hakiim thought it time to interrupt. "Enough, Pinki
You play very nicely, but the gentleman has already told u
he has no use for a musician."

Rashiid cleared his throat and turned his bulk toward th
slender Moor. "That is not precisely what I said, merchan
I said if he is willing to do other work as well, and as he ha
been offered free, I would feel it only Allah's will that I giv
him a home."

Within moments of Raphael's picking up the ud, Hakiir
had evolved an estimate of his value which was roughl
three times the value of Djoura. With this in mind he re
plied, "Your charity does you great credit, ben Rashiid, bu
there is no need. A good caretaker does not try to sell
horse to a man who wants a camel, nor a camel to a mar
whose need is for a goat."

Rashiid's deep hazel eyes had a hot glow in them, lik
those of a man who has been allowed to handle a ruby an
whose lust is thereby awakened. Hakiim knew that loo

well, for it was his goal to produce it in every customer with
whom he dealt.

But though it seemed Rashiid was willing to pay full asking price for Djoura, that would not half compensate
Hakiim for throwing away the musician. Besides, there
were some questions to be asked about that one. Hakiim
turned to his partner quite calmly and scratched his left ear,
a signal between them which had always meant "back out of
this sale."

Perfecto scarcely looked at him. Instead the Spaniard
rested his eyes on emptiness as he said quite formally, "We
have offered the gentleman a sale and he has accepted."

Now they were bound. Hakiim's lips moved in a curse.
'We have offered," indeed! HE had offered, and now
Hakiim was out a large sum of money which might have
done much to ease the last few weeks' headaches and speed
him on his homeward voyage.

While Hakiim sat with angry eyes averted from the company, regretting monies he had only contemplated having
for the past five minutes, Rashiid chuckled complacently
and Ama danced her success.

She was a charming little thing and moved her feet most
cleverly, despite the handicap of her condition, until she
spun around to come face-to-face with the black slave she
had just purchased, and whose existence she had completely forgotten.

There was something in the set of that face that called an
end to the girl's capers. She backed slowly into the shadow
of her husband once more, and peered instead with large
eyes out at Raphael.

"I am your mistress. My name is Ama," said the very
small and young person, and then with no pause she flipped
round on her stool to present the back of her sleek head.
"Do you like the way my new maid has done my hair?"

It was a complex arrangement of many little braids which
had been then woven together in drooping swags. Gold
coins hung at intervals, gleaming against the dark mass.

Raphael smiled at her, thinking that if Ama represented
the circumstances of his life as it would be, it would be

quite endurable. "I like the style," he answered. "It looks like this . . ." and his fingers echoed the complexity of Ama's hair on the strings of al ud.

"I'm not sure I do." Ama swiveled back, brisk as a sparrow on a branch. "She pulls tight—and the way she looks right AT me! She is a bold woman. Maybe Nubians are always bold women. My nurse wasn't, though. She was nice.

"The coins are her idea. I had to make holes in the middle of them, so I guess they can't be spent anymore. Djoura said copper, but gold is always better, don't you think?" Her eyes (not bird eyes, soft almond eyes) flitted briefly to Raphael.

"Your hair is even fairer than gold: not like copper at all. So strange! What did you say your name was?"

All this was said very rapidly, as Ama's quick, darting eye looked here, there, and everywhere around the mimosa trees and over the fish pool, resting at last on the musician she had come to bother.

His blue eyes (which Ama thought even stranger than his yellow hair) rose to hers. Had they not been so large, perfect, and deep blue, the little lady would probably not have given him time to answer her question; she rarely felt the need of answers.

But as it was, she fell quite suddenly tongue-tied as he spoke. "I don't think I told you. My name is Raphael."

Ama fitted the name in her mouth as though it could be tasted. "Raphael! Raphael! What a wonderful name. But Djoura called you something else—less wonderful. What was it?"

"Pinkie," Raphael admitted. "To Djoura I am Pinkie."

Ama fingered the red clay beads that bound the ends of her braids. Her sweet child's brow pulled down. "I don't like that. You should have a name as beautiful as you are. I will make her call you Raphael, I think." Then Ama went off into a moment's brown study.

"Or I will have my husband, Rashiid ben Rashiid, make her do it. He likes Djoura, I think. I don't think I do. Do you?"

Raphael opened his mouth to reply, but it was not necessary, for Ama went on, "It is funny, isn't it, that my husband's name is Rashiid ben Rashiid, when his father's name is Pablo? He comes to visit us sometimes and then they speak Spanish. I can speak a little Spanish: Fatima's maid taught me. Until Rashiid bought Djoura I didn't have a maid. Becuse I am the second wife. In fact, I was almost Fatima's maid, until I got—until we knew I was going to have a baby. That made almost ALL the difference. Now, Fatima might as well be MY maid—but don't tell her I said so or she'll pull my hair for me!

"Sometimes I say bad things in Spanish to surprise the servants. Then I can pretend I didn't understand what I said. I do, of course. Don't tell anybody. Do you speak Spanish?"

In the time it took to draw the next lungful of air, Ama forgot what she had been saying. "Play for me."

Raphael had been attempting to play ever since Ama had joined him on the bench by the fish pool. Now he was given at least a moment to start. The wooden instrument keened under his fingers. He sang, and the words went:

My father is a sparrow in the leaves, in the tangle of
leaves.
I hear him in the winter in the bare trees. He calls me.
But I—I have forgotten the language of flight.

By dint of great effort, Ama stayed quiet so far. Then she interrupted. "That sounds classical. It doesn't rhyme. I know what it means, though, because I listen to songs a lot. When you say your father is a sparrow you mean you don't have a father, or that he does not admit to you. And when you say you don't remember how to fly, you mean you are a slave."

Raphael looked startled. His left eyebrow shot up, and it seemed he was about to contradict his young mistress. But instead he replied, "Everyone must take his own meaning from a song, or it would not be a song."

"But I'm glad you are a slave," continued Ama, after pausing to examine his answer and finally throwing it away

as a bird will throw away a prize it finds inedible. "I'm especially glad you are a . . . a boy, and not a man. Or else I
would not be able to sit here with you with my veil off and
show you my hair. With men, everything is all very difficult.
They are strange beasts—men, don't you think? All they
think about is leaping on you like a bull on a cow—or I have
never seen a bull and a cow, but I'm told it is the same. And
so we have to stay hidden all our lives, lest we be disgraced.

"Disgraced!" she repeated, frowning solemnly and dab-
bling one pretty toe in the water.

"Rashiid, my husband, of course, is not like that. Not
exactly like that. He is almost human. But all THAT, you
know, is not very much fun." Ama's eyes roved uncertainly
from a bronze-backed carp to Raphael's attentive face. "Is
it?"

Raphael laid the ud in his lap. He did not pretend to
misunderstand her. "I do not know," he replied seriously.
"About men with women." Ama snickered.

"Of course you don't."

Her slave's expression did not lighten. "But as life comes
from Allah, every part of it must have some beauty in it."

Ama gave a tiny sniff. "Don't talk like a book!"

Then, in the next moment, a spark appeared in her
brown eyes. Assuring herself that the garden court was
empty except for Raphael and herself, she said, "Let me sit
on your lap."

Dutifully the slave put his instrument aside, and little
Ama snuggled up to him. Raphael stroked her as one would
stroke a cat, and suddenly, for no perceivable reason, he
laughed out loud.

Justly he could call himself Rashiid ben Rashiid, for he
was a self-made man, come far from his father's mule stud.
He had left Granada early, having a dislike for livestock and
mules in particular, and made his money in lower Egypt,
coming home with a regular income and a new name. Once
home he bought a house and planted orange trees (whose
fruit was forbidden by law to the infidel) everywhere. But
Rashiid had not completely buried Paolo, son of Pablo. For
one thing Pablo himself still lived, and for another it was

much more profitable to do business with the *giaour*—the Christians. They were less likely to complain to the Hajib when affairs went badly. Therefore the household of Rashiid lived by compromise.

There was a featureless white wall with tile eaves peeping over, which in size suggested a building of Moorish type—facing inward over its central court—and palatial dimension. This was an illusion, however, for most of what was visible from the street was the wall of the enclosed garden, flecked out to look like house frontage, with arches, doorways, and little stone steps. The house itself, while sizable, sat huddled in one corner of the lot, revealing its peasant origins in every squat line.

To make up for the limits of the house proper, the garden was scattered with little round and thatched outbuildings which resembled mushrooms springing from the irrigated soil. These, though necessary, looked terribly native.

There were no separate women's quarters, because there was no room for such, and also because Granada (being half Christian) tended to be lax in the observance of the Islamic proprieties. But because Rashiid ben Rashiid did not want to be known as lax in observance, it was necessary for his wives to pretend occasionally that they were not about when they WERE about. For this purpose were maintained certain hidey-holes in various parts of the house to which they could escape in the event of orthodox visitors.

These provisions made life a bit difficult for Fatima and Ama, not to mention the Spanish maids. But the two Islamic women consoled themselves with the knowledge that though they were married to a convert, the very inconvenience they were put to proved that they themselves were still persons of quality.

Djoura (though possessing proprieties of an entirely different nature), put the closets into similar use. She would retire to them and pretend she was not there, especially when she heard Ama's piping, querulous call. There was one retreat at the end of one of the inside walls of the house which she preferred, for it had a rough, dimpled window through which she could see everything within the walls, from the bondsmen's barrack (very small) to the stable

which housed Rashiid's one horse: an immaculately kept
Egyptian gray which he never rode. Between these two
outposts lay the garden itself, where the orange trees
bloomed and perfumed vines twined around the fish pond.
This little body of water was perfectly round and sat like a
pockmark in the dusty skin of the garden. It had no natural
source and had to be topped off daily with water brought in
on donkeys (never mules).

It was there that Djoura's eyes were bent, as her chin
rested on the thumb side of her fist, which pressed in turn
on the clay windowsill. The coins above her forehead rus-
tled like leaves in the day's airs. The white muslin costume
which had become Djoura so well had somehow disappeared from the wash, and she was back to wearing her
traditional fusty black. With stony, set face she watched
Raphael dandle his little mistress on his lap.

Ama was an irritation: a spoiled little fluttering thing and
a stumbling block toward certain long-range goals. It was
part Djoura's intention to gain a reputation for trust and
biddability, and to that end she acted her role before
Rashiid very effectively.

Her very contempt for the man—pompous, damp, and
fleshy as he was—lent her zest for the part, and the knowledge that he desired her lent her confidence. Yet Rashiid's
lust was a danger, too, which Djoura did not underestimate.
He was in all ways disgusting.

Ama—curious and willful as she was—could not be dis-
missed with the same sniff and a sneer. The little woman
was ubiquitous, and enough like the black Berber in mind
that she could not be readily cozened. Djoura could not feel
contempt for Ama. But she could hate her. And she could
be jealous.

Look at the little chicken, bouncing on Pinkie's knee—
bold as a child on an aged donkey. Wouldn't she get a big
surprise if she could see the fellow without his trousers. If
she kept behaving so shamelessly, she might get a surprise
some day: every man had his limits.

Even Pinkie. Djoura bit her lip, for Pinkie worried her
more than Ama did: more than anything else did in this
place of rich food and sloth. Ever since she realized that the

fellow was no more a half-wit than a eunuch, her concern for him had grown heavier and heavier.

More and more she doubted he was a Berber at all, despite his knowledge of both tongue and music. He sang other songs besides the desert chants, with what seemed to Djoura equal facility: songs in Spanish and songs in languages of which the woman knew not even the name. And the placidity with which he had sunk into this life of captivity was dreadful. What Berber could seem so content wearing the iron collar?

Djoura had never asked Pinkie directly where he had been born or who his people were; first, because it was rare she found the time and privacy for such conversation, and secondly, because she didn't like such questions herself. When the woman closed her eyes at night she would still often see her father's mare scrabbling up the mountain trail toward camp, dragging his headless body by one stirrup. Behind the horse had come the riders of the Bedouin Arif Yusuf, following the bloody trace through the sand.

And then Djoura would be visited by an image of her mother, with veil thrown back, swinging a grass scythe in deadly circles around her head, wearing an arrow through her cheek like an ornament.

A man born a slave had shame in his past. A man enslaved had defeat. It was never good to ask. Yet as Djoura watched Fatima (fat, harmless Fatima, whom even Djoura could not dislike) come puffing out of the middle door of the main house, gesticulating and babbling to Ama in Spanish, she knew she would have to make more certain of Pinkie—since they were going to escape together.

Evidently the first wife didn't like Ama's antics any more than Djoura did, for the two of them were at it now, their shrill, staccato words falling like a shower of stones on the garden.

And here was Pinkie, sent off to the house with a flea in his ear. Now was both time and opportunity. "Hsst! Pinkie!" he called out the window.

He approached, his odd, narrow-featured (to Djoura) face looking as mild as if no one had ever raised her voice to him

in his life. "Get in here," she hissed, backing from the
rough clay opening.

"Through the window?" the blond asked, and in reply
Djoura snatched his hand and pulled him over the sill. He
rose from the floor, looking only slightly surprised.

"I didn't want anyone to see us together," she explained.
"Enough talk goes on already, you can believe!"

Then her voice roughened and she pointed her index finger at him. "You listen to me, Pinkie, when I tell you to
leave that nasty little thing alone, if you value your future."

His eyebrows (and even Djoura had to admit that Pinkie
had fine eyebrows) shot up. "Ama? Do you mean . . ."

"I mean the baby girl who calls herself my mistress,
Pinkie. If Rashiid (Allah shrivel his big belly) finds out
there's nothing but a pair of cotton trousers between his
favorite wife and a man's . . . whatever . . . you'll soon be
no more than you claim to be!"

His blue eyes shifted uncertainly. "Djoura, what do you
mean by what I 'claim to be'?"

Djoura struck her palm against her forehead. "I think
you're simple after all, Pinkie. A boy, is what you seem to
be!"

"A boy?" he echoed, looking down at his long legs and
well knit body.

"A permanent boy. A eunuch," Djoura hissed with feroc-
ity.

Understanding awoke for Raphael. "They think I'm a eunuch? Why? Nobody asked me. Nobody even looked."

She blinked. "Woodenhead! I make sure they didn't! I
spent the last week standing in between you and discovery.
You can bet I told that oily Hakiim you'd lost your bollucks.
Made fun of you for it, too. And I didn't stop flirting with
this hog-boweled Rashiid until we were out onto the
street."

"Why?" he pressed, as mildly as ever.

Djoura sat herself down on the only stool in the room.
"First of all," she pronounced very slowly. "Those two deal
in boys—eunuchs. If you hadn't been one before, you
would have been as soon as they found out. And even if they
didn't for some reason, no one would buy you entire unless

they wanted to put you in a mine somewhere, or out in a field with iron burning your neck and wrist.

"No one. NO ONE would have bought you and I together had they known you were entire!"

Two small lines of worry appeared between Raphael's eyes. "But Rashiid has bought me already. If he thinks I am a eunuch, he is wrong, and perhaps I should tell him so."

Djoura hushed him and looked wildly around. "Never! You must never tell anyone or let them know. Not if you want to escape the knife!"

"That is very awkward," Raphael said simply. He laced his fingers over his knee and sat with his back against the wall. "It is like a lie."

"Hah!" She swallowed a laugh. "Nothing is a lie, if it helps a Berber win back her freedom!"

"It will help you win back your freedom if I let them believe I am a eunuch?"

She nodded decisively. "And yours too."

A look of pain and fatigue touched his fair features and he looked away from her face. In that moment Djoura became satisfied that Raphael, too, remembered freedom. "But he does not believe me," whispered Djoura to herself. "He does not believe I can arrange it." For a moment her own doubts knocked. But the Berber stiffened her jaw, and her ebony hand reached out and touched his.

"Pinkie," she said gently. "You must trust me. I am your only friend."

Raphael looked quickly up. His hand reached down to the hem of his trousers and he felt something that had been inserted between the stitches. "You ARE my dear friend, Djoura, but I have another."

The woman snorted. "Who's the other, then. Ama?"

Raphael's face lit softly. He held a pebble in his hand. "No. I meant someone I have known a while. His name is Damiano."

This was new. Djoura blinked at the news before replying, "And where is Damiano? Where was he, that he was not there to help you when all the sense was beaten out of you and you were sold to a crab louse like Perfecto? I don't call that much of a friend who—"

For the first time, Raphael interupted Djoura. "He does not live anywhere. He is with Allah. And yet he is a great help to me.

"He gave me this." Raphael proffered the pebble reluctantly, as though afraid she would dash it out of his hand.

Djoura, examining the thing in the half-light which came in through the irregular window, recognized it as the pebble Pinkie had refused to take out of his mouth that first morning in the hills, and had carried all that day locked in his battered hand.

Carefully, she gave it back to him. "Not much of a gift," she said gruffly, but despite her words she was touched. She let out her breath in what was intended to be a snort, but turned out a rather wistful sigh.

"Who whipped you like that, Pinkie? Your old master?"

He shook his head. "It was my brother who commanded it done. We are old enemies." And after a moment's quiet reflection, Raphael added, "I don't think it is over between us: my brother and I."

"Ah?" This was interesting. It opened up new images of Pinkie. Poor men had less reason to attack their brothers than did great ones. If he were not such a good musician, Djoura might suspect her pale friend of being wellborn. "Your brother betrayed you? Then you had no master, before?"

Raphael's smile was private and gentle. It called out an answering one from her. "None save Allah."

Djoura giggled and placed her head close to his. "'There IS no master save Allah . . .' We understand that, you and I!"

"So!" The deep voice from the doorway startled them both. "You would teach our boy the *sa'lad:* the statement of faith?"

It was Rashiid himself, and he did not look particularly happy at the words he had half heard. He glowered down at Raphael's head. "Ama tells me your name is actually not Pinkie but Raphael."

The blond rose smoothly. "Yes, that is true."

Djoura blinked in surprise. Having once decided to call her charge Pinkie, it had never occurred to her to ask if he had another name.

Rashiid did not like the response. He felt patronized, and obscurely threatened. In fact, there was something about Raphael that had begun to bother Rashiid: the unclean smoothness of his cheek, perhaps, or the fact that his pretty face stood at man's height and stared at him with mannish directness. Rashiid—or rather Paolo, son of Pablo—was not used to eunuchs, and he did not like standing too close to this ambiguous creature. But it was up to Rashiid to set an example here, in the presence of the girl, so his hand flicked out. "You say, 'Yes, MASTER. It is true, MASTER.'"

Raphael's tongue touched a bleeding lip. "Yes, master. It is true, master."

"And I want you to remember, boy: you are no battle captive, you are Saqalibah. You can say the sa'lad until you are hoarse and you will still be Saqalibah."

"Yes, master," said Raphael very mildly, but his eyes were as unafraid as those of a cat. Those eyes made Rashiid shift from foot to foot.

"You could bow to me, also," the householder growled sullenly. "Never hurts."

Then Rashiid cleared his throat. "I came to tell you that I'm giving a dinner tonight for some very important people. The highest quality, from Tunis, so bring the ud, not the lute.

"And—" Rashiid looked from side to side. He didn't know quite what he wanted to say. How did you ask a slave to be cooperative without showing weakness? He hated to show weakness.

"And don't make me ashamed of you," he concluded lamely.

"I will try not to, master," replied Raphael, and he bowed. Rashiid paraded out.

Djoura touched Raphael's damaged lip. "Raphael? That is your true name?" He nodded.

"That's a silly name, especially for a pink fellow like you." The black's hand was gentle, but her face was as hard as a carving in onyx. "Once we are free," she whispered as she

dabbed at his cut with her sleeve, "we will come back and
kill that one."

"Now THAT is silly," returned Raphael.

The sea was Hakiim's hope; once he reached the water,
temperatures would be temperate and the air moist. But
the sea was a very long way away, many days by muleback.
Heat had crumpled the airs of Granada so that no line could
be discerned between earth and sky, and the air itself
smelled like ashes. The Moor had one hand on his mule's
girth strap, and was peering into the high distance when
Perfecto addressed him.

"You think I'm crazy, no doubt," grunted the round-faced
Spaniard. "You must think I'm crazy, after the way I acted
with the eunuch."

But Hakiim glanced at his partner's expression, and for
the first time in weeks he tended to believe that the man
was NOT crazy, for this hangdog attitude was every inch the
old Perfecto. The black glint was gone from his small eyes
and his fat-shrouded jaw no longer clenched and un-
clenched.

"I never thought you were crazy," answered Hakiim,
with more regard for the amenities than for the truth. "I
merely thought you . . . ill-advised."

Silence fell, impossible for the Moor to endure. "It
seemed that first you wanted too much for the eunuch, and
then, as soon as he was found to be of value, too little. That's
all.

"But it is done, and no great loss." He raised his foot to
the round wooden stirrup.

Perfecto put one hand on Hakiim's shoulder. "Old friend,
I can explain."

Hakiim smiled uncertainly. He no longer wanted explanations, but to be out in the clean air, away from Perfecto
and Granada both. "I am to meet a troop of *fursan* outside
the Alhambra at noon. They will let me ride with them all
the way down to the sea, but I must not be late."

Hakiim's sleek and restive mule pawed the desiccated
earth with his hoof. In reply Perfecto thrust one finger at
heaven, swaggered behind the house, and returned with his

wn beast, already bitted and saddled. "I will ride with you
) the Alhambra," he said. "That will give us time."

Hakiim was not happy, but he was one of that sort who,
/hile not especially kindly, has a great deal of difficulty
eing rude. He allowed Perfecto to mount beside him.

The mules danced their first few steps, finding their bal-
nce under saddle. The Spaniard coughed and cleared his
hlegmy throat. "It has to do"—he chewed his lip silently
)r a moment—"with a promise I made once. That I would
) something for someone. If it needed doing."

Hakiim frowned. He suspected Perfecto of talking non-
ense. Like a child. Like a Spaniard. "To do what, and for
/hom?" He led his animal along a street so narrow that
edestrians darted into doorways to alow them to pass.

Perfecto's animal followed. The Spaniard's reply was inau-
ible and so Hakiim turned and asked him to repeat it.

"It does not matter to whom I gave the promise, does it?
t was a promise and I was therefore honor bound."

Hakiim, as a dealer, thought this attitude was so much
ung of the mule. What was more, he was certain that Per-
:cto had no more illusions than he himself. But as he
rned to say something of this nature, they rounded a
ump in the road, and a white donkey, carrying a man and
vo sacks of wood, rammed nose-to-nose into his mount.

There was a great thrashing and hawing, and Perfecto's
nocent mule received a kick in the chest from Hakiim's.
Vhen the incident had resolved itself (the donkey rider
acking his animal along the alley and into a cul-de-sac)
erfecto pointed urgently along a cross street that led out of
ie gates of Granada.

"Here. You will arrive at the fortress at the same time as if
)u had cut through the city. AND, we will be able to hear
urselves talk."

"I don't want to be able to hear ourselves talk," whis-
ered Hakiim to himself, but he turned the mule's head.

"As to what the bargain—or rather the promise—was,
ell, that was to depend on circumstance. As it happened,
was necessary that I sell this man in Granada."

It was cooler outside the wall, and undeniably freshe but Hakiim's mood was unimproved. "Not man, Perfect but boy. And how can you . . ."

Quite calmly the Spaniard corrected his partner. "N boy, Hakiim, but man. The blond was never a eunuch."

Hakiim let the reins slide down his mule's neck. F some moments his tongue forgot speech. "And you kne it?"

"From the beginning. But I knew that you would be ver unhappy with the idea of selling an entire, so I thought better to pretend."

Perfecto, jogging along on the mouse-gray back, looke more complacent than ashamed.

Hakiim thought furiously.

"I should have suspected something when the Berbe woman refused to be sold without him."

Now it was Perfecto's turn to raise his eyebrows. "Berbe woman? Djoura?"

Hakiim made a negatory wave. "She . . . always claime to be a Berber. Pay it no mind."

But Perfecto's little eyes squinted littler. "Are ther then, black Berbers?"

"A few," Hakiim admitted. "In the west and south. Bu that doesn't mean that she is one . . ."

Perfecto gave a heavy sigh. "It would be a dangerou thing, to sell a woman of Berber tribe as a slave, in a lan where the Berbers have the sharpest swords," he said.

"You are referring to Tunis?" Hakiim mumbled nervousl

"I am referring to Granada," answered the Spaniard.

The wall of the city rose to their left, gray but gleamin like milk in the sun. Below was a bank of shale tha crumbled down to a series of turtle-backed hills. Th sprawling fortress called the Alhambra, red walled an white towered, gleamed from half a mile away. Hakiim too a deep breath of sage-dry air and listened to the cicadas i the dust.

But for Perfecto, now, he'd have solitude.

"There is a world of difference between selling a Nubia who CALLS herself a Berber and is not, and selling a ma

YOU call a eunuch, and who is not. What will happen when Rashiid finds out he has been tricked?"

Perfecto urged his animal close beside. "Tricked? It was not I who told him Pinkie was a boy, but Djoura herself."

Djoura. Hakiim's brow knotted. "Yes! Our black lily must have known. Was she in this business with you?"

Perfecto spat off to the side. "No. Djoura is only perverse.

"And Rashiid can have no complaint to us, since Pinkie did not cost him one shaved copper!"

Hearing an unmistakable jingle, Hakiim turned his head. Perfecto had taken out his moneybag and was shaking it in his hand for emphasis. Hakiim's own profits were kept in a discreet bag-belt which wrapped his body beneath his shirt. It was a heavy belt, but not so full as this moneybag.

A sudden guess made Hakiim blurt, "So you were paid for taking the eu—the blond."

Perfecto laughed, and at this moment Hakiim's mule stopped dead and pawed the black shale with his foot three times.

"A bad omen," grunted the Spaniard. "When a mule does that. Take a good look before stepping onto the ship you engage, old friend!"

Then he added quickly, "No, I was not paid for taking the Saqalibah, or at least not in gold. I told you I did it for someone to whom I owe a number of favors."

Hakiim was getting tired of being told that "Which makes me suspect the fellow was no more a legal slave than a physical eunuch," he replied. "Tell me, Perfecto. Who puts you under such strange obligations?"

"I will do better than tell you," the Spaniard proclaimed. "I will introduce you."

This was too much. As though Hakiim had any desire to meet Perfecto's low European friends . . . "No time," the Moor said shortly.

"All the time in the world," replied Perfecto, and he laughed.

"Go meet the devil, you damned paynim!" the Spaniard bellowed, swinging his moneybag (heavier than gold), down on the back of Hakiim's neck.

* * *

These visitors were so fancy that not only Fatima and
Ama had to be hidden but the furniture as well. The nor-
mally concealed household bedding, however, was subject
to a good deal of attention, as the dining room was strewn
with pillows and the spread long ago embroidered by
Rashiid ben Rashiid's mother hung dimpled from the ceiling. (This use of her handiwork would have surprised Lu-
crezza, wife of Pablo, very much.)

Ama found this all very hard, as she perched on a heavy
oak table in her hidey-hole at the corner of the house. Since
all the floor was taken, she was forced to crawl along the
tops of the piled European furniture. Like a cat. And there
were no cushions to make her position softer.

Better to be an old drudge like Fatima and supervise the
cooking in the kitchen house than be locked up like this, in
stifling heat with nary a toy or amusement all evening.
Djoura was scrubbing pots, and even Raphael had been
taken from the little wife of Rashiid, for he was to play for
the guests.

Ama felt a stab of resentment. Wasn't it she who had
sensed the value of the musician, when Rashiid hadn't
wanted him for free?

And for that matter, wasn't the blond a mere European?
Why did Raphael get to attend the party, while her pure
Moorish bottom rested on the hard wooden furniture her
people despised?

Ama would turn the tables on all of them, she promised
herself. Big tables, like the one she sat on.

Hasiim Alfard, lean and dry-faced Berber of Morocco,
looked to go the night without cracking a smile. His two
lieutenants, Masoud and Mustapha, sat like dusty shadows
at his feet, and unbent no more than their *qa'id*.

Rashiid's reaction to this was a grin like that carved on a
turnip-face. He knew such an ingratiating and constant
smile displayed a certain feeling of weakness before his
powerful guests, and so he wiped the expression from his
face again and again.

But it came back unnoticed, and in fact, there it was now, splitting his wide face and revealing teeth of various assorted shades. "You find it crowded in Granada, Qa'id Hasiim, after the tents of your people?"

Hasiim's right hand dipped into the spiced lamb, went to his mouth, and rinsed itself in the crockery bowl before he replied. "I find it . . . dirty," said the Berber. "But then, what can I expect? It is Granada."

The dry man (only his lips were moist, wet with the grease of Rashiid's expensive hospitality) turned slowly away, distracted by the ud player in the corner.

"Dirty?" echoed the heavier man. "Ah, yes. Unfortunately. But you say rightly, my honored friend; it IS Granada." Rashiid erupted in fruity chuckles. "My own people . . ."

But the qa'id turned back to the food as though Rashiid were not even present. It meant nothing to him that Rashiid had "people," such as the gentry of Granada counted them. In fact, he might as well have admitted to Hasiim that he had been born with the name of Paolo. He would have found himself neither more nor less respected on that account. The city man was not a tribesman of Hasiim's, and that was all that mattered.

The Berber pulled a piece of gristle from the lamb on his trencher. He examined it, frowning hugely.

Rashiid sweated. In all his years in business he had failed to learn that one cannot impress a fanatic any more than one can impress someone else's watchdog. He tried.

"It is so hard," he began, "to maintain the mosques decent and clean in a place like this, in a city where no one knows how to keep Ramadan properly, and infidels wandering the streets freely as the faithful."

Once more Hasiim scooped, bit, chewed, and swallowed before answering. "There is no need for mosques," he said, his voice totally devoid of expression. "In our hills there are no mosques."

Rashiid cleared his throat, but said nothing. He had begun to lose hope for this particular gathering. Why had he invited this fellow anyway, with his stiff-necked puritanism and unwillingness to be pleased?

The answer surfaced unbidden: because Hasiim was o
very high lineage, and his cavalry was barracked in the Al
hambra. These fursan were among the most powerful and
fanatic of the Berbers, who were the most powerful and
fanatic among the Arab conquerers of Spain.

The man of Granada felt an almost unconquerable desire
to sit in a chair. Forty-two was too old to be squatting on the
floor like a peasant.

Music intruded into his consciousness. The melody of the
blond slave's music soothed his nerves as nothing else
could. At least he need have no fear for the quality of his
entertainment.

As a matter of fact, Hasiim was listening to Raphael with
peculiar, brooding intensity. So were his silent fellows
Rashiid waited until the end of the piece before he spoke
again.

"Handles the instrument well for a straw-haired barbar
ian, doesn't he?"

Hasiim's eyes (brown and shallow set, like those of an
Arab horse) flickered. "There is no music worth making ex
cept that which glorifies Allah," he stated. "And there is no
instrument worthy of praising Allah except the voice of a
man."

Rashiid felt a mouthful of eggplant stick halfway to his
stomach. His face prickled all over. He turned to Raphael
who sat tailor-fashion on the hard floor behind the guests.

But there was no need to direct the slave, for at Hasiim's
words Raphael had put the wooden ud down at his feet.
"Shall I sing, then, for you?" he asked, his blue eyes staring
directly at those of Hasiim.

Rashiid's terror of nerves resolved itself into a fury, that
the boy should dare speak to an honored guest in that familiar voice.

But Hasiim forestalled his discipline, replying, "Yes, of
course, if you can do so without impropriety." (For among
the things which do not impress a fanatic are manners.)

Raphael closed his eyes. He took a breath, let it out
slowly, and then began to chant the same evening song he
had shared with Djoura on his first day in chains.

In the kitchen the woman heard him. She raised her head and her hands clenched the handles of the cauldron she was dragging from the fire (black hands, black cauldron). Her eyes stung with tears she did not understand.

In the chamber of cushions, no man spoke until the song was over. Then Hasiim stood up and walked over to Raphael.

"You!" he hissed. "Could it be you are a Berber?"

The blond smiled as Hasiim lowered his leather-tough body beside his. "No, I am not. But I sing that song together with my friend, who is a Berber."

"His name?" pressed the other, for Hasiim knew the name of almost every desert soldier quartered in Granada.

"Her name," Raphael corrected him gently, "is Djoura."

Now, in spite of himself, Hasiim Alphard smiled, and his face creased into dozens of sun wrinkles. "And how, in the name of Allah's grace, did a barbarian like you meet a Berber woman?"

"We are slaves here together," the blond replied innocently.

"No, a Berber cannot be a slave," stated Hasiim, as though saying, sheep cannot be green. "Not even a Berber woman."

"Djoura is," Raphael dared to say. "She is cleaning pots in the kitchen right now."

There was a hideous silence.

7

Saara's second procession through the worm hole was less eventful. The dragon was gone, but Gaspare stepped out into the cleft of sunshine, where that creature had so long been chained, and squinted. And sniffed.

"Doesn't smell bad, considering."

Saara didn't bother to turn. "Why should it, when he wasn't fed for twenty years?"

Gaspare made a worried noise at that, and followed Saara into the next dark tunnel. "Speaking of which, do you think we can trust its—his—promise, not to eat Festilligambe?" His words rang and echoed through the darkness so that they were barely understandable.

"He didn't eat you," was the Fenwoman's reply, and then she put her fingers to her lips for silence.

Gaspare didn't see the finger. Indeed, he saw very little of anything in the deepening gloom, and soon began to stumble. The witch was forced to take his hand.

It was long, this tunnel, and as sinuous as a serpent. But like a serpent it was smooth. It became more and more difficult for Saara to walk cautiously. But the amiable builder of the tunnel had been chained in the middle of it since its first construction. The Liar might very well have made changes; the very regularity of the walls and floor might well be designed to delude the wanderer away from caution, so she goaded her ears to hear and her skin to feel.

While feet are moving, time is passing, but neither Gaspare nor Saara had any sense of time's progression, and the weariness of their black march turned into irritability.

Gaspare fell, twisting his body like that of a cat in his effort to keep the lute from striking the ground. The instrument was saved, but its back-curving neck smacked Saara sharply on the thigh as it fell. She hissed her annoyance.

Gaspare himself whispered his curses to the floor, but as he clambered to his feet again (disoriented in the darkness), he remarked very calmly that a witch ought to be able to call fire to hand at need.

Delstrego had.

Saara was still massaging her leg, but this implicit criticism stung her worse than the blow. "I have heard a little bit too much about Damiano Delstrego lately," she said between clenched teeth. "And what a great witch he was. There is a difference between accomplishment and simple talent, you know. Or perhaps you don't know!

"Of course Damiano could call fire. He had fire coming out of the top of his head! But it took me to teach him to make clouds."

Gaspare snorted. "So who wants to make clouds, except a peasant in a drought?"

Both had forgotten the necessity for quiet and for caution as well. Gaspare strode bullishly down the corridor, one hand tracing the right wall for support.

Until he fell again.

Saara heard the thunk, followed by a small weary whine like that of a child. All her anger melted away.

"Don't get up," she told Gaspare, and she lowered herself beside the young man. "And don't talk. Give me a minute to think."

Damiano ran through Saara's memories like a bright but tangled thread. Her powers had been his, for a while, and his powers had been hers, for another while. Bodies, too, had shared as they might.

For a short time. Such a short time.

But surely Damiano's favorite magic should be accessible to her. To make a fire without anything to burn . . .

She fished into the unsorted depths of her mind and came up with brown eyes. A lot of curly brown hair, in snarls.

There was a dog, an angel (in all this she mustn't forget Raphael), a girl's face with blue eyes, a wonderful face with braids and green eyes (oh no, put it back, put her own face seen through Damiano's eyes at the bottom of the blackness), a plow horse with raw and pussy shoulders, seen once outside of Avignon . . .

There. There it came, with the image of the abused, fly-bothered beast. Hot anger welling up out of the floor of her mind . . .

"Lady Saara!" yelped Gaspare, scooting across the floor away from the smoldering woman.

"Hush," she chided him, and she turned down all the vents of her emotions. Her dress—last of the two she owned—was discolored, and it smelled of burning hair. She sighed.

But at last Saara raised one hand like a torch.

"There, Gaspare. Behold the world around us!"

"Wonderful," replied the redhead, staring not at the cave but at the flame itself. "Though Delstrego's was blue and did not flicker."

When they found their way under sky again, the sun was already descending. A path worn into the mountainside led away from the tunnel, treeless, grassless, winding up to a broken tooth of a peak above.

So high had they come that the air was thin and it tasted of ice. Gaspare began to shiver.

"There is steam ahead," murmured Saara, who rarely felt the cold. "Hot springs, maybe. Either that or someone is boiling a kettle." She peered narrowly at the single fang above them. It was a bit familiar-looking; seen from farther to the west, it might become quite familiar. She examined it keenly for any sign of entrance. Blood rushed to Saara's cheeks, not entirely because of the wind.

"Does—does not the Devil . . . have cauldrons?" stuttered Gaspare in her ear. "Could it be?"

She shrugged. "If so, it means we have come the right way." With a sigh and a stretch, she strode forward.

The steam wavered in the frozen air. One more rock and they would see it. Hot springs? There was no smell of brimstone in the air. Cauldrons? She herself had spoken of the Liar's cauldrons of steam, but they were part of the world of Lapp children, not of grown witches who themselves had a power of hot and cold.

She stepped carefully around the last rock.

No cauldrons. No hot springs. Just the glistening length of black serpent with floral head and eyes like miniature suns and the hot, moist air of his body hitting the cold.

Something else black was amidst his coils.

"I could not help but notice that you produce fire, too, madam. I could see your spark down the length of the passage. You are a remarkable human in all ways!" chuckled the dragon. He greeted her with a white and steaming smile. "I believe, however, that you left something behind."

It was Festilligambe the dragon indicated. The horse stood spraddled with head and tail drooping, ears flat out sideways, and made no move.

"You found him!" Saara padded up and began to climb over the smooth-scaled sections of dragon. "I didn't think anyone would ever find him again, the way he ran when he saw you."

"He was nervous," drawled the huge creature, revealing his canines further.

Saara came up to the gelding and stared into his black, blank eyes. "Well, he is not nervous now," she commented. "Is he alive?"

"I believe so," replied the dragon, and he, too, turned to examine Festilligambe, but he did not let his armored head get too close.

Saara lifted the horse's unresisting chin with professional interest. "A spell?"

The dragon wiggled, causing Saara to sit down hard. "Please, madam! Do I look to you like a wizard, that I should be casting spells hither and yon? It is only that I am a dragon—that alone produces such an effect on certain animals."

Saara spared him an eye as she got to her feet. "You ask me what you look like quite a lot," she said. "Don't you know what you look like?"

"Mere rhetoric." The dragon used the Italian word, since the Lapps had none fit to the purpose, but he glanced at Saara sidelong, as though he suspected her words to him of having more than the obvious meaning.

Saara put her hand on Festilligambe's withers and shook her head with regret. "I don't know what we're going to do with him," she said. "What good is a horse, for attacking a fortress at the top of a mountain? Especially this fortress."

The jeweled eyes met hers, and in a moment Saara understood what the creature had meant by "that alone produces such an effect on some animals." For a long moment neither the green eyes nor the gold eyes blinked, and at last the creature laughed softly. "I think," he said, "that we should leave the horse here and come back for it later.

"Along with the little flame-head."

"We?" Saara stepped back and sat down on a length of swart tail, moving the spines out of the way.

"We. You and I, woman," added the beast. "Who else has a hope of succeeding against the fallen Star of Morning?"

Saara grinned at the huge, expressionless mask of a face. "And have we a hope, Black Dragon?"

A red split tongue played over the teeth. "Perhaps not."

"Then why do you want to come?"

The dragon turned his head away, to where a tiny and very brave Gaspare was struggling up and over his outermost coil. "Because you freed me. I owe it."

"I release you from the debt," Saara said formally.

The head twisted back along its own neck. "You cannot," the dragon hissed. "It is MY debt.

"Mine!"

Gaspare acceded with surprising grace to the scheme; perhaps it was because it was the dragon, rather than Saara, who explained it to him, saying that he should take the horse and explore farther along the road, while Saara and the dragon prowled the air.

Gaspare did not feel comfortable throwing temperaments in front of a ninety-foot-long steaming creature with teeth like scimitars. But he had enough boldness left in him to inquire how the dragon was to fly, lacking wings.

The great creature curled once around his muzzle before answering. "That is a reasonable question, little naturalist. I don't fly like a bird, you must understand. I swim. I ride the wind. And I can do this because I am hot."

Gaspare frowned thoughtfully into the gaudy, metallic face. Having endured heat, cold, devils, and a shape-changing witch, there was little that one dragon, however well equipped, could do to overawe him. "Delstrego had a power of fire," Gaspare remarked, "but I never saw him fly."

Curiosity lit the amber eyes. "Delstrego? Delstrego you say? Who or what would that be?"

"Never mind," Saara broke in. "If you stay around Gaspare, Dragon, you will hear a lot about Delstrego. But now is not the time. Let's go." In another moment there was only a dun-colored dove on the cold stone path, its wings lifted for flight.

The dragon peered at it closely, as a man might focus on a flea. "More magic," he breathed in tones of disgust, then added more politely, "I fear that in that shape I will fry you without even knowing it, woman of the north.

"Besides, you might have difficulty keeping up with me."

Saara blinked back. "Then how?"

The dragon slid his chin along the ground. Scales rippled in the light of the setting sun. "Behind my head," he hissed.

Using the corona of spikes for footholds, Saara hoisted herself up and looked. There, directly behind the last crimson starburst was a length of smooth neck which did not support a dorsal spine. It fitted Saara like the back of a very round horse. To her surprise she found two small raised scales with handholds cut into them. She fit her fingers with difficulty into them.

"You have been giving rides to . . . children?"

He raised his head off the ground. Saara, used as she was to flight, felt her stomach lurch. "No. Not a child. A small man. A man of India. A little ugly man with a face like a frog's."

Coils scraped by Gaspare, not touching. The dragon oozed a short way down the mountain slope, head elevated. Saara was no more than one more spine on the spiny head. Suddenly the air wavered strongly. As the smell of hot metal reached Gaspare's nose, the beast was aloft.

It squirmed in the air, like the flecks of paper ash tumbling out of a chimney. Gaspare's heart was in his throat as the black tail sliced the sky over his head. The whip shape in the air loomed even closer; perhaps it was out of control and would crash with Saara, crushing himself and the dazed horse in the process.

But no, the writhing of the body continued, but the head of the beast was stable, erect . . .

Riding the wind.

Warm rushes of air bathed Gaspare as Saara and the dragon shrank into the blue sky.

"I never was close enough to see the portal itself," spoke the beast. Saara felt the deep voice through her legs and seat. "Lucifer met me on the mountainside, whereupon I played the part of the credulous fool!

"It had been so long, you must understand, since any creature had dared attempt mischief upon me . . ."

"I can well believe that," screamed Saara into the wind
that buffeted her face. Her words swept behind her, but the
dragon appeared to hear. "But didn't you sense that he was
evil, not to be trusted?"

The beast snorted a gout of flame. "To which sense would
I be indebted for this information, madam?

"Sight, possibly? I tell you he looked like a man of substance. Sound? His voice was good enough. Smell? All
mammals—forgive me my bias—smell rather strongly to
me."

Saara only laughed. She was finding the sense of flight
without work quite exhilarating, and the dragon's upwash
made the air around her comfortably warm. "I mean the
sense of your power—the magic sense."

A shudder passed along the dragon's length and the
scales under Saara roughened slightly. "I know nothing of
such, and wish to know no more."

"But you're a dragon!" the woman blurted.

From the splash of flame at his mouth, it appeared the
creature had cleared his throat. "I am a natural being," he
replied with forced control, "possessing (I have it on good
authority) the imperishable essence of truth.

"Magic, on the other hand, is illusion. Delusion."

Saara, feeling an argument in the making, kept her
mouth shut, and as they floated up beside the nameless
peak of rock, and the dragon continued his story.

"He said he could direct me to Signor Alerghenni—the
man whose teaching I sought—but that it was necessary for
me to delve a tunnel through a certain rock.

"Sages have asked their devotees for stranger things,
so . . ."

"So you created that hole in the mountain?" Saara was
impressed.

"Such as it is, yes. With no attempt at aesthetics, and not
with the idea I was to live in it for twenty years, but I did
cut it."

Suddenly a wave of breath-stealing heat washed over
Saara. "I cut it and then, when the trickster betrayed me, I
cut it in two, letting in the sun. But I could not break the
delusion that held me there."

And then the dragon laughed, causing Saara's body to tremble on its hard seat. "Trapped in delusion. Such an old story!"

It was intoxicating for both the long-prisoned dragon and his rider: swooping at the gray tooth of rock, swirling great loops in the thin freezing air. But Saara did not forget to watch, either for a tall window in the surface of the peak or for some sign of its deadly householder.

"Perhaps it would be better," she spoke into what she hoped was the dragon's ear, "if we landed and worked from the rock itself. We would not be as easily seen."

"Crawling over stone like a lizard?" the dragon drawled. He wrapped his tongue around his muzzle once again. "All very well if you're not in a hurry." And he continued his sailing progress.

At the top of the peak there was no fissure of any kind in the rock. They worked their way down in great circles.

The sunlight failed and the flat blue sky deepened with that immense suggestion of distance that stars give. Instead of darkening, the peak went white.

Saara felt a touch of dizziness, for though she was used to flying, she was not used to being carried. The long whip-body swung lower and lower, faster and faster. They were almost back to the road.

Suddenly Saara felt it; something bad was below. Something cold and bad. She leaned out over the dragon's neck, hoping she was not about to be sick.

"I see it," replied the great creature, though Saara had not had time to speak. "A bar of light. And more."

Now Saara was horribly dizzy: dizzy as a mote spinning on the end of a string. She felt around her a touch of invisible, filthy fingers.

"It is he. The Liar," she whispered through her nausea.

Beneath Saara the black dragon was like so much steel cable. He said nothing more, but sank swirling down upon the road, not fifty feet from the soft-lit window in the rock. Elegantly, insouciantly, Lucifer stood at the lip of his tall window and watched the dragon's arrival.

They had found him. Or had he found them? Saara knew a moment of worry on that subject.

The Devil had chosen to dress himself in white—white velvet—and his gold hair shone like coins. With both arm crossed over his slender chest, he leaned against the bald rock of the mountain peak and looked the dragon up and down.

"So. The watchdog has slipped its chain." Then, stepping forward on his small (oddly small) feet, he added, "And i had't even the wit to run away."

When the dragon opened a long mouth, dim red light suffused the stones. "Base delusion!" he hissed, word muffled by fire. "How fitting that you dress in death's color You spawn of chaos by error! Begone!"

Then Lucifer laughed outright, supporting his chin in one hand and that elbow against the palm of the other hand

"This is no watchdog at all, but a parrot!"

Perhaps this was a miscalculation on Lucifer's part, or perhaps it was part of some long and subtle plan of his. Perhaps he wanted to induce the dragon to cover his head o gold curls and his clothing of white velvet in a deluge o liquid flame. But whether foresight or folly, the Devil vanished beneath a molten spew that burned the air and melted rock beneath him.

He vanished and reappeared, rising phoenixlike in a shape that mirrored the black dragon in length, shape, and deadly armament. But whereas the dragon was black, Satan was white: a stainless, powdery white, tipped with gold at every claw and spine.

These two beasts flexed metallic crowns as they stared at one another. The black dragon reared, rising as effortlessly as a bubble in water. So did the white. Together they lifted slowly: two marionettes on a single wire, two heads balanced on serpentine necks which rocked back and forth in time, keeping even the distance between them.

"Clown!" drawled the snowy dragon. "Wind kite!"

The beast of black iron showed its teeth. Saara crouched behind the dragon's multicolored head shield, gripping the pierced scales with all her strength.

She was no more than a flea in a battle of armed and
armored knights; invisible, powerless, ignored by both con-
estants. She suspected that the Devil did not even know
he was there.

But she was not forgotten: not by the armored knight who
carried her. For as the two dragons rose and the white
spewed fire, the black dragon arched his head back, sparing
his rider the force of the flaming blow.

At the same time his whiplike tail lashed forward, slicing
at the ermine belly of his opponent. The Devil howled and
struck again.

Saara closed her eyes, for the heavens were wheeling
above her too closely. Her feet slipped from the dragon's
metallic sides and there was nothing holding her on except
the grip of her fingers.

Whirling, twisting like two strands in a rope, the dragons
rose. The sharp peak of granite fell away beside them. The
air was lurid.

But though the black dragon was huge and ancient, he
was a creature of the earth, with terrestrial limits. He bent
back before the limitless onslaught of Lucifer's flame. He
threw back his head for a breath of air uncontaminated by
his enemy's reek, and at that moment the white beast
struck, slashing with scimitar teeth at the iridescent black
neck. The black dragon hissed pain and fury.

The floating rope of two strands bent, became a wheel:
black-hubbed with a rim of shining silver. The white serpent emitted a blistering laugh and slashed again, using
flame and tooth together.

Saara, though she could not see, could guess the deadly
situation. "You can't get close enough to use your own fire!
Because of me," she shouted thinly into the furnace-
crackling air.

"No matter," replied her mount quite calmly, though his
mouth spattered flame as he spoke. "There are other weapons at hand." And once more he slashed out at Lucifer, not
with his tail alone, but with his whole length, from the base
of the neck.

The air cracked like thunder as seventy-five feet of edged
violence snapped through it. It caught Lucifer at the crease

where his near hind leg joined the body, leaving a shar‹
pink line which darkened to red. Then as the white drago›
pulled back, guarding the wound, the black released hi‹
bottled fires.

Blazing acids, not sulfurous but smelling of iron, spat‹
tered and stuck to the snowy scales. Wherever the‹
touched, the stainless surface bloomed into whorls of color‹
red, green, and blue like oil spilled on rock. Then, as th‹
flame went out, the circles darkened.

"Ho, Demon," boomed the black dragon. "You hav‹
smudged your funeral whites."

Lucifer coiled and faced his enemy. All was still for a mo‹
ment, with the two beasts circling each other like twi›
moons. Then the Devil whispered, "I needn't bother t‹
dress well for YOUR funeral, brute."

Snakelike, Lucifer struck. The black dragon twitche‹
back with the same speed, but as he did so he felt the gri›
of his hidden rider loosening. He slipped back under he‹
but in that moment the claws and jaws of the white drago›
found their hold, and the two were locked in awful embrac‹
in the skies.

Saara heard the armor of her champion crack and shatte›
She saw moonlight on a tooth as long as her body, before i‹
sank into the black neck not five feet from her leg. Sh‹
smelled blood.

And the massive head of the black dragon lashed left an‹
right, ineffectually, unable to catch any part of the enem›
which was grinding into his windpipe below.

Saara cursed. She released her hold and slid down th‹
shining black scales until the white muzzle (now staine‹
red) was near beside her. She stood, propping hersel‹
against the first of the black dragon's dorsal spines.

"Yey! Liar! You fly-blown pisspot! Look here!"

And the white dragon's blue eyes searched up and down‹
left and right, before he focused on the mite before hi‹
nose.

"No matter how long you wash, you still smell like a sick‹
dog, you know," commented the little witch. Then sh‹
added, "And though you fancy yourself a trickster, I have‹

found you the easiest dolt in the world to deceive." She let
go her hold on the spine and flung herself into space.

Lucifer twisted his jaws around and spared one claw to
catch the plummeting human. But no sooner did the black
dragon feel his enemy's grip slipping than he himself
struck, with a fury of contained hate. Not only did the Devil
miss Saara, but he lost his killing squeeze on the black
throat, and in another moment his clutching claw was
pierced by teeth as sharp as slivered glass.

Meanwhile, the shape plunging in blackness wavered
and was replaced by a ball of downy feathers. The owl Saara
had become tumbled and lost a few secondaries before re-
covering in the air, then rose again to soar in wide circles
around the battle.

What she saw was a different scene from that she had just
left, for the black dragon had a wealth of stored fires and
twenty years of stored hate. Once free of the necessity to
protect his head, he fought with a savagery that seemed
beyond the reach of pain.

He had Lucifer's foot in his mouth and one claw beneath
the Devil's long jaw, holding both tooth and fire useless.
The white dragon, at the same time, had wrapped his serpentine tail around the black's muzzle and was striking
viciously with its edged tip at the other's eyes.

Saara circled, hooting dim, owlish encouragements to
her champion, who had now forced his other claw to the
Devil's throat and was attempting to strangle him. The
white dragon was kicking the black's belly like a fighting
tomcat.

Regardless of the dripping wound in his neck the black
dragon held on. He caught one of his enemy's punishing
hind feet in his own and twisted the white's lower body
around so that he kicked only air. When Lucifer's front
claws found the tear in the flesh of the black dragon's neck
and worried it open, he not only ignored the pain, but was
not aware of it at all.

Could a mortal creature, however strong or ancient, destroy a spirit? A great spirit? The dragon considered this

question in a dry and academic manner while his mouth
uttered his rage and talons squeezed and squeezed.

Although the Mahayana philosopher, Nagarjuna, admitted various levels of spirit and matter, nothing among them
was imperishable (except the atman, or breath, according to
certain other Indians). Therefore this dragon before him
(who might contain breath, but was certainly not purely
breath) might well be perishable.

But the Japanese, now, like Dogen, tended to put change
above all, and did not exclude breath from its dominion.
THAT would imply that this white dragon neck between his
claws was susceptible to infinite alteration, no matter what
its spiritual character.

Where does the flame go, when a candle is blown out?

The dragon, deep in such reflections, snapped his mouth
over that of his white enemy, both pinning its jaws shut and
cutting off air. He threw his shoulders into the cause of
metaphysical experiment until the silver throat caved in beneath him.

The pale body writhed wildly and was still. But a voice
from the air spoke, saying, "I think I am getting bored with
all this."

The white dragon went out.

Like a candle.

The black dragon floated through the air as limply as a
weary swimmer. His fire-washed sides were dull under the
starlight, and black blood oozed down his length, dripping
at last from his tail to the earth far below. His head snaked
left, then right, but his amber eyes found nothing.

Except a tiny feathered shape that darted in above the
lofting heats and sat on his nose. "Quick! There. Follow
while he flees, or it will be for nothing!"

"Follow what?" asked the dragon patiently. Saara sprang
from his muzzle to his outstretched hand. She took human
form and pointed at nothing-at-all among the stars.

"There. The bright shadow. Can't you see?"

Snapping his tail behind him, the enormous beast shot
forward, enclosing Saara in a cage of black tines. "Certainly
I can see. I see Betelgeuse and Rigel and a host of lesser
luminaries, and I see the moon in her half-phase. I see the

Mediterranean Alps beneath and I see your little friend dis-appearing into the window we have sought so long. What else should I be seeing?"

"The Liar! He shines like rotting fish.

"Follow where I point," added the witch, as she saw that the dragon had no more eye for magic than had Gaspare.

"Now up!" she shrilled, and suddenly, "Turn, turn to your left! Sharper."

The dragon obeyed, though growling softly to himself. The earth beneath them reeled repeatedly, with white stone and black pine tilting like beer in a rolling barrel. But Saara was too intent for dizziness now. "Up, up!" she cried ferociously. "Faster or we will lose him."

But the dragon's climb slowed, though his tail beat the air below them so fast Saara could barely see it. It slowed and stopped, and finally they began to fall.

"Too high for fire," whispered the dragon faintly, and they floated, loose as a rope in the ocean, down toward the gleaming earth below.

There were some moments of silence, during which Saara stretched out on the five-fingered hand of iron. "So it is," she admitted ruefully.

They sank, weariness establishing its mastery over both of them. The dragon began to ache.

"That was a famous battle," Saara remarked. "If I were a poet, I would make a saga about it."

The dragon, however, growled glumly. "What does it matter how it went, when I failed you?"

The witch sat up and peered behind them at the black and starry sky. "Failed me? How? Did you expect to split the sky in two? You would have done that before killing the Liar, who was never born."

"Then what were we after?" The yellow eyes, bigger and brighter than torches, looked down at her.

"The answer to a question," replied Saara, who con-tinued to stare into space. "I must find Raphael, the Eagle Chief."

The dragon puzzled. "But we failed in that too. He gave us no time to ask, and now he is gone beyond chasing."

"No," the tiny woman corrected him. "He is not beyond chasing. In fact he is coming back at this moment."

Then the stars spun about as the black dragon swiveled in place. "Where?"

"Coming," repeated Saara, calmly. "He wears no shape." Changing her own shape once again, she darted, a round fluffy owl, behind the dragon's head spines. "I will tell you where he goes," she whispered, "and what he does."

"He is below you," said the owl. "What do you see?"

"Nothing."

"Then what do you feel?"

The dragon slashed with his tail. "Loathing," he hissed through set teeth.

Again the owl peeped and chattered. "Now he is beside you. Can you sense him?"

The dragon's back scales scraped together. "I feel only . . . disgust," he said, but Saara thought he might have used another word but for pride.

"Now he is abo—" hooted the owl, but at that moment a shape hurtled toward her, and Saara threw herself fluttering to the left.

It was an eagle, and it was shining white. It pursued the rotund owl in the air with a skill equal to her own. Twice it chased her around the dragon's very head, pressing so closely she had not the time to hide herself among the projecting spines.

The dragon craned his neck wildly, but the birds were too tiny and too close for him to touch. Like a hawk mobbed by ravens, he sank away from the combat in the air.

But owls do not give battle with eagles, or at least not for long. One of the eagle's talons struck, taking a handful of feathers from the owl and scattering them. She flapped, off-balance, toward the dragon's protective head. The satanic eagle followed, growing closer.

The dragon saw his chance and took it. He opened his mouth and let the owl flutter through. His crocodilian jaw snapped shut on the eagle. The wounded owl fluttered down on his hand.

"Now I will not ask, but demand," said Saara, whose dress hung in tatters stained with blood. She motioned to be brought nearer the dragon's mouth.

"Liar!" she called. "Now you will take us to Raphael. You will release him from his bondage. Or you will spend a long time in a very dark place!"

There was silence, and the dragon clenched his jaw. Then he gagged, for suddenly out of his mouth and nose was pouring streams of matter.

They were hideous, the white-blue of phosphorescent, decaying flesh, and they crawled. They erupted from the dragon's mouth faster than he could spit them out, and they scrabbled over his body. They came down his hand and claw and reached Saara.

They could bite. They could burrow into flesh. Saara screamed, while the dragon belched helpless fire that lapped his sides but did nothing to discourage the infestation. In a panic of horror Saara watched the scum of pale blue disappear between the dragon's scales.

He writhed like a back-broken snake. In a moment surely he would close his hand and crush her. Saara herself lay in a ball on the black palm of the dragon's hand, clawing at a body that had gone slippery with blood.

Like thistledown the black dragon floated down through the high airs. He touched the stone of the peak and rolled as limp as a leather strap, all the way down to the road.

8

Where had his pride gone, Gaspare asked himself. He had not felt so shaken since the bad days: the days he tried never to think about, the days before Damiano, when he had been nobody, with bare feet on the streets of San Gabriele.

He watched the Lady Saara ascend into the sky on he serpentine steed, knowing he had been put on a shel while she and the dragon were out to confront the Devil Yet proud Gaspare—man of many tempests—had sai nothing against the plan. Yes, he would continue along th road, in the unlikely event the Devil had placed the en trance to his eyrie in plain sight. Yes, he would watch th befuddled horse.

Truth was, Gaspare was fit for nothing else, for he had ru out of strength. Entering the worm hole had drained him c bravery in no ordinary manner, while his encounter wit the dragon itself had left him with a dull feeling that any thing might happen next and there was naught that coul be done about it.

The high air (or lack of it) was much to blame for th redhead's shakiness, but, child of the mountains that h was, he did not connect the peaks around him with his in tense desire to sit down on the road and shut his eyes.

He leaned against Festilligambe: not a good idea, for th horse was in no condition to support his weight. "Come, ol outlaw," grumbled the redhead. "Wake up and show som fight!"

Festilligambe hauled up one ear, but made no other re sponse to Gaspare's urging. Staring into the gelding's roun brown eyes, Gaspare thought he saw reflections of amber.

"What has he done to you, ass-face? You look like ol Lucia after her third tankard." The youth twisted Fes tilligambe's black tail (heavy by nature, thinned by too much standing near the fire) as though the horse were a pig A groan was the only result.

Festilligambe's paralysis conquered Gaspare's. His spirit rose to contempt for the addled beast. "Snap out of it horse. It was just a big lizard, you know. A dumb brute like yourself."

Suddenly there came a whistling shriek from somewhere above and ahead, accompanied by booming curses and fol lowed by a great hiss of engines. "Or a brute, at any rate, Gaspare added with less cockiness. "Come on. We can' stay here."

To his left rose a slope of rock and rubble, rising to the sharp tooth of the mountain. On the right the slope fell again in increasing steepness. Gaspare did not move to the gravel-scattered edge to look over, for there was an uncomfortable cold wind.

Ahead of him a spur rose at the right of the road, amidst the scree, so there would be protection from both sides. Protection from the wind, at any rate. Gaspare tweaked Festilligambe's ear and prodded one thumb knuckle into his ribs, but the horse did not respond. At last he drew back, cocked his foot, and spun around, landing an impressive roundhouse kick just below the gelding's limply hanging tail.

Slowly the horse swayed forward. Slowly he began to move.

Gaspare entered the protection of the rocks. When the road veered away to the left, following the base of the peak, he clipped the skin of Festilligambe's nostril between two fingers and led him around.

A shrieking roar blasted the rocks. Gaspare gazed up in time to see the dragons, white and black, rise twining into the high air. A horrid glory of flame brightened the evening sky.

Gaspare fell to his knees, not knowing it was Satan himself who assaulted his friend in the air, but knowing it was terrible. "I am useless," he whispered, his teeth chattering. "By God and all His saints, I want to hide!" He hid his face in his hands.

The bellowing faded as the combatants rose farther from the road itself. Gaspare, folding his hands in half-shamed prayer, looked ahead and beheld the yellow light of a lamp.

In front of him, along the road itself, was a window. It extended from the gravel and dust of the earth to a peak at least twenty feet up, and the stone trim around it was as neat and pretty as that of a church. It was the kind of window one could walk through, having neither shutter nor glass. Inside it was a room.

As Gaspare stood perched on the sill, a light spatter of flame licked the stone of the road behind him. Acid hissed and crackled against stone. The youth hopped through,

down the two-foot drop to the interior floor, which was tile·
quite fashionably in the Italian manner.

"So," he said. "Even as Delstrego described it."

Delstrego had visited the Devil. He had told Gaspare a·
about it. But the redhead hadn't listened, exactly, becaus·
it had been back in the days when he thought Delstreg·
was . . . well, confused.

But he DID remember that the Devil's high chambe·
had been big—so big that a man might sit on a table as larg·
as a ballroom floor. "Not quite as Delstrego described it,·
Gaspare amended.

Here was a table. Gaspare put his hand upon it. Abou·
two arm spans by one-and-a-half, he judged. On it were tw·
things: a rather impressively made model of a fortress, and·
bowl of grapes. Besides the table, the only furnishings i·
the room were a single high-backed chair, various loud an·
busy scarlet embroideries on the walls, and a red leathe·
bag hanging from the ceiling lamp.

Gaspare's curious fingers played with a tiny steel shutte·
which hung on one of the few windows of the model. I·
worked. He peered inside the arched windows on the tin·
cupola which topped the model. There was something in i·
but he couldn't make out what. By habit he plucked a grap·
from the bowl and brought it to his mouth.

But there was something about the fruit, somethin·
greasy, perhaps, or was it the color which was not quit·
right? Gaspare put it down again and danced nervousl·
through the room.

No doors, just three other windows. Two of them looke·
out onto blackness (night fell so abruptly in the mountains·
Gaspare peered out of the fourth window, hoping to sp·
Saara and her dragon.

After a brief glimpse he backed away again, reeling. Ga·
pare's stomach didn't feel too well. He cursed a prayer, ·
prayed profanely (from the time he had been a stree·
urchin, the two actions had blurred into one for him), an·
returned his attention to the toy on the table.

IT had no doors either. "No doors," he mumbled. "N·
way out."

"Go out the way you came in: that's my advice. And do so as quickly as possible," said the red leather bag hanging from the lamp.

Gaspare leaped squealing into the air and his arms flailed. One hand struck the bag, which was soft and saggy, and which began to swing back and forth. Two blue eyes, on stalks, moved in opposition to the swaying. "Don't do that," the bag complained. "You might hurt the image."

Gaspare blinked from the speaker to the work on the table. "I'm sorry," he blurted. "Who . . . what are you?"

It had a mouth, set above the blue eyes. It had a blobby big belly, with sticklike arms and hands tied together behind it. (Tied in a bow. With red string.) It had feet set at the very top of the belly, one of which had been tied with red string to the lamp cord.

"I am Kadjebeen," stated the bag. "I am an artisan."

Gaspare made a discovery. "You're upside down," he informed the bag.

"Yes, I am," replied Kadjebeen equably. "I'm being punished."

"For what?" asked Gaspare, but before the demon could answer, Gaspare had untied the sticklike arms and was working on the knot in the lamp cord. Such was his attitude toward punishment.

The little horror was lowered to the table. It rolled over so that its blue scallop-eyes were upmost. "I was supposed to have someone whipped half-to-death." His small raspberry-colored mouth emitted a sigh.

"What is 'half-to-death'?" Kadjebeen asked Gaspare, but did not wait for an answer before adding, "Life is neither distance nor volume, that I can take out my weights, levels, or my measures and get it exact. What was I to do?"

Gaspare didn't answer. The demon massaged his button head in both hands. "Better to be conservative, don't you think? I mean, one can always whip a little more, afterward, but if the man is dead, one can scarcely whip a little LESS, can one?

"Besides . . . I did so admire those wings."

Gaspare, who had been listening to Kadjebeen's complaint with a certain lack of sympathy, suddenly lunged forward. "Wings? Angel wings?"

Kadjebeen cringed back, hiding his eyes in his hands.
(One in each.) "What'd I say? What'd I say? Don't hit me!
I'm only an artisan!"

Gaspare repeated his question more moderately.

"I don't know what kind of wings you're talking about.
These weren't like regular demon wings. Not leathery.
They had feathers like birds'. Whitish."

"Raphael!" cried Gaspare, and when Kadjebeen threatened to withdraw once more, he shook him.

"Yes, yes! Raphael was his name. Nice guy, he seemed.
Well put together. Looked a lot like the Master."

Seeing Gaspare's exultant face, he asked, "You interested
in wings too?"

"I am . . . interested in Raphael's wings," warbled Gaspare, dancing another little dance of excitement. "Raphael
is my friend. My teacher. We have come from San Gabriele
in the Piedmont, looking for him.

"Through cold and wind," Gaspare chanted. "Past dragons and enchanted boulders we have come, and not all the
Devil's wiles could stop us!"

Kadjebeen sighed again. "Then he must not have been
trying very hard."

Gaspare was stung. "I'm sure he was! If he had any sense
he was, because we are justice itself on his trail."

The skin at the back of his neck twitched, as Gaspare
remembered where he was and to whom he was speaking.
"You . . . LIKE him? Your wicked master? In spite of what
he did to you? You'll tell Satan I was here, and everything I
said?"

Kadjebeen's eyes made independent circuits of the room.
"Like . . . the Master?" Then in a rush he replied, "Of
course I don't. Who could like him? But I'm sure I will tell
on you. He'll torture me till I do."

The round demon sighed. He walked over to his toy and
fiddled with it in proprietary fashion. "And then he'll torture me some more, I guess."

Gaspare's courage, working as it did by law of opposition,
rose as the demon quailed. "It doesn't matter if you do tell,
you miserable insect. We've come for the angel and won't

leave without him!" He pirouetted around the table, slicing most gracefully with an invisible sword.

"Well, I'm very sorry, then," mumbled Kadjebeen.

Between one florid step and the next, Gaspare stopped dancing. "Sorry for what?"

Kadjebeen was sitting on the table. He had both hands laced around his middle. Now his color was returning, and he looked more like a raspberry and less like a bag. "Because the Master gave him away."

"Gave him away?" echoed Gaspare. He struck his bony fist on the tabletop. The greasy grapes bounced. "He gave away an angel of God?"

"Watch out for the image," mumbled the demon reflexively. "It's a perfect correspondence, you see, and one has to be careful." Then the demon realized that Gaspare's attention could not be diverted from his goal.

"Yes. He melted off his wings and gave him to one of his toadies—uh, servants. Perfecto the Spaniard, the man's name is. I imagine your Raphael is in Granada now."

Observing the dusky flush of Gaspare's face, Kadjebeen added, to console him, "The wings were gone by then, anyhow."

Gaspare's impersonal glare sharpened. "You must take us to him!"

The demon squeaked, and drew in both hands and feet, so that nothing but his trembling eyes disturbed his rotundity. "Oh, I couldn't! The Master would never let me! He'd be so angry if he even knew you'd asked!"

Gaspare, whose own fear had somewhere been left behind, strode to the window, where the dazed horse stood placidly, seeing nothing. All sounds of battle had faded, but in his heart was growing a conviction that the battle was already won: a conviction which had nothing to do with Saara's magic, or the length of the dragon's teeth.

"Your master, little insect, is nothing but scum!"

"Oh dear, don't," quailed Kadjebeen, as his ears and eyes rotated nervously. "He is the Prince of the Earth and very sensitive about it."

"He is the Prince of Cowardice," Gaspare declared. "And all his victories are cheats."

He spun theatrically and smacked his chest. "I myself te
you this, you poor deluded slave. And I should know, be
cause I AM A VERY BAD MAN!"

Kadjebeen stared at Gaspare with an increase of respec

"Or I WAS a very bad man. But with the grace of Go
and the help of His angel Raphael, I am trying. It is hard,
added the youth, staring with wide green eyes at the roun
body on the table, "when you are born with low instinc
and have habits both worldly and violent, but it is possib
to throw off Satan entirely. Even you could do it."

His gaze on the demon lost certainty. ". . . I think."

"This Raphael person," Kadjebeen thought to mentio
"didn't last very long against my Master."

Gaspare frowned, remembering Kadjebeen's part in tha
deed. "Raphael sacrificed himself," he said with dignit
"For MY sins, I am told.

"And I . . . I will release him from bondage. I have th
greatest witch in all Europe at my side. We cannot lose.

Kadjebeen's stalked gaze shifted to Festilligambe. "Th
greatest witch in all Europe is a horse?"

"Uh, no. This is Festilligambe. He is probably the faste
horse in all Europe. He is certainly the most troublesome.
A glance at the slack-jawed, lop-eared face forced him
add, "He is, however, not feeling his best.

"My companion, the Lady Saara, is at this moment cha
ing your foolish master's legions from the skies, while I hav
the responsibility to locate and rescue Raphael."

"He's in Granada," repeated Kadjebeen helpfully.

"So." Gaspare cracked his knuckles, one by one. "Take
to Granada."

"I couldn't . . ." began the raspberry demon, but h
changed his mind in midsentence. "I would like to, but
don't see how . . ."

"And you call yourself an artist!" Gaspare's voice, not na
urally resonant, rang strangely loud in that stale, tile
chamber.

"An artisan," Kadjebeen corrected him. "I build thing
Images. As a matter of fact, I am the greatest maker of im
ages that—"

"Artist, artisan . . . Bah!" Gaspare brushed the distinction aside. "Don't you know that all the arts are blessed, and Satan is their enemy? Raphael is the greatest musician ever created, as well as the most beautiful; it is out of jealousy that Satan has done him hurt. I myself—"

"I myself am tone-deaf," interjected the raspberry demon. "As well as ugly. But go ahead—you were about to tell me what YOU were greatest at."

"I was not," grunted Gaspare, instantly deflated. "I'm not the best at anything, although my old friend and partner . . . Oh, never mind." For to Gaspare's mind came the words the ghost had said at the top of the hill in Lombardy. "Don't strive to be the best, or you will wake up one day and know yourself no good at all."

There was no sound to be heard, except the droning sighs of Festilligambe, who seemed to be waking up. Suddenly Gaspare wanted to be out of this square room with windows that made no sense and air like doused ashes. Even if its owner never returned, it was no good place to be.

"Granada, you say?" He spared a last glance at the demon. "Then to Granada we will go, on the back of the greatest dragon that . . ." Gaspare swallowed.

"On the back of a dragon." He leaped lightly onto the sill. Festilligambe nickered sleepily. Gaspare dragged him along by the mane. "Come on, ass-face. We have what we came for . . ."

It was black outside, and all noise of combat had ceased. A dust of stars whitened the sky. Gaspare lifted his head, and cold wind caught his russet hair.

Where were Saara and the dragon? Gaspare felt pregnant with news and wanted to communicate it. Surely they had not chased that stranger dragon so far they could not get back to him? All pretty white and gold, it hadn't looked like a beast with much fight in it.

As he stood in the mountain darkness, huddled against a black horse for warmth, Gaspare heard an awkward scuffing behind him.

A squarish black shape was following his trail on spindly pink-purple legs. It looked like a bedding box with the hindquarters of a chicken. For a moment Gaspare's hair

stood on end, not out of fear but disbelief, until he recog
nized the object as Kadjebeen's toy palace, propelled b
Kadjebeen himself.

"I'm coming," panted the demon, unnecessarily.

"With that?"

Kadjebeen hugged his masterwork with arms too shor
for the purpose. His eyes drooped protectively over the top
"It's mine," he mumbled. "I made it. Best thing I eve
made. It's an image of the whole palace. Even His Magnifi
cence has never appreciated how perfect a job it is."

Gaspare only sighed. Together he, Kadjebeen, and th
horse stepped out of the shelter of the rocks.

There, on the gray-lit slope of the peak itself, lay a lon
body like a length of rope cast off by some giant. Moonligh
glistened on it, for it was coated with some sort of slime
and small, scuttling things went in and out of the great
scimitar-lined mouth, which leaked steam. Yellow eye
shone faintly, staring at nothing.

Caged in one iron paw, undamaged but motionless, was
small shape in a scorched blue dress.

Gaspare stopped dead, causing Kadjebeen to bump int
him. The horse reared in panic.

Then Gaspare ran wildly over the rubble and stone, u
the slick and gripless slope of rock, toward the fallen drago
with its phosphorescent infection. He reached the black
clawed hand. He squeezed between the bars.

With both hands Gaspare wiped the ooze from Saara'
eyes. He wept and cursed together as more came out of he
nose and lips. Her flesh looked and felt like wax.

The creeping disease touched Gaspare.

Kadjebeen stood alone on the road, leaning on his work
He was feeling very low.

The fellow had seemed so certain of himself, with hi
greatest this and his fastest that. It had been a long tim
since Kadjebeen had met anyone except the master himsel
who was so self-assured. He tried to remember when an
where he HAD met another like Gaspare. His memorie
were sadly jumbled.

But the raspbery demon was sure of one thing. He really
didn't want to hang from the ceiling anymore.

Amid the cries and weeping, as Kadjebeen leaned dis-
nsolately on his image, he heard a familiar sound. From
mewhere nearby, his master Lucifer was laughing. Kadje-
en listened, and in his present discouragement he had
e idea Lucifer was laughing at him.

Long white wings: light, intricate, craftworthy. Melted
e ice.

"No!" He shouted petulantly. Then louder. "No. I'm
ed of it. Always the best work is broken and the worst
alted. Always the back of the hand! Well, I won't any-
ore. I won't!"

And Kadjebeen, in excess of rage, sprang up in the air on
s bandy legs and came down right on the cupola of his
asterwork—the image of Lucifer's Hall.

He let out an "oof" and an "ouch," for the little object was
inted. But it was also fragile, and it splintered beneath
s jelly-shuddering weight.

From the mountain beneath came the thud like that of a
amming door, magnified many times. Kadjebeen
amped. Something shifted in the rock itself. The air
pped.

But Kadjebeen hopped again and again, smacking his
boed surface against paper-thin walls. The image gave
y.

The fortress of Lucifer gave way. Rock shuddered, deep
the earth. The thin air was loud with broken deceits and
e cries of demons with their leashes snapped. The yellow
ht shining around the corner went out.

A fungoid silvery growth appeared on the black coils of
e dragon, as Lucifer dragged himself frantically from the
sh of his victims. His shape solidified, grew hair, was
essed in white velvet.

He hurled himself through the air toward the gate of his
lace, at the small figure standing by the shards of delicate
ne.

It was not bulbous, not colored like a raspberry. It was a
an, or the shade of a man: short, wiry, but not uncomely,
th very strong arms and hands. His face was bearded and
s eyes round and blue.

"No more, my Master," said the shade, and the voi
came to Lucifer from far away. The spirit pointed to its eye
its body, and to its mouth. "No one is made so badly as y
would have them believe," it whispered, and the beard
mouth smiled. Slowly the large, sail-white wings spread b
hind it and tested the air.

Smiling, the shade raised its strong arms and squar
workman's hands. It rose and faded into a sky awash wi
the stars.

Flaming with curses, Lucifer fled away to recapture h
scattered devils.

As a half-moon rose from behind the rock-tooth, t
yellow eyes of the dragon answered its light. The bladed t
twitched.

And Gaspare, in the pergola of the dragon's upturn
hand, held Saara until she was warm again, and her ey
opened.

9

Though the glassy night was the most comfortable time
late-summer Granada, the servants in their barracks we
too tired to stay awake for it and Rashiid and his wives we
too well-fed. Only Raphael sat up, crouched half-naked b
side the fish pond, and the fish circled at his feet. He w
talking with Damiano.

"You look much better, I think," the spirit was sayin
"Except for your nose."

"My nose," repeated Raphael. He touched that memb
for identification and winced at the result. "It hurts. And
whistles when I breathe through it."

Moonlight had bleached the gold from his hair and r
duced the glorious color of his black eye to mere shadow
He glimmered as insubstantially as his friend the ghost.

Damiano's cloudy suggestion of a face drew closer and darkened in sympathy. He said, "I can hear it. A very musical sound, as befits a teacher of music. But I know a cure for the problem."

"Tell me!" Though weeks of humanity had taught Raphael some sophistication, his face still reflected his every feeling, and now his perfect blue eyes (one of them rimmed in purple and green) pleaded with Damiano.

"It takes bravery."

Raphel nodded soberly.

The spirit's umbrous wings folded back. He added, "It is not a magical but a musical cure."

This did not seem to surprise Raphael at all.

"Take your hands," began Damiano, "and clap them in your lap." The blond did so, but quietly, so as not to wake the slaves in the barracks.

"Now keep the rhythm and follow me, clapping whenever I clap." The ghost went clap, clap, clap in his lap, making hardly a sound, and then raised his arms above his head and struck his ectoplasmic hands together. Raphael accompanied him in (of course) perfect time.

Three claps more above the knees and three in front at arm's length and three more in the lap and then in front of the face, one, two, and . . .

Perhaps Damiano gave a nudge, or perhaps Raphael, in the heat of the performance, wasn't thinking quite what he was doing, but the third clap came hard and symmetrically down on his injured nose.

He gasped and rose half to his feet. "I hit myself!" he cried aloud, and then, as greater understanding came to him, he added, "You MADE me to hit myself!"

The spectral form wavered, perhaps through shame. "But your nose: How is it now?"

Raphael gave a careful sniff. "I smell blood," he said, with a hint of petulance. "But I think . . . I think . . ."

Again Damiano leaned close. "I don't hear anything."

Raphael, too, listened. "No. Nothing. The whistle is gone."

"And your nose is straight again. You'll be as handsome as ever."

The blond's fine hands were locked protectively around the middle of his face, but his eyes turned to Damiano with sudden interest. "Am I handsome? I never thought about it."

Sadly Damiano smiled. "You've never been a mortal before. Now you'll think about things like that: Are my teeth good? Is that a wrinkle or a spot forming by my eyebrow? Is that fellow a bigger, stronger, better man than I? It's the mortal condition; we don't seem to be able to help it.

"And another part of being mortal, Seraph. Hating. Do you hate your master yet?"

Raphael squatted down again. He lifted his eyes to the stars while the warm wind stirred his hair.

"My master? I feel bad that he hit me. He had never told me I was not supposed to mention that Djoura was a Berber in front of other Berbers. And how was I to know that Djoura's father had been sworn to Qa'id Hasiim years ago?

"And though I know Rashiid had reason to be angry—he felt compelled to give a great gift of money to the Berbers in the Alhambra, as well as losing what he'd paid for Djoura—still, I'd rather not have to see him anymore. Somehow I don't like looking at him or hearing his voice."

"Understandable."

"Is it?" Raphael's left eyebrow shot up in a movement familiar to his student. "I don't understand it. After all, Rashiid will be Rashiid whether in my sight and hearing or not.

"But that is nothing like hate, I know, for I have felt hate. One doesn't have to be a mortal . . . There is one I hate and have hated for a very long time." Then Raphael took a deep breath through his newly repaired nostrils.

"And anyway, this blunder of mine led to Djoura being freed, and freedom was what she most wanted, so I'm glad of it."

"Freedom is what we all most want," murmured the thoughtful spirit, and for a moment he faded into moonlight. When he raised his face to his friend again, there was a hint of fire in his dark eyes.

"Raphael, you must remember who you are!"

The man looked only weary. He turned his head away. "I
member, my friend. My confusion is nearly gone.

"I remember every voice in the choir. And the song, in all
 parts—how could I forget that? But my memories are
ly memories, and don't move me."

The voice of a single frog hidden in the weeds of the pond
enced Raphael for a few moments. Then he said, "More
al to me than heavenly music is the fact that my nose
irts, and is dripping blood, and that I know I must dig at
 e latrines tomorrow, as well as play the ud."

Damiano nodded. He dipped one vague hand into the
ack pool water, passing it through several little perch in
 e process. Neither hand nor fish were the worse for it.
ou don't talk about God—your Father—anymore."

Raphael's eyes slipped down, from his friend's face to the
idisturbed surface of the water. "You mean Allah. Here
 e is Allah, and the people of Granada use His name in
ery third sentence. And they all seem to know just what
is will is on every issue. All but me, of course.

"Allah and I have not been introduced."

"You are bitter," whispered the ghost.

Raphael smiled and his battered face was transformed.
'm not, really." He put his hand into the waistband of his
ousers and pulled out a little pouch. "I have a pebble,
ami: the one you gave me. I take care of it."

The moon had rolled away and only Jupiter and the Dog
ar made light enough to outshine the approach of dawn.
 that season and latitude Sirius never set.

Raphael was sleeping like a dog, however, curled against
 e cold with a protective hand on either side of his nose.
ven as he slumbered, the little perch of the pond did not
·lax their honor guard, and the carp at the bottom hugged
 e bottom and sides of the tank as though to push their way
rough soil to the transformed angel.

Soon the dozen men in the barracks would be expected to
ake up and be useful. They slept all the harder now in
 pectation.

But in the main house little Ama was awake; she had had
 wake up to vomit, which was her recent custom. As al-

ways, concluding this task left her fresh and airy, ready fo
the day's experience. And now she tiptoed out the whit
doorway, sure of her path despite the lack of light.

Ama was wearing white. She came sans veil and her hai
was undone. She looked more like Rashiid's little daughte
than Rashiid's young wife. She found Raphael on the benc
beside the fish pond. Finger-length perch darted in ever
direction.

"Ho, slugabed! Wake up. Wake up and do my hair."

Raphael opened both eyes. He yawned, winced, an
touched his upper lip. He chafed his unclad arms.

"Since because of you I don't have Djoura anymore, yo
must be my body servant," Ama persisted. Then she gig
gled. "You're much nicer, after all, though you're the wron
color."

She leaned over him and peered closely at his face
"Wrong colors, I should say. How shocking!" Ignoring hi
incoherent reply, Ama pushed his knees off the bench an
sat herself down facing away from him, presenting he
abundant hair.

"My husband is a brute; I have always known so. H
would hit me, I'm sure, if my family were not so importan
I'm glad they are. My uncle is a *nakib;* he has the fealty o
two hundred men. But not so much money.

"Why do you sleep outside, Raphael? It gets cold in th
morning. It's cold now.

"You know how Djoura used to sleep? Fully dressed, i
all those dusty black gowns of hers. Looked like a hill o
mud, she did, with her veil over her black face. But she wa
warm, I bet.

"What did you say?"

Raphael had been about to tell Ama why he slept on th
bench by the fish pond: a story which involved his first an
only night in the barracks (fully dressed, like Djoura), whe
because of his humming and his muted conversation wit
an unseen visitor he had earned eviction. But as he ros
from his hard cot he thought of something else to say.

"I don't know how to do your hair, mistress," the slav
admitted. "I have never done a lady's hair before."

Ama shrugged and set her small mouth. "You know how to make braids, don't you? Braid it."

Raphael set to work. His hands were good, and he was, of course, an artist. He worked neatly but without great speed, and Ama wiggled. After a few minutes, she wiggled backward into his lap.

"Rashiid is angry with me too. Isn't that absurd? All because I'm the one who wanted the black. How was I to know she was of an important clan? It's Rashiid's own business to know those things; I'm just his wife, after all."

She darted an avian glance back at the blond. "I wish I weren't his wife. I wish I was YOUR wife instead!" Then Ama giggled at her own conceit. "The wife of a eunuch! Wouldn't that be an easy job?"

Suddenly the girl spun about on Raphael's knees, pulling her black tresses from his fingers. Her face was inches from his. With her fingers she combed his yellow hair over his eyes and began to twist it about. "Your turn, Pinkie . . . I mean Raphael.

"You'd make such a pretty girl yourself, except that you're too big, of course, and too skinny. But I like your eyes, and your mouth is so sweet." She kissed his not-quite-awake face.

Color had descended from the sky: the green of the pond, the blue in Raphael's eyes, the hidden russet in Ama's hair. "Shall I marry you, Raphael? Shall I forget about Rashiid and marry you? You can be my little wife!"

Ama forced her treble voice down to a masculine growl as she repeated again and again the phrase "my little wife." She had quite a talent for imitating Rashiid, both in word and gesture; Raphael found himself being possessively pawed all over. It was rather pleasant.

"I have only seen one eunuch before," whispered Ama, breaking out of her husbandly character for a moment. "He was the little boy of my uncle's household in Algiers, and he had two red scars in this shape." She lay one finger crosswise over another. "He would cry if we tried to touch them.

"Here, Pinkie. While no one else is watching. Take your trousers off and show me."

Raphael's fair forehead drew down and he prisoned Ama's exploratory hands in his own. "I'm not supposed to do that," he said.

With a force of outrage she yanked free of his grasp. "Not supposed to . . . Who said you're not supposed to? I'm your mistress and I say . . ." Ama grabbed the waistband of Raphael's cotton trousers and pulled until the cord broke. The baggy garment slipped onto the bare wood of the bench.

Little Ama looked first surprised and then quite confused. She was speechless. Under the intensity of her stare Raphael grew nervous. He also felt quite warm, somehow, though the sun had not yet crested the wall. He attempted to gather the cloth again at his hips, but Ama forestalled him.

"Either a eunuch looks just like a man, once he grows up, or . . ." Her small round eyes rose to his. "Are you a whole man after all, Raphael?"

"Yes," he replied. "But no one is supposed to know that."

Ama rolled her eyes. She edged away from the slave along the bench and folded her hands on her lap. Her feet swung to and fro, not touching the ground. "By the light of Allah!" she whispered, and then, "Rashiid is going to be sooo angry!"

Raphael found he was more nervous than ever, though not nearly so warm. "I did not ever tell him I was a eunuch," he ventured to say to the girl, but she only muttered and shook her head.

Then with her typical unpredictability, Ama squeezed Raphael teasingly in a place he did not expect. "I won't tell," she promised, grinning sidelong. "Not if you're nice to me." Then she turned and darted, perchlike, past the fish pond and away.

In the harbor of Adra, the big-bellied ships bobbed and wallowed in the swell. The longshoremen sang in Spanish and the wind tasted of salt.

Djoura hated it: both the Spanish and the water-laden air, which made her nose run. She despised the whining Northern Arabic of the mariners who warbled and yodeled to each other in the hold, securing their cargo of oranges. She had great contempt for the official Granadan bookkeeper, a sunburned Spaniard who sat on a small date keg by the gangplank, in case the owner of the boat should try to load anything in evasion of the export duties.

Djoura sat behind the gay-striped partitions in the stern of the ship which was to take her across the Mediterranean, and she thought furiously.

It had been a pleasant shock, in the beginning, when the tribesmen burst into the Spanish pig's hot kitchen, scaring his old wife into hysterics and pulling her out of the grease and soot. It had also been fulfilling to see Rashiid babbling apologies—not to her, of course, but to the Berbers he had so grievously offended.

Djoura had not expected these pale Berbers, strange to her, to take such an interest. It was only just—only Berber—that they should, of course, but still, Djoura had lived her life in the real world, and no one else in her five years of slavery looked past her skin color to see that she was of the free people, and that her captivity was an outrage.

And this, besides, was not the manner in which Djoura had planned to regain her freedom. Where did they think they were sending her, anyway? Not a soul had bothered to share with her that information. The black woman knew well she had no living male kin. She had seen her father's headless body, and her single brother—well, if he had lived, he would have found her by now.

Perhaps they would dump her with the first black Berbers to pass through Algiers. Then what would she be? Little more than a slave, again.

As a slave, she had known herself a Berber, and therefore not truly a slave. Now, kinless among her own race, she would be a free but homeless female, and therefore not free at all.

Djoura cursed the pride which had forced Hasiim to "rescue" her—a woman in whom he had no interest, and to whom he had never bothered to speak.

And always Djoura's circle of thought returned to her Pinkie, whom she had groomed for the role of her male "protector" in their escape from Rashiid's household, and who was the unwitting cause of all this upset. How had he suffered for his interference? Surely that greasy swine had not let his loose tongue go unpunished . . .

Poor Pinkie: How long would he be able to hide his secret among that household—without Djoura? He would be a real eunuch soon enough, and with stripes to boot.

Ah, but maybe that would be just as well. Pinkie was so naïve: too childlike even to consider vengeance. And he wasn't much of a man, to look at: pale, beardless, baby-haired. He wouldn't mind as much as some. Assuredly he would not kill himself from the shame of castration, as many men would. Djoura sighed. The wind caused the hangings of her enclosure to flap and billow, reducing it to an unconcealing framework of ropes: a seclusion as ineffective as was this "rescue" from slavery.

Then, between one moment and the next, Djoura knew that she could not leave Pinkie to his fate.

For hadn't she named him her brother? And even as a brother must avenge his sister or die, so must she, Djoura, return for the poor pale singer she had adopted.

Besides, she missed him.

With dignity, the woman rose to her feet. Brass coins jingled sweetly around her ears. A pillar of black, she strode out of her enclosure, ducking under the supporting tent rope.

The bookkeeper with his tally sat on a keg at the head of the gangplank. He looked up with surprise to see the woman standing before him. In faulty Arabic he told her to return to her place.

In response Djoura mumbled something inaudible. She crooked her little finger and whispered again. Rising halfway to his feet, the embarrassed official presented his ear for some petty feminine revelation.

Djoura put one large hand firmly over the man's money pouch and the other firmly against his chest. She heaved.

With a weak cry the bookkeeper fell backward from the keg into the green Mediterranean. Djoura paraded down the plank and into Adra.

10

"Though heat rises," the deep, pipe-organ voice beneath them intoned, "the upper regions are colder. This is true over all the earth."

Gaspare was not satisfied. He shifted his grip on Saara's waist. (He had shifted his grip so many times that she was developing the horse's trick of swelling her middle whenever the girth tightened.) "I'm more inclined to believe you just haven't gone high enough to find the layer of heat that surrounds the earth."

There was a short silence from the dragon. "I have never read that there is such a layer," he replied at last.

"Stands to reason," attested the youth, kicking the metallic black neck absently.

"I rather think a look at the simple geometry of the situation will explain the phenomenon, youngster."

"Geometry. Is that a foreign word?" Gaspare mumbled distrustfully.

The dragon sighed at Gaspare's ignorance. Saara sighed also, for she had a headache. She had carried it since waking on the mountain's stony side with Gaspare shaking her. She wondered how the dragon (old as he was) could have recovered so quickly.

When Saara as a child had a headache, her mother had used to roll an egg against her head, until the ache went into the egg. Then she would bury it beneath the snow of the yard: egg and ache together.

She wished now she had an egg. She wished she were home.

Home? Yes, and she didn't mean Lombardy, but the far Fenlands, where her Lappish people dug their houses, pressed felt, and followed the herds of sturdy deer through white winter. For the first time in many, many years, Saara the Fenwoman thought of home without remembering Jek-kinnan and the faces of her dead babies, strewn across the floor of the hut.

Her children were dead, and Jekkinnan too. So, for that matter, was Rogerio, and her old enemy Delstrego senior. All dead and folded away. (Like egg white in a cake. Like an egg itself buried in the snow.) Soon she, too, would be folded into history: that was the rule ever since the Spirit sang earth into being.

Damiano was right; the summoning made the separation of the living and dead worse. Saara felt renewed pain, for she would have liked so much to have shown Lappland to Damiano. He would have liked it, for he liked anything pretty.

If she lived through this, she told herself, she would return to the Fens and see it again—the red autumn, the white winter, the crying geese in the springtime—for the sake of Damiano Delstrego, and perhaps he would know the beauty through her eyes.

Padding barefoot down an alley wet with offal, Djoura's every movement was regal. The night air might as well have been thick with jasmine as with garlic and piss, for Djoura's free soul was touching the high winds freighted with clouds.

For over a week she had been alone among the rocks in the climbing desert which stretched between the ocean and high Granada. She had bought a mule and then sold it again, prefering her own feet for transport. The customsman's gold had permitted her to eat well. Now she had reached Granada.

For the first time in her grown life Djoura's steps had not been ordained by another. These nights were the first in her life that someone else had not decided where she should sleep. She had slept in haystacks and under upturned wagons. She had slept under the moon.

Tonight Djoura did not sleep at all, but paraded past mud brick and stucco, through the capillaries of a city she did not know, toward the liberation of another besides herself.

The poor were curled dozing in doorways all around her. Good for them—it was certainly better to sleep in a doorway than in the rank holes within doors. Djoura stared down at the sleepers from a great height. Her veil was back and her hair gleamed with a constellation of coins. From within one house—a heavy, feverful pile of mud—came singing. It was bad singing, out of tune and with strictly private rhythm. But Djoura took it in and let it add to her own strength; she swelled with power as she walked.

"I am so tall now," she whispered to the air, "that there is no chain forged which could span my neck. And should some clever man forge such a shackle, he would find no ladder big enough that he could reach up to put it on.

"And if he DID reach me, I would crush him in this hand, for his trouble," Djoura continued. Her black hand moved invisibly through the heavy shadow. Eyes, teeth, and coins glimmered. "I grow larger at every moment.

"Like the earth after rain," she murmured on. "Taller and stronger, stronger and taller." Her round nostrils flared like those of a high-blooded horse.

"I am Djoura, the black one, the free. The breaker of chains. I am Djoura: my will is a sword!"

And the walls on either hand fell away from her as though she had pushed them down. Djoura stood at a large crossroads, under moonlight. She raised her arms and made the moonlight hers. Her layered clothing cast a terrible shadow on the paving.

Even Djoura herself blinked, surprised at the way the world was acceding to her new-won mastery. The moon touched her face like a rain of white feathers.

Djoura cupped her hands to the moon. She danced (with African straightness, lest she spill the moon from her hands) and laughed, crying, "I am mad, mad with my own strength! Moon keep me up, for if I stumble, I must knock a house down!"

And though the woman was far from stumbling, she did spill moonlight as she spun. Cold light spattered from the coins on her head over every rough cobble, and her wide skirts made a shadow like a spinning black planet.

There was one other sharing Djoura's star-washed stage, though she hadn't noticed him. This was a small man, long nosed, thin, dressed in Bedouin white muslin. He sat waiting on the dry fountainhead that marked the center of the square, and what he was waiting for is of no importance to us.

His legs were neatly crossed. To Djoura (when she at last perceived him) he looked impossibly droll, sitting there so neatly and so still under the savage moonlight, so as she passed him she reached up one long African arm and clenched her hand. "I have caught the moon!" she whispered to him, making her eyes round. "I will hide it in my bosom now, and no one will know who took it but YOU!"

Following her own words, she thrust her hand into her bodice, lifted it out, and shook her fingers in the small man's face. "See! I have hidden it. I don't have it anymore!" She floated away, then, laughing high in her nose.

The man sat without moving. His mouth had gone faintly sour, and his eyes were fixed on the wall opposite him. But after Djoura had passed, fading into another dark alley, he raised his sight to heaven. "There is no God but Allah," he intoned, "and Mohammad is his Prophet."

"Yes, a fish," Raphael admitted. "A fish, or a small bird. This orange tree, too, whispers His name to me, but only after everyone has gone to bed."

"His name?" whispered the soft voice that came from the shadow.

"The name of my Father, whom they call Allah: the name I can't remember from moment to moment," Raphael replied. Then he pushed a weight of pale yellow hair from his eyes. "But none of these speaks as clearly to me of Him as one look at your face, Dami."

Either the ghost laughed, or the wind made a rustle in the tree. "Thank you, Seraph. Though I have no more face than the green earth and your memory give me, still that is good to hear."

"The green earth?" Raphael moved closer to the voice of his friend. "I am made of the earth too. This—here—is the earth . . . See?" He lifted one fair arm and clenched and

pened the hand. "It is earth itself my desire is causing to
ove. Flesh is earth, like wood, like fish scales.

"And it is me." The deep blue eyes (not angel's eyes any
onger but Raphael's eyes nonetheless) shone with par-
cular intensity. "I am growing increasingly . . . what is the
ight word . . . TENDER of this body."

Brown eyes, created of Raphael's memory, answered his
aze. "You take your exile well," Damiano commented, his
ords dusted with soft irony. "But I think you'll get very
red of your body if you sit up every night, talking to ghosts
nd orange trees."

Like a child, Raphael drew his knees up to his chin and
rapped his arms around them. He closed his eyes content-
dly. His form was obscured in a veil of light and shadow:
amiano covered his teacher with dusky wings. "Take it
ell? My exile? What else should I do? I am bound to this
esh. It colors everything that happens to me, and time
oes the rest; time is always around me, with the drip of the
ater clock—plink, plink, plink. Get up, void, eat, work,
lay for Rashiid, sleep (or try to). Is it time, flesh, or slavery
hat rules my life? I think if I were not a slave, with some-
ne to tell me at every moment what to do, time would
onfuse me utterly.

"I do get tired," he admitted. "But it is not because of
our visits that I get tired, nor yet from talking to the or-
nge tree. It is because my mistress keeps me awake every
ight."

There was a moment's meditative silence. "I have heard
f men having that problem," Damiano replied finally, in a
areful voice devoid of expression. "I have never heard they
ere to be pitied, however."

The man who had been an angel sighed. "I am not really
simpleton, Dami; I know when you're making fun of me.
Vithout cause, I assure you."

The ghost grinned. Raphael's answering smile was slow.

"It IS a problem. Ama sleeps during the siesta (which is
omething I'm not given time to do), and she cannot sleep
ll night as well.

"She wants to play with me then. She wants to sit on my
nee while I comb her hair. She wants to complain about
er husband, and she wants me to tell her stories.

"What am I to do? I am her servant, and besides, she
very sweet. But sometimes I'm asleep when I should b
doing something else. Yesteray I fell asleep during my ma
ter's dinner."

"Did he beat you?" came the concerned question.

Raphael shook his head. Night-silvered hair spilled ove
his shoulders and cast milky lights on the water. "No. H
only threatened to." Raphael gazed upward at the full moo
and yawned so hard he squeezed the moon out of his eye
"I can never predict, about Rashiid."

The spirit also laughed. "So! Sleep now, then. I'll play fo
you—I'll play especially dull music. You'll have no choic
but to nod off."

It was not dull music, nor was the lute poorly played.
was to Raphael very dear music, for he had taught it to h
student and Damiano had changed it and added to it until
came back as a gift to the teacher. And Raphael listened i
no danger of falling asleep, for he was traveling a long way i
his thoughts.

Chained to a framework of bone: prisoned in time. No
miserable, however, even though the damp reache
through his cotton shirt like searching roots and his eye
were grainy.

For Raphael's head was full of music: music which too
time—man's master—and played with it. It curled aroun
his mortal bones until they shone with light. The walls o
Raphael's prison dissolved under the gentle siege of Da
miano's lute.

But his reverie was a slave's reverie and he did not forge
that in the morning he would have to help Fatima bake th
breakfast breads. Nor that he would then wake up his mi
tress and attempt the duties of lady's maid. There would b
digging, or picking, or pruning, and during the hot hour
Rashiid would want his music. Sand the morning's dirt
pots, crank the great fan in the north chamber, then dinne
and more lute playing (unless there was someone to im
press, Rashiid preferred it over the ud). And tomorro
night his sleep would be interrupted or forestalled as it al
ways was, by little Ama, restless as a bird.

He carried all these burdens with him through his joy, like a man dancing with a sack of rocks on his back.

And his sad smile, as he gazed into the darkness where he could not see his friend, was ancient.

Raphael heard a noise through the music. He turned his head to peer over the packed earth of the yard, but he knew already what it was. Ama was coming out.

She walked on her tiptoes, not out of stealth but out of bouncy habit. Somewhere she had found a completely unorthodox, unsuitable scarlet shawl, and she had wrapped this thing around her head and shoulders, making her appear more birdlike than ever. She blundered over a garden rake on her way through the yard.

"Hisst! Hisst!" She scrambled around the edge of the fish pond, calling in too loud a whisper. "Raphael. Pinkie! Where are you? Don't tell me you're not here; I won't believe that!" Her padded skirt caught twigs off the ground. One foot sent a litter of gravel into the water.

Raphael crawled to his feet. He looked questioningly in the direction of Damiano, but the bodiless playing continued. "This is she," Raphael explained, speaking without sound. Damiano made no reply.

He stepped over to Ama. "I didn't say I wasn't here."

She gave out a treble yelp, shied away from him, and dipped one foot into the cold water.

Raphael caught her, and for a moment she struggled in his grasp. Then she was giggling, and she put her arms round his neck and kissed Raphael. She kissed him wherever she could reach: on the left corner of his mouth, his nose, his chin. Her kisses were short and sharp: like bird pecks.

He put her down on the pathway and turned, self-consciously, to the spot the music came from.

"Don't mind me," came a ghostly whisper. "I doubt very much the child can see me." Damiano struck up a saraband.

Ama was rubbing her mouth thoughtfully. "Raphael! Do you know you have a beard coming?"

Confused both by Damiano's and Ama's words, Raphael put his own hand to his face. "A . . a beard?"

Ama bent him down with a hand behind his neck. S
ran her fingernails backward over his cheek with female e
pertise. "Yes. You're growing a beard." She snickered, can
up on tiptoe and poked him under the jawbone. "Well, wl
not? We both know what you are—or aren't!

"My secret stallion!" Ama bubbled over with connivanc
as she added, "But how we'll hide THIS from Rashiid
don't know. Unless we pluck them all out, of course."

"Sounds painful," murmured Damiano from nowhere
particular.

The slave, too, made a tentative demur, but Ama was ha
ing none of it.

Raphael shot his friend a pleading glance as his mistre:
dragged him toward the house. The ghost, however, mac
no move to interfere.

By the light of one candle it was very difficult to find th
fine yellowish hairs on Raphael's cheeks. Sitting on her sul
ject's lap was also not the most convenient way to set abov
the task. But there was only one stool in the women's hide:
hole (now that Moorish visitations had become much rare
and Ama was used to working in bad light. She was expe:
with the tiny brass tweezers.

"There's one," she hissed, and the implement hovere
closer. The tweezers struck with the speed of a hawk an
Raphael flinched just perceptibly.

"Poor Pinkie," Ama crooned, and left a kiss on the spc
she had stung. The kiss took much longer than the pluck
ing.

Raphael looked around at the candle-dancing clay wall

"Perhaps I should simply tell Rashiid that I am not a eu
nuch at all," he ventured to suggest. "It is the simpl
truth."

Ama drew her breath in in a hiss. "Raphael! Then yo
would BE a eunuch for certain. Do you want that to har
pen?"

He squirmed in his seat, considering the question. "No,
he replied with some decision. "I don't know quite why, bu
that is a very repellent thought."

"Or maybe he would merely kill you in his rage!" Ama
dark threat dissolved into a giggle. She plucked and kisse

ree times in succession. Then she kissed three times
ore. "My dear Pinkie. You're funny, with your 'simple
uth' and all!"

Ama was so small and warm and cuddly that Raphael
und himself hugging her. Her hair was against his lips. He
roked it. She lifted her face to his.

The only other woman who had ever touched him had
ad hands less soft than these. Black hands, which had
athed him and combed his hair. Hands that smelled like
n and sand. Raphael heard Djoura's rich, brocaded songs
his ears as he held the little Arab girl.

His embrace grew tighter, with an urgency that seemed
nposed upon him from outside, against his will. Ama
ressed her round, fragile body against his. The last kiss did
ot end, but wandered from her mouth to her neck.
aphael's flesh was singing like the strings of a lute struck
ll together. So this was lust, he thought to himself.

This beautiful thing. Lust. A grin stretched tightly across
is face.

"Why aren't you looking at me?" hissed Ama in his ear.
Why are you sitting there smiling into space like that?
Don't you like to kiss me?"

Raphael had to swallow before talking and still his voice
was thick. "I do," he said, smiling shyly. "And I don't know
hy I was staring out; I just was."

"Then kiss me again, and keep your eyes closed," she
nsisted. Raphael obeyed his mistress, and she in turn took
is hand in her smaller one and placed it where she thought
est.

The stool Raphael had been sitting on had gotten lost
omehow. They were sinking to the floor. And the floor was
varm. It was as though the earth were turning soft and
ilky: like flesh.

But behind his closed eyes the flesh he stroked was not
mber, like that of Ama, but ebony, and the mouth that
ouched his was heavier. And more proud.

"I want you to be my husband," Ama crooned, burying
er face against Raphael's breast. "You are so beautiful. So
gentle!

"I don't love Rashiid; I hate him! He is a bear. A stup
pig! I want YOUR love."

Raphael's blue-black eyes clouded over. He struggled u
from the floor, pulling his mistress onto his lap once agai
He nestled her sleek head beneath his chin.

"Poor Ama," he whispered. "My poor, dear Ama."

Ama struggled free. "What do you mean, 'poor Ama
You are supposed to say, 'lovely Ama, beautiful, generou
Ama'! Are you not my slave, after all? Is it not I who a
conferring honor?"

She stood, and thus was slightly taller than he wa
seated. Her taper threw a writhing shadow on the wall be
hind. Raphael saw a small candle flame in each of her shi
ing brown eyes.

"I . . . I called you poor Ama because you said you we
unhappy," he said simply.

Ama settled her clothes, like feathers, into place. Sh
leaned forward to him, hands on her knees, and kissed th
tip of his nose. "Ah, but you can make me happy!" she whi
pered, and her ready grin was back.

"See this?" She let the brilliant shawl fall about her fac
"Isn't it terrible? Spanish. I wore it for you!"

Raphael took the fabric in his hand. He didn't think it wa
terrible at all, even if Spanish. It suited Ama's olive colorin
very well. He thought it would look good on Djoura too.

"How can I be your husband when you already have
husband?" he thought to ask.

"If Rashiid will be angry to learn I am a man, will he no
be much angrier to find you want to . . ."

Ama cut him off with a grimace. "Rashiid is not to know
mooncalf!"

"This is Rashiid's house. You are Rashiid's wife, and I a
Rashiid's slave." Raphael folded his hands between hi
knees and let his head hang forward. For a while h
watched the play of shadows on the tile floor. "I may be
simpleton, as everyone says, yet I know we cannot ac
THAT part for long here without the master discoverin
us."

There was total silence from Ama, which lasted unti
Raphael lifted his eyes to see she was crying.

He opened his mouth in incoherent apology, but Ama spoke with trembling voice. "Don't you love me, my ankie, my Raphael? I have loved you since the first time I saw you. It was because of you I made Rashiid buy that nasty black Djoura, and . . ."

"Djoura isn't nasty," he began, but seeing Ama's expression, immediately took a new tack.

"You are very dear to me, mistress. You are my closest friend in this place, and . . ."

"You have closer elsewhere?" Her dimpled chin jutted forward.

Raphael was not allowed to reply, for Ama found her own answer. "Djoura! That's why she wanted you sold together; she said you were her brother, but what she meant was quite different, I'll bet! I'll bet you lay together every night you could!"

"That isn't true," he said, but as he spoke his mind filled with unbidden images, with the Berber's song all mixed with Ama's warm skin and the divine irresponsibility he had just learned to call lust. Therefore his words did not carry authenticity to his mistress's ear.

"I'm going to tell Rashiid you attempted to force yourself me!" the girl declared.

"Please don't," Raphael said weakly.

"Why not? Why shouldn't I?"

"Because it's not the truth."

This plain response seemed to daunt Ama. "Well, I'll just tell him you're a whole man. That's the truth, and will be the same in the end."

He reached out a hand to her, but hers hid behind her back. "But you said he would do me harm."

Ama snorted and looked down the length of her nose at the fair face before her. "A moment ago you were the upright one: the one who wanted to tell him. And you a mere Christian—a giaour! Trying to make me feel low. Well, where's your courage now?"

The entreating hand dropped to Raphael's lap. "I never said I was courageous, Ama. In truth I am not very brave at all."

He blinked confusedly and rubbed his face with bot
palms. "Nor very clever, I don't think.

"But I do know this; if I lie with you, mistress, it will lea
to great unhappiness, maybe death, for us both."

His blue eyes gazed so steadily that Ama turned her hea
to one side. "I'm not afraid."

"I am," whispered Raphael.

Ama ground her teeth. "Then be afraid of this, Pinkie
Unless you're a lot . . . nicer to me by tomorrow night,
have every intention of telling Rashiid what I know abou
you."

Ama snatched the candle and stalked out of the room.

He sat with his forehead propped on his spread finger
tips, his elbows on his knees. "How have I gotten mysel
into such a sticky web, when to my best understanding
did nothing wrong at all?"

It was the sort of question a man asks of the air, but i
Raphael's case the air replied. "Know your own duty; that'
all that's asked of you, and it's simple enough, isn't it?"

Raphael lifted his beautiful, offended face. By the velvet
movement of a shadow it seemed his friend was standin
just outside the window. "No, it is not! Simple? How ca
you say . . ."

Damiano's vague form wavered, shruglike. "That's wor
for word what you said to me once."

"I did?" The slave hoisted himself out of the window
again, and took a calmative breath of night air. "How dared
open my mouth about mortal concerns, having never bee
a mortal of any sort?"

There were the stars, up above his head in a Spanish sk
untainted by clouds. There was the full moon. Unaccount
ably, Raphael thought of Djoura. "A mortal of any sort," he
repeated, lamely, to those stars.

"Yet your advice was always of the best," Damiano
chuckled, in a voice as soft as the wind. "You told me t
dress myself to attract girls. You cut my hair becomingly
You even won over my sweetheart, who felt she had reason
to hate you.

"In fact, Raphael, mortal or no, you have always known how to please the ladies."

The blond turned to stare at Damiano, which was difficult, since he had no clear idea where he was. "You were listening!" he blurted aloud. "To Ama and me!"

There came a soft rustling, not like that of orange leaves but like that of a man shifting from foot to embarrassed foot. "Yes, I was listening. Shouldn't I have been?

"After all, I hadn't said I was going away, had I?" Then, in tones airy and droll, he added, "Perhaps I should write you a note to tell you when I'm nearby. I remember someone suggesting that policy to me once."

The ghost's voice had taken Raphael to the garden wall. He slumped against it, feeling its coolness as a relief more than physical. "Don't make fun of me, Dami. If I was officious in the past, you can console yourself with the knowledge I'm wretched enough now."

Damiano stood beside him in an instant, perfect from his rough hair to his large mountaineer's boots. His square hand (nails cut blunt on long musician's fingers) rested on his friend's shoulder. "I'm so sorry, Seraph," he said. "I was only trying to make you laugh.

"Is it what your mistress said that disturbs you? Is it her displeasure, or do you fear your master will really do you harm? I have some advice on that point, if you'd care to listen."

As Raphael opened his mouth to tell Damiano that he was quite definitely afraid of what Rashiid would do, another answer came to his lips. "It's not any of that."

The cicadas were droning like a headache, like sleep. Rashiid's unused mare moved restlessly in her confined quarters, kicking at a board.

"When Ama . . . embraced me, I really wanted to . . . to . . ."

"Of course you did," said the ghost.

"No, you don't understand. I wanted to . . . replace her with someone else. And make love to her instead."

This statement hung between them in the air for some moments before Raphael added to it. "I miss my friend Djoura."

"Ah." Damiano's voice held understanding, but he could not resist adding, in the next breath, "Wasn't she the one who used to kick you at night to make you stop singing?"

"She only did that once," the slave replied with offended dignity. "And I understand now. Her whole plan was to keep everyone from finding out. That I am not a eunuch."

A ripple of pigeon gray against the white of the wall showed that the spirit had ruffled his wings. "Well. That leads us back to the original problem. The fact that you are not a eunuch."

Raphael, feeling very uncertain of himself, listened in his friend's voice for clues. "Is that what you think, Dami? That the problem is simply that I OUGHT to be a eunuch? Perhaps, then, I should allow my master to . . ."

There was an explosion of immaterial feathers. Damiano's twin sails snapped upward, hiding the moon and stars. "Seraph! Teacher! Raphael! What are you saying?

"You must not permit yourself to be so maimed! Nor, for that matter, should you continue as a slave. Nor languish without your lady friend.

"And THAT'S the advice of Damiano, the intrusive spirit. Take it or leave it," he concluded, less passionately.

Raphael couldn't help casting a furtive eye over the dark garden, even though he knew Damiano's outburst had made no sound another could hear. "But Rashiid is my master," he answered. "Under the laws of man. And Djoura—she is freed and gone from here."

The ghost allowed his smoky wings to sink back again, until they obscured his outline, but a pair of quick Italian eyes darted from the wall to his friend's wan face. "Laws of man," he echoed, rumbling in his deep, mumbling, Piedmontese accent. "Hah, for the laws of man!" A complex, obscure gesture accompanied the words.

"Raphael, you know me for a witch, don't you?"

The blond's eyes (not quick; not Italian) deepened in memory. "I know what you were in life, my dear friend."

Damiano lifted one eyebrow and one wing, in unconscious imitation of his teacher. "Well, Seraph, alive or dead, I'm about to work a great magic for you. To help alleviate this problem."

Raphael managed a smile. He let his back slide down the smooth wall until he was sitting on the turf. "Which problem, Dami? That of my freedom, or of my . . ."

"They are linked," the ghost replied shortly. With a face so full of gravity it wore a scowl, he floated back from Raphael.

Great dusky wings stood out sideways, as stiff as heraldry. Two rather large hands were lifted in front of Damiano's breast. He raised his flashing eyes to the heavens. "Habera Corpus!" he intoned. "Ades, Barbara, Ades!"

His shadowy hand was lit suddenly and only for a moment. The air smelled of lightning.

"Witness," cried Damiano, pointing inexplicably at the top of the garden wall. "Witness my power."

Raphael looked, saw nothing, and gazed confusedly once more at the spirit.

Who completed the ruination of the effect by winking.

But at a sound Raphael's head turned again to the wall, just in time to see Djoura, bareheaded but draped in her numerous garb, put one foot and then the other over the top and drop to the dry garden earth beside him.

Raphael's welcoming embrace was oddly hesitant and awkward, for the juxtaposition of what he had imagined with what he had never dared made him shy. But the black woman was too full of her own mission to notice.

"Don't ask questions," Djoura hissed into his ear. "I have walked all the way across Andalusia to rescue you, so you must follow me."

With a glance back toward the spot where he had last seen Damiano and another at the figure of the boy who lay snoring at the bolted garden gate, Raphael did follow Djoura, up and over the garden wall.

Now I am a renegade, he thought, crouching in the obscurity of the roadside, looking back at the pale height of clay he had just scaled. Just like Lucifer: a renegade.

Not quite like Lucifer, he qualified, as a firm dark handhold pulled him on. Lucifer would never let anyone lead him by the hand. The snores of Ali the doorkeeper faded in his ears.

For five minutes he scuttled after his liberator, along al
leyways he did not recognize, passing squares where ever
now in the second hour of morning they encountered peo
ple who had risen already for the next day as well as people
who had not yet been to bed.

He was prodded to walk upright. He was made to stroll
Djoura, stepping meekly behind him, twisted her bony
knuckle into the small of his back to induce him to behave
"You are free, Pinkie! Walk like a free man!"

Raphael was walking the only way he knew to walk. Or
impulse he turned on his heel and came round beside the
woman. He lay one arm over her shoulders.

"If I am free, then this is how I please to walk," he re
plied reasonably. "And if I were wholly free, I would no
walk at all, because I need so much to speak with you, my
dear Djoura."

The Berber wiggled out of touch. "None of that! What are
you thinking, man? You'll have us both pilloried, holding or
to me in public."

Raphael smiled ruefully, feeling not very free at all. Bu
he trotted along, talking over his shoulder, while Djoura
drove him from behind.

"Did the magic pull you from your Moroccan home
Djoura? Or were you still on the sea when the call came?"

Djoura puzzled at his phrasing. "I escaped from the ship
before it sailed the harbor. I tossed a customs man into the
water, took his wallet, and walked down the gangway ar
hour before sailing.

"Pah!" She spat dry and catlike upon the street. "Tha
ship was like a prison, and I've had enough of chains. And
have no family left in the south.

"Besides." Her voice dropped in timbre and her eye
snared moonlight. "I had to come back for my pink Berber."

A grin spread over Raphael's face: a shy grin as tight as a
shrunken suit of clothes. All he could say was, "I missed
you, too, Djoura." But that smile and the warmth which
accompanied it dissolved as he thought further.

"But if I am running away from my master and you are
running away from your home, then where are we going
TO?"

The black woman snickered. "How about your home, Pinkie? Don't you have one, somewhere, with a mother who would be glad to see her little boy again?

"Along with his charming friend?"

Raphael stopped dead in the exact middle of the street. He made no answer, nor did he glance at Djoura, but stood with his hands clenched at his sides and his head bowed. He bit his lip. Djoura was standing before him, a concerned look in her coffee-colored eyes. "I know already that you are not a Berber," she said diffidently. "It was the music you play that confused me. But I have heard you play the music of many places, since, and that doesn't matter."

"It doesn't? You came back for me anyway?" They were quite alone on the street. Raphael touched her face. The look she gave him back was haughty, as though to say the reasons she did the things she did were hers to know.

"Djoura, I don't know how to find my home anymore. My memory has been . . . damaged. But I know the earth is filled with pleasant places to live. Come with me and we will find one we like."

"That is for me to say," replied the woman, shooting him a glance over a lopsided smile. "I am the one with the wallet," she added, letting coins tinkle softly beneath her clothes.

But she let him kiss him in the darkness that came after the moon's setting.

11

The great military entity that was the Alhambra was not about to bestir itself in the cause of the wounded pride of the Qa'id Hasiim Alfard: not though he had a thousand horsemen under his command. But Hasiim had also within his regiment a few dozen men tied to him by blood: tribesmen and sons of subordinate tribes. These had allegiance of another order.

Days before Djoura arrived back in Granada, Hasiim was aware of her escape. When the fursan courier relayed this message to the qa'id, he did nothing but shrug. But Hasiim's many eyes and ears were opened.

Djoura led her blond companion through a tangle of sleeping streets. There was no indecision in her step, for what is the use of indecision when one does not know where one is going? Raphael, too, followed without hesitation, for it was all one to him. The light (hardly more than symbolic) iron ring about his neck had been hidden beneath swaths of fabric.

Black fabric.

"In the north," murmured Djoura over her shoulder, "it will be necessary for me to pretend to be giaour—a Christian. You will show me how."

Raphael considered this silently, while he gazed down at the uneven street in front of his bare feet. "I'm not sure," he said at last, "that I can do that convincingly."

"Because I am black?" Djoura countered, with rising belligerence. "Or because I am too much of Islam?"

Raphael shook his head. "Because I myself don't know how. There are so many dogmas AND sacraments, and one need only do or say one word wrong to get into a great deal of trouble. I have not ever studied . . ."

The Berber woman snorted. "Yet you yourself are a Christian, and have managed."

"I am not a Christian," he stated, and for easier conversation, Raphael fell back beside the woman. "That much I DO know. There is a ritual called baptism which one must undergo to be a Christian, sometimes by immersion and sometimes by sprinkling. I have never been baptized."

"That you remember . . ." chided the black good-naturedly. "But you don't remember much."

She took his hand. "Ho! You are so cold, Pinkie. Is it because of your weak skin?"

At her touch (And it was not cold at all. No, underneath all her tentlike layers, Djoura was very warm.) Raphael had begun to tremble slightly. He turned his hand beneath

hers, and moved his sensitive fingertips over the surface of
her palm, her thumb, her wrist . . .

And he said nothing at all.

Dawn was near, but the darkness now was almost complete. Djoura stopped in her tracks, suddenly indecisive.
"We'll give you another shawl, Pinkie. That will keep you
warmer."

He allowed her to drape another musty garment over his
shoulders. "Djoura," he whispered, when all was arranged
to her maternal liking. "Could you call me Raphael?"

She stiffened and barked a laugh. "That again?" When he
neither moved nor responded she continued more seriously. "That is a very important name in the desert,
Pinkie. A fearful name. Raphael is one of the great djinn,
which a good Berber—a good Muslim—must never bow to
worship."

Then it was Raphael's turn to laugh. "I don't ask you to
worship me, dear one, but only to call me by my name."
And when Djoura didn't reply he took the opportunity to
kiss her softly upon the lips.

Djoura stood still for a moment, then made a very small
noise in her throat and turned her head away. Stepping
back, she protested, "I don't want to be pawed around by a
simpleminded man!"

"I am not simpleminded, Djoura," he replied with no
hint of offense. "Only new here.

"And I love you. When you left the household . . . ."

"That was YOUR fault, with your big mouth . . ."

"When you left I missed you terribly, and then when Damiano brought you back . . . "

"When WHO brought me back?" the woman almost
wailed. "You ARE an idiot, Pinkie." Djoura caught her
tongue, then, and with unexpected consideration corrected
herself, "Raphael. I came back by myself, with no help from
anyone!" She turned on her heel and paraded forward
again, going nowhere in particular with great determina-
tion. Raphael took hold of her skirts so that he would not
lose her in the dark. "I'm glad," he began again. "Either
way. That you came back for me."

She sniffed. "You are my responsibility."

The man's steps slowed. "That's all? Your responsibility?" His fingers slipped their hold. Raphael came to a disappointed stop in the middle of an empty street.

Djoura, feeling his absence as quickly as she had his uncomfortable presence, turned around again.

"Curse it all, Pinkie! You only think you love me because I wiped your ass for you when you were sick and pushed food in your mouth."

Raphael had one hand resting on each of the woman's shoulders. "What is the difference," he whispered softly, "between thinking you love someone and loving them? I love you because you are kind and hate to be known as kind. Because you are brave . . ."

"Brave, huh? Because I kicked you?" Her voice held a shade of embarrassment.

"Ah, but you won't kick me again, will you?" His grip slid down to the woman's elbows. He took her hands.

Djoura was suddenly aware that Raphael was taller than she was. And the awkward, gangling Pinkie of her memory had to crumble before the presence before her, that held her hands in a grip no longer cold.

"And because you sing, Djoura," he continued, as though he had not been interrupted. "When I was newly a . . . a slave and I tried to refuse this life, I heard you singing."

In a small voice, very unlike herself, Djoura said, "I only did that to bother the woman sellers."

"You did it beautifully," Raphael insisted. "It was the voice of . . . of Allah, to me. It still is."

Once more Djoura snorted, but she allowed Raphael to slip his arms around her. "I have grown very bad at hearing HIS voice, Djoura, except through others.

"But what does all that matter? In the end I don't need a reason to love you, except that you are Djoura and I am . . . myself. Whatever you call me."

The Berber woman allowed her head to rest against his collarbone. She rested her hand on his shoulder. Although she was no less uncomfortable, she felt no desire to move. "Ah, Pink—Raphael. I know you are no simpleton. In some ways you are as wise as a scholar. And my singing is like a bird's peep next to yours.

"If only you weren't . . ."

"Yes?" His voice was tender but worried. "Weren't what?"

"Weren't such a funny color!" Djoura burst out, and then he giggled. They both giggled together. It was a laughter that grew almost rowdy and then was cut off knife-sharp.

They stared at one another, mouths still open, silent.

Raphael pulled her closer. "You can't see my color in the dark," he murmured close into the woman's ear.

The arms Raphael and Djoura wound around one another were hard through labor. It grew very warm on that tenebrous windy street.

"I think it is getting hotter, even up here," stated Gaspare. Saara had one hand gripping the dragon's pierced scale while the other held the young man's hands together in front of her waist.

He leaned out over the dragon's side and the updrafts of the great beast's movement caught his red hair. Nothing but Saara's grip held him on. "This is a long mountain range, dragon," Gaspare observed idly. "What comes after this?"

"Granada," replied the black dragon.

The first light was miraculous but frightening, for although it enabled their feet to move with careless speed, it exposed them to the cruel, awakening world.

How white was Granada, where the sun had bleached even the urine-stained walls to fairness. And how large, for they had been shuffling through half the night and had never reached the north city wall. It was as though Djoura's stern leadership had taken them in circles.

The odor of lamp oil and that of candle wax floated out of the bare little windows along the street. Soon sandaled feet and bare feet trod the cobbles and the clay beside theirs. Raphael was once more pushed out in front. Djoura's eyes sank to the earth, doelike, submissive. She prodded her leader with one concealed knuckle.

"I don't know where I'm going, Djoura," he said amicably. "The street keeps curving to the left."

"It can't do that forever," the Berber woman hissed. "Te
me what you see."

Raphael cleared his throat. "I see . . .

"A shop with a brass cup hanging out in front. Anothe
with a wheat sheaf (very dry) impaled above the door. I see
man in trousers striped with red."

"Keep walking as you talk."

Raphael strived to obey. "I see a crack of the sun, alon
that cross street. Shall we take it?"

"The sun or the cross street?" countered Djoura. The
giggled together—again.

"Now the sun is gone again. I see an ass pulling a cart
sand—get over to the side, here. And I see three wome
with very large bottles.

"Children. More women. A black man in the doorwa
with green-striped trousers."

Djoura had to sneak a glance. "A eunuch," she an
nounced, flat-voiced. "Nothing to me."

"Now the sun. Another ass. Watch the man lying in th
street."

"Drunk." Djoura stepped carefully around.

"Two more asses. A man on a horse." Raphael was pant
ing with the effort it took to speak while picking their wa
along a street where every house was vomiting forth its in
habitants.

The street DID continue to turn left. It seemed to be
circle. What use was it to travel in a circle like this? An
why would anyone build a circular street?

Raphael was about to suggest they turn at the very nex
cross street, and go right, toward the outside of the circle
Instead he stopped dead.

"I think you should raise your eyes, dear one," he whis
pered.

Djoura lifted her eyes toward the odd-dozen black-robe
men on their little desert horses who were sweeping ar
rogantly along the street, sending men, women, and th
tiny donkeys fleeing toward doorways.

In front of them came a small fellow, mounted barebac
on a horse he was having difficulty managing. Djoura recog
nized him at the same moment he recognized her, and sh

aw him pointing and heard him say, "That is her. The black
nfidel who worshipped the moon before my eyes!"

But Hasiim the Berber did not need such identification.
Ie spurred his mare forward.

Raphael was watching the man come, followed by a mass
f pounding hooves which could smash human flesh into the
lay of the road. Had Djoura not snatched him by the hand,
e might have stood there until overtaken, for he had no
xperience in running away from things.

Nor was running a very useful endeavor, for the horses
vere faster than any barefoot man, let alone a woman
vrapped in heavy skirts. But Djoura slipped around a corner of the street and pulled him into a doorless entryway.

"Fly-caked pigshit!" she hissed violently. "Infidel, am I?
Vell, this infidel is going to spit him like a fish!"

Raphael heard horses racketing toward the narrow corner. One came through. Another tripped—slammed the
un-baked wall. A man screamed and the beast went down.

Toward them danced an hysterical Arab horse, with its
ight bit clenched firmly in its teeth. It tossed its head while
he small citizen of Granada bounced unhappily up and
lown on the animal's withers. His right hand held a cavalry
cimitar out in the air, where it wobbled dangerously. His
eft was caught in the horse's mane. He did not look at the
ugitives at all.

Without hesitation Djoura struck, pulling man from
nount and the sword from the hapless fellow's grasp. The
reed horse bolted forward along the alley, leaving the
houts and screams of the inhabitants in its wake. The dis-
rmed warrior crumbled into a ball before Djoura, also
creaming. She lifted the scimitar above her head, then
topped still, an expression of disgust on her face. Finally
he kicked the fellow out of the way.

Raphael stood next to Djoura, watching the struggling
nass of fallen horses and riders which blocked the alley
ntrance. One animal urinated in its panic: the air grew
our.

In the sunlit street a small white mare whirled. The black
obes of her rider billowed as she was spurred toward the
ongested corner. Then lifting into the air like a deer she

leaped the whole mass and came down perfectly balance
in the alleyway only fifteen feet from Djoura.

Hasiim reined his mare expertly and her hind feet pull
under her. Dropping the reins along the mare's neck, I
lifted his sword in a practiced hand.

Djoura hefted hers like a club.

The white mare sprang forward. At that same mome
Raphael stepped out into the alley between Hasiim ar
Djoura. He raised his empty hand toward the beas
"Dami!" he cried. "Old friend, help us! Help us if you a
near. If you can. Remember the horses in the pass of Aost¿

There was nothing to see. No shadow more nor le
haunted the alley. Raphael's hope shrank and he chide
himself for expecting too much of a friend who had, aft
all, passed beyond earth's turmoils.

But the horse—Hasiim's war mare—stopped dead in h
tracks. Hasiim was slammed hard against her neck. Sl
lowered her head. Nickered softly.

In the moment of the Berber's amazement, Raphael w
up behind him. He took Hasiim's sword arm in both of I
and struck it against the alley wall.

Hasiim cursed his mare's infidelity. He cursed enchar
ments. He dropped the sword.

Raphael took it in both hands and was off.

Outside the alleyway and in the wider street beyond, tl
desert horses stood locked in a pleasant dream. Neith
spur nor quirt led to more than a fly switch of the tail. Tl
horses who had fallen now climbed to their feet and stoc
together, completely blocking the entryway.

The townspeople of Granada remained where tl
onslaught of the fursan had driven them, watching fro
windows or huddled in black doorways, and what emotio
this humiliation of the Berber cavalry raised in their sever
Muslim or Christian breasts were theirs to cherish.

Raphael passed the sword from one hand to the othe
until suddenly its weight settled in his grip and he kne
what to do with it.

THERE WERE FOUR OF US: MICHAEL, GABRIEL, URIE
AND MYSELF. WE DROVE HIM OUT—HIM AND ALL HE H¿
DELUDED TO STAND WITH HIM.

Raphael darted back to Djoura, and their two swords ~~i~~ced the light.

"What was that?" hissed the woman. "What happened to ~~h~~is horse?"

Raphael opened his mouth, but hardly knew what to say. ~~A~~ . . . deed is redeemed: a deed done years ago, in the ~~h~~igh mountains of the north. It is my friend who has helped ~~u~~s—he of whom I told you. The pebble."

"The pebble?" Djoura's startled eyes shifted from the ~~d~~anger ahead to the strange fellow beside her.

"Off your horses!" Hasiim spoke in the hill Arabic of Mo-~~r~~occo. (Down the darkened alley Djoura heard him and ~~c~~ursed in the same tongue.) "Off your horses and after me!"

A more slender shape appeared among the equine sil-~~h~~ouettes blocking the corner. One man squeezed through. ~~A~~nother.

With no other coign but a bolted doorway from which to ~~fi~~ght and over a dozen swordsmen slipping toward them, ~~t~~he fair man and the black woman turned together and fled ~~d~~own the alley.

It was dank: the cobbles both slippery and odorous. ~~D~~joura ran with a focused, arrowlike urgency, like a person ~~w~~ho knows refuge is just ahead. Raphael followed her in ~~s~~imilar fashion, not because he believed there was such a ~~r~~efuge (no, he knew it was only Djoura's unquenchable con-~~fi~~dence which led them) but because he did not want to lose ~~h~~er. The woman's dusty black skirts were hiked, and her ~~s~~cimitar bobbed in her hand. This weapon scattered once ~~m~~ore the mothers, children, and men without employment ~~w~~ho frequented the alley. Again shrieks and bellows.

The fugitives passed the small man's horse, the runaway, ~~a~~s it was being led by eager dirty hands through a doorway ~~o~~f clay daub toward some illicit fate. The sound of foot pur-~~s~~uit echoed behind them, giving wings to their own steps.

Then they were out in the morning sun again: first ~~D~~joura, whose clothes drank the brilliance and gave ~~n~~othing back, but whose head flashed with coins, then ~~R~~aphael, wound—no, tangled—in shawls over his striped ~~h~~ousehold trousers, his fair hair flying like a horse's mane.

Their eyes watered in the light and before them rose a wall
the north wall of the city of Granada.

It was impossibly high, and here and there the poor ha
built mud-wasp huts of clay against it, narrowing the stree
to a mere donkey track. Djoura turned to the left and as sh
bolted forward she shrieked, "The gate! We must find th
gate!"

Raphael's breath rasped in his throat. He felt his nos
bleeding again. He pressed behind Djoura through a block
ade of dirty children, while a dog with pointed ears and
curling tail barked sharply at the confusion.

Was that a gate ahead, round arched and trimmed with
tile? It was: the north gate of the city, as high as a house
and the wall around it was ornamented with lapis cut int
the words of the Koran. Djoura sprang toward it an
stopped, for in its shadow were framed five swordsmen
with the Qa'id Hasiim in the front.

Raphael crashed into Djoura from behind. He put on
arm around her shoulder and glanced about them.

On their right the city wall, far too high to climb. O
their left, a potter's shed. The street was littered with cla
pots and with broken fragments of clay.

What had this wild flight gained them, besides burne
lungs and a head full of panic? No matter. Djoura was no
about to flee again. She backed against the white wall
where a buttress stood out a few feet. There she was a
obvious as a fly on sugar, but there was no longer hope o
hiding. Shouts from left and right told her she was sur
rounded by her enemy.

But then was there anyone on earth who was not Djoura'
enemy? Not the people of her home, anymore, nor th
Spanish giaour who stared at her now from buzzing clump
in the street. Only Pinkie—Raphael—with his weak ski
and strange eyes as blue as a blind man's, who stood by he
now, back to back, with his scimitar fluttering in his hand
lightly as a bird. She pressed against him.

Hasiim's men erupted into the sun and when they spie
their quarry at bay they gave out a noise like hounds. The
came with the fury and undiscipline of men who are no
used to fighting on foot.

And they slid to a confused halt, for there was no flaw or
opening in the defense of the blond European who stood
with back against the chiseled wall. And the black woman
beside him, with her weapon held up rigidly like a heads-
man's sword . . . All knew she was mad, and in league with
spirits besides, but who knew what strange arts she possessed to do harm?

Hasiim then came forward, for he was a pure Muslim and
without superstition, and he had a wealth of injured pride
to avenge. He glanced from Raphael (with only professional
interest) to the black Berber. He was armed once more.

Raphael shifted his balance so that he faced Hasiim and
stood slightly to the front of Djoura. He caught the warrior's
eyes with his own and held them. Djoura, seeing that her
ankie knew more of this business than she did, took one
step back. Then Hasiim struck: a feint toward the black
woman which ended as a stroke at Raphael's wrists.

He met steel, and the blond flexed his blade in a tiny
circle. To Hasiim's immense surprise he felt his weapon
loosen in his grasp. The scimitar hit the earth. Hasiim flung
himself back.

To take a breath. To consider. To demand another scimitar
from his milling followers.

Raphael did not drop his eyes from Hasiim's. He saw the
Arab blink, shift from foot to foot, breathe a prayer to Allah.
HIM AND ALL HE HAD DELUDED TO STAND WITH HIM.
Satan himself had given back before four angels. What hope
had a mortal warrior, however skilled? Raphael looked at
Hasiim and knew he could destroy the man. He stepped
out from the buttress, his scimitar drifting like a leaf in the
breeze.

The Berber's eyes widened. Raphael met those eyes.

And Raphael was lost.

This man was not Satan nor had he been bought by him.
He was a stubborn and prideful mortal—a man not to
Raphael's taste. A dangerous man. But Raphael gazed at
Hasiim and felt a peculiar painful pity.

This hesitation gave Hasiim—who felt no similar emotion
while glaring at Raphael—time to strike another sweeping

cross-hand blow. Raphael countered, but did not press the advantage.

With a strident ululation, another tribesman stood beside Hasiim, sword at the ready. In this man's face Raphael read plain fear, mastered by the desire to please his commander. This second warrior slashed fiercely at Djoura, who raised her blade against the attack. But the swordsman feinted away and licked in beneath the woman's awkward guard.

Raphael snapped the man's blade in two. Djoura opened his face.

Hasiim, losing patience, shoved his subordinate aside and rushed his opponent as though he himself were still on horseback, slashing in even diagonals as he came. Raphael flung himself down on one knee before Djoura and his scimitar flashed broadside, clashing against Hasiim's weapon. Then he sprang up again and knocked the qa'id backward before he could disengage. Taking the swordsman's wrist in his own, he twisted the hilt of the weapon, trying to pull it from Hasiim's grasp.

They fell and struggled, breath hissing into one another's face. Next to Raphael's head a sword struck the ground and sparked. Hasiim's eyes shifted. He cried a few words in his Berber dialect and the attack was not repeated.

Only a few inches above Hasiim's face hung that of Raphael. It was pale under its sunburn, bearing no sign of anger or outrage, but rather the sad concentration of a tutor with a very slow pupil. And from Raphael's neck dangled, like some rough piece of jewelry, the iron slave collar. Hasiim grabbed it in one hand, while the other hand dropped his blade and fixed itself against Raphael's neck. With one hand he pulled, while the other pushed, crushing.

Arching back, the blond put his knee against Hasiim's chest, while he worked his two arms between his opponent's stranglehold. He made no effort to use his sword against Hasiim. His breath came in a choking hiss. His vision sparkled.

He broke the hold.

Raphael stood above the fallen Hasiim, who looked up with fanatic indifference, expecting death. He did nothing

but his sword twitched like a cat's tail, warning off the fursan
who had witnessed this crude duel.

A voice was calling out to Raphael: He didn't understand
at first. "Drop your sword, giaour. Look up and drop your
sword."

Raphael did look up. Around the frosting-white tiled
wall, behind the Berber fursan, stood a semicircle of humanity. Raphael stared from face to face.

There shuffled a poor Spaniard with confused, rolling
eyes, bearing baskets of fish and of peppers. Next to him
stood a proud Moorish householder in silk and muslin, his
hands upon the jeweled hilt of a scimitar which had probably never seen use. Here was a woman so veiled neither her
age nor race could be guessed at, another woman with
tawny hair, sans veil but with the ring around her neck. Two
teenage eunuchs, well dressed, who stood carefully not
touching anybody. A dark peasant ignoring the squirming
horned kid in his arms to stare, stare, stare . . .

Each casual figure engraved itself into Raphael's stunned
brain, as though within the astonishment, fear, or unholy
excitement expressed in these faces he would find the clue
to every mystery. But finally his eyes found (as they were
meant to) the five soldiers who stood with their legs braced,
their wicked small bows drawn and aimed at both Raphael
and Djoura.

The woman did not move. Neither did she drop her
weapon. The steel of her sword sent glints of silver over the
white mosaic wall, joined by the spark of gold from the
coins in her black hair. Her face not black now but suffused
with a ruddy blush, and when she spoke to her companion
her voice held a furious elation.

"When I cry out, Raphael, then we will go forward together. We will give them reason to fear us!"

His face filled with pain. "But they will kill you, Djoura!"

She snorted in her habitual arrogance. "What are these
but dogs? They will kill us anyway. This way . . .

" . . . is freedom." She took one step forward.

But Hasiim, who had risen cautiously to his feet, heard
her fierce whisper. He replied not to Djoura, but to
Raphael. "My men are not dogs. I say they will not kill you:

neither of you, unless you make it necessary. The woman I have promised to return to her own people and I will do so.

"You . . ." He stared at the fair figure. Raphael's borrowed clothing had all fallen off and he stood now wearing nothing but his eunuch's trousers. The scars on his back were visible around his sides and shoulders like the tendrils of red clinging vines. "You we will return to your master, and what he may do to you for this scandal is none of our business.

"Though I say," and here the Moor paused. "Though I say that if I thought I could buy your loyalty with your sword arm, I would trade ten good horses for you."

Raphael said nothing in reply. Slowly he lowered his blade. Djoura turned upon him a look of infinite bitterness.

"It gets hotter and hotter," observed Gaspare, shifting his sweaty seat from side to side. "If we have to go much farther south we'll all burst into flame!"

The black dragon smiled: an action which caused Saara's thighs and knees to tickle. "That is mostly my own personal heat. It is actually quite cool at these altitudes, even in the south.

"I could cool down by going slower, of course . . ."

"Don't listen to the boy," snapped Saara, who felt she had been sharing this aerial perch with Gaspare for too long entirely. "I'd rather have the speed. I feel time is pressing."

The dragon's sigh was more disturbing to the riders on his neck than his smile. "I won't ask you why," he drawled. "It' probably some sorcery and I'd rather not know about it . . ."

Saara opened her mouth to say it was not sorcery at all, but just a feeling she had, but the dragon was not finished

"Besides, if I'm not out of my reckoning, that white shimmer where the mountains slope down is Granada itself."

Gaspare craned over Saara's shoulder. It seemed they had finally reached the bottom of the Sierra Nevada. Good Mountains were nothing special to Gaspare. "Even if that is not Granada," he called into the black dragon's ear, "I think that the horse has to do something."

"I know, I know," came the lugubrious hiss.

* * *

They set down to discuss plans upon a rock rubble only a few miles north of the city. Since the dragon was quite capable of firing any house or dry field he touched while at flight heat, it required some thought how to rescue Raphael without setting all Granada ablaze. The horse was released to gather what nourishment he could find.

But instead of offering suggestions, Gaspare stretched himself out with his back against a stone while he played the lute. Saara only paced.

Both of them heard a terrific racket, as though boulders in the nearby landscape were being crumbled into powder. Gaspare started up. It was the dragon, giving himself a good scratch against the rocks.

Gaspare's rhythms were almost as hard to listen to. Saara could not rest. She could not even sit down.

"He can alight on a tile roof," stated the witch. "That way, even if he does set the timbers ablaze, he can knock the house in and contain the fire."

"Fine by me," mumbled Gaspare. "Of course the inhabitants of the house might disagree . . ." He raised his eyes and seemed to see Saara for the first time.

"What's wrong with you, my lady? You act like you have ants. Can you feel Raphael's presence from way out here?"

"No," Saara said shortly. "I don't know WHAT it is I feel." She shot Gaspare a glance under lowered brows.

"I told you, didn't I, that I was going to go home after this?" Gaspare lifted a surprised face.

"What else should you do, lady: stay in Granada?"

Saara grimaced. "I mean home. To the Fenlands. If I live. Home to my people, the Lapps."

Gaspare put both hands around the neck of his lute and corrugated his young brow massively. "By sweet San Gabriele, Saara, why do you want to do THAT?"

She took offense. "Don't speak of my home in that tone of voice, youngster! You've never been there to judge it."

With a single gesture Gaspare discounted that fact. "I know it is not civilized," he replied. "And so no place for the greatest witch in all the Italies. And Spain."

Saara's ire dissolved in Gaspare's predictable flattery. She produced a nervous grin. "It is a peaceful place, Gaspare, where the greatest enemy is winter. And beautiful, too, for in the autumn . . ."

". . . all the grasses and moss turn a scarlet red, which covers the steppe and shines against the blue sky or the gray clouds like sunset," said the voice, the familiar soft, deep voice which was not that of the dragon. "And the snows in winter take the color of the curtains in the sky, so bright that the dark time grows light enough for one to walk about and marvel."

"Dami!" cried Saara, and her voice caught in her throat.

"Here," he replied, and there he was, clear and only slightly shimmery, sitting on the hard ground between the witch and Gaspare. His storm-cloud wings were scarcely visible behind the mortal image.

Saara put her hand out, but stopped before touching. "I . . . wanted you to see that. I thought about you and the russet time . . ."

"I know," he whispered and gave her a very comfortable little smile. Then he turned to Gaspare and let him share the wordless joke. Then he stood up, wings rising behind him.

"Listen to me, my friends. I am here to interfere in the affairs of the living, as doubtless I should not!"

Damiano's amused smile faded into seriousness. "If you wish to be of service to Raphael, you must go into the city now. Move quickly. South of the central square you will find a broad avenue lined with orange trees. On this street is a house with a carved gate of cedarwood in a white wall. Enter in.

"There are also within Granada right now some fine horsemen riding fine horses very slowly. These are a sample of my interference, and as such may be of interest to you. But finding the house with the gate is more important.

"Go now; you are needed." The ghost did not fade; he was simply not there anymore.

Gaspare rose as though on a string. He filled his considerable lungs with air. "Dragon!" he bellowed. "Come quickly!"

* * *

"A ghost?" repeated the dragon.

"The ghost of Delstrego," replied Gaspare importantly. "And he said to hurry."

The black dragon took to the air lithely enough, springing off his coiled tail, but he refused to be hurried in speech. "I wish I might have seen that."

Saara had to chuckle. "I thought you would disapprove terribly. Magic being delusion, and all that."

The great beast considered. "There is that. But spirits have their place in the natural order. If I disapproved of spirits in general, why would I then be adding my small energies to the rescue of one?

"Besides, madam: if this specter had knowledge to communicate . . . real wisdom, perhaps . . . What is it he said again?"

Gaspare repeated Damiano's message, word for portentous word.

They came to the city and passed over the wall. The dragon swooped down in a stomach-twisting dive in order to inspect the place more closely. With its regular low rows of daubed buildings and crowded streets (smelling even up here in the air) it looked like—first, a hive of bees, and then like a hive of disturbed bees. "People can see you," shouted Saara. "They're terrified!"

The dragon writhed contemplatively. He slowed his progress so as to examine the length of one avenue broader than its fellows. "So it seems," he murmured silkily. He rose a few yards higher.

"That edifice just beyond the city," he explained for his riders' sakes, "set like a pearl in the red sand. That is the Alhambra, military center of the State of Granada, as well as the residence of Muhammad V, lineal descendant of Muhammad ben Yusuf ben Ahmand ben Nasir, who founded the present dynasty. It is generally accepted to be one of the most beautiful constructions in the world, and into its stones have been set the words of Ibn al-Khatib, that most martial of Islamic poets . . ."

"Fly!" shrieked Saara, whose sense of urgency had become almost overpowering. "South!"

"I AM flying," declared the dragon patiently. "And hysteria will make me fly no faster. Besides, if we went faster, I should have missed what I now see below—that small force of either Bedouin or Berber cavalry, whose horses plod with their little teacup muzzles scraping the dirt of the road. Did not the sage spirit speak of such?"

"But he said the house on the street of oranges first, the cavalry after!" Gaspare insisted. "I heard him distinctly."

Still the dragon, hanging high above the street, vacillated. "Yet we HAVE the cavalry, while the house on the street of oranges is theoretical only. And the prompting of spirits is a very subtle thing. Perhaps we should first investigate . . ."

"I've had enough of this," said Saara, and without further ado she turned into a dove. Gaspare, left without a handhold, squeaked and grabbed for the dragon's coronary spines. "Me, too! Take me with you, Saara," he bawled.

Unruffled the dragon said, "Youngster, I am more than willing to set you down."

12

The dove scouted, dipped, and led the horse on. Gaspare clung like a monkey to the lean black back, with nothing to restrain Festilligambe but a tattered rope bridle. But the young man's cross-continental ride on a dragon had burned away all the nervousness he had once felt around horses.

They passed the central square—a little plot of green cleverly irrigated and tended with immense labor—and found the avenue that was edged in fragrant orange tree without trouble. This way was wide and fairly empty. The few people they did pass were dressed well in Saracen style. They failed to notice (or pretended to fail to notice) the sight of a horse chasing a little brown bird along the avenue. Gaspare, not knowing which of these strollers might have had a hand in Raphael's imprisonment, cursed the overfed lot of them equally.

He sought the house with the white wall and carved wooden gate. Odd. ALL the houses had white walls and all the white walls had wooden gates. They were almost all carved, too, with inscriptions in Arabic, meaningless to a young man not even literate in his own language. The words of the dragon flashed into his mind. "The promptings of spirits are subtle." Damiano, too? Gaspare had clean forgotten that the ghost had specified cedarwood as the material of the gate they were seeking. But then, neither would he have been able to recognize cedarwood if he had remembered.

Saara, however, fluttered straight toward a gateway of mottled yellow and orange, which was set into a featureless wall surmounted by red tile.

She stood beside Gaspare. "It's bolted. There's something going on inside: I hear voices and the sound of a bellows. Can he jump it?"

Gaspare turned Festilligambe and trotted across the street. Then he stared at the looming wall of wood and daub. "Sweet San Gabriele," he whispered. "Never."

In his frustration he turned on Saara. "He's only a horse, you know: not a Cathaysian dragon." Then an idea occurred to him.

"Delstrego—Delstrego could have made a flame to burn this door away from in front of me!"

Saara, who had been about to return to bird form and dart over the wall, found herself stung by Damiano's name. "Oh, he could, could he? Well, Gaspare, you stand right there and you will see what I, whom yourself have named the greatest witch in all the Italies OR Spain, can do!"

Gaspare waited nervously.

The desert horses were aware of a presence in the air before their riders. Their dreams of honeyed grass dissolved into the terror of rabbits beneath a hawk.

The black dragon's interest in the beasts, however, was only aesthetic, for he had recently consumed both a large fat mule and several wild Andalusian cattle (scrawny, but serviceable), and dragons do not eat as frequently as men. And neither did the Berber riders interest him greatly, for he did not see among them any select individual whom a spirit might have thought worth noticing.

There was the little fellow who, once thrown from his horse, waved a spindly sword into the air . . . But the dragon was hoping for something more flamboyant.

And his sun-bright eyes noticed very soon that the little troop, which had been riding south, toward the Alhambra, held a prisoner—just one. A woman whose ebony skin gave off the same rich highlights as his own scales, and who wore a corona of gold tips (again like his) in her hair.

The dragon chortled with delight at this exotic find. He plucked her from among her captors with the care a collector will give to blown glass.

Simon the Surgeon stared from Rashiid to the cup in his hands. "It is the common practice," he observed. "Without the draught many more of them die. Since he is full grown and unwilling as well, there is a good chance that this one might."

"Indeed he might," said Rashiid, with rising inflection. "Indeed he might." The rotund householder's eyes were shining; his hands were knotted fists at his sides.

Rashiid was angry. Being awakened to take delivery on a runaway slave that one had not yet noticed was missing—that made one angry.

It also made one feel a little bit of a fool.

Stripping the boy for flogging only to discover that he was no boy at all but a man intact—that added to both the anger and the foolishness in no small way.

But sending for the local surgeon: saying to the functionary, "Come," and having him come, and saying to the assembled household, "Stand," and having them all stand—that was a thing to comfort one with one's own power. Rashiid's mottled hazel eyes were gleaming with that power, and the assembled household shifted from foot to foot, its

any subservient eyes turned to the sky, the pond, the
hite garden wall . . . Anywhere but to Rashiid.

Anywhere but to the man tied to the hitching post.

Raphael, too, stared past his master, to the white clay
all of the house. But his eyes were not focused on the
ouse. His head was turned slightly, as though he were lis-
ning—listening to something important, yet expecting in-
rruption at any moment from a fellow who tended to
terrupt. Who had a reputation for interrupting important
mmunications.

Who was a bit of a fool.

"He very well might die," Rashiid repeated again, for
mphasis.

Simon shrugged and put the cup down on his work-
nch. He was neither overawed nor afraid of Rashiid, for
mon was a free man employed to do a job. Since the great-
t part of his work was done at the market, where buyers of
ung beasts wanted them castrated before taking them
me, this wealthy cityman was an unlikely source of busi-
ss. His tempers could not do Simon harm. The surgeon
nsidered telling him not to get in the way.

No—Rashiid was the employer, and there was no use bor-
wing trouble. Simon put the cup down.

He signaled his apprentice to step up the bellows pump-
g.

Some practitioners castrated with hooks and some used
mps and a few used a loop of shrinking leather, but Sion the surgeon had a curved knife with a handle of wood,
d this served for almost any occasion from gelding to
odletting; one could even shave with it. He thrust this
ade into the coals so that its single stroke would both cut
d cauterize.

The second wife of Rashiid had been standing with her
der housemate: soundless, white-faced, one knuckle be-
een her cupid's-bow lips. Her round eyes had grown
ore than round, watching Raphael bound to the post.
atching the coals laid and the fire draw up. Now a waft of
t, metal-scented air came to wrap around her where she
od. The fire spat back at the bellows and the blade itself
ade a noise as it heated.

Ama fainted into Fatima's arms.

Rashiid saw his wife crumple. He subdued an impulse
go to her. It was first pride that caused him to ignore t
incident—the unwillingness to break this moment of pow
with softness of any kind—but then a horrible surmise e
tered his brain and Rashiid's face went hard as stone. I
Ama give thanks to Allah that she had been discovered to
pregnant BEFORE this boy who was not a boy arrived.

Raphael's blank eyes saw only the face of Djoura at t
last moment he had seen her, before they had bound h
and thrown him over a horse. Her scorn withered him st

For Raphael had no great confidence in the choice he h
made; perhaps the mortal-born woman had been right a
they should have died together under the blue and wh
tiles of the wall. Now she would be taken back to Afri
where she did not want to go, and he . . .

Raphael heard the knife moan in the orange coals and
knew dread—dread of loss and further shame . . . Dread
a life compassed by drudgery and by whippings, played o
to a dull rhythm of days. Dread of simple pain.

Surely Djoura had been right.

But though the song was of pain and fear, still Rapha
body was singing. That body had a will of its own, and
heard it telling him what it feared most was to die.

Raphael listened to the voice of his body with his he
turned slightly to one side and on his face was a distar
concentrated expression. But when Ama slumped in
Fatima's arms he saw and he opened his mouth, as thou
he were on the point of saying something.

HAD he spoken, it would have been to tell her that
knew she had not betrayed him to Rashiid. That he did r
blame her for his fate. But Rashiid, Ama's husband, sto
between them, so Raphael said nothing at all.

The knife came out of the fire, not red-hot but hot enou
to twist the air around it, turning morning mist into stea
Simon approached Raphael and peered appraisingly ir
his eyes.

In shock already, the surgeon said to himself. Bad ri
Aloud he called, "Bend him back."

The calloused hands of the head gardener came around
Raphael's neck and shoulders and stretched him back over
the hip-high wooden post. One hand covered his mouth.
Another squatted behind him and held his knees.

He could see nothing but the hairs on the gardener's
arm. He heard the man's heavy breathing. He felt his own
body stiffen and he wondered at this, for he had not told it
to do so.

Next came a fearful deep noise like wind and a great
thudding and crashing. Raphael did not know what caused
this, whether the gardener's shoulder against his ear, an accident with the surgeon's coals, or his own body's confusion.
But the howling continued and suddenly he was released,
reeling at the end of the chain which bound his hands to the
post.

The household of Rashiid was scattering like so many
birds and crying in a dozen voices. The surgeon's terrible
knife lay abandoned on the ground. Rashiid himself was
waving his arms wildly and his face was contorted.

In the middle of this uproar a horse plunged and reared: a
black horse. Upon his back was a tall, gangling rider with
red hair. He was shouting something inaudible, and so was
Rashiid. A flutter of feathers sank down by Raphael's feet
and rose up again as a woman.

She sang a word and his chains fell open to the ground.

The horse seemed to be moving all its legs indepen-
dently, like a spider. It sailed over the threshold like a leaf
in autumn.

Gaspare wondered if he were going to stay upright at all,
or the vicious cold wind sucked him along willy-nilly. He
spun over packed ground, narrowly missing the wave-
washed surface of a pond, with his hands full of horse's mane
and rope. He lifted his eyes.

It was Raphael and yet it wasn't Raphael whom Gaspare
saw: naked, squinting with confusion, gape-mouthed, lost
in the middle of all the screaming Saracens. There was the
angel's hair, perfect face, slender figure—but all pinched
out of mere human clay. Gaspare sat the capering horse
with unconscious expertise, his eyes locked on Raphael's

confusion. He saw his teacher fall to his knees. Rage fille
Gaspare, mixed with nausea, that he should have to se
Raphael reduced to this. With a choked scream he thre
Festilligambe into the tumult.

Raphael blinked at the horseman almost half-wittedl
But then the naked man's eyes focused on the head of th
lute projecting beyond Gaspare's right shoulder, and men
ory awakened. "Hoa!" shouted Gaspare, and he pulled o
the reins.

But the horse had his own memory. His black ears swi
eled to the human beside his withers. He nickered unce
tainly. Then Festilligambe lifted his fine dry head an
bellowed like a stallion from joy.

Raphael, grinning at this salute, hoisted himself up b
hind Gaspare.

There was another hand on the bridle: the same callouse
hand that had held Raphael only a minute since, the hand
the head gardener. Gaspare kicked at it and the horse a
tempted to rear. Rashiid, seeing this, ran from the doorwa
where Gaspare's first rush had pressed him and put his ow
white-knuckled hand on the headstall. Festilligambe thre
his head futiley from side to side. His tragic large eye
rolled, showing white all around.

Gaspare dropped the reins and took instead two handfu
of the gardener's hair. Dragging the man half off the groun
the redhead bit him in the ear. His uneven teeth groun
together until the gibbering fellow dropped his hold. But
the time it took to accomplish this action three more me
had taken hold of some part of the horse's anatomy. On
grabbed Raphael's bare leg and began to pull him to th
ground.

Saara had not been idle. Though weary from her win
summons (but she HAD to show Gaspare) she had scra
bled over the turf among fleeing feet and horse's hoove
Now she came up with Simon's bitter-edged knife. Han
dropped away from Raphael. From the horse.

Rashiid, for whom the capture of the horse had mea
victory won from defeat, turned at the disturbance and d
not see the knife at all, but only a child-faced woman wi
brown hair in uneven braids and a dress which did not cov

er legs. She reminded him a bit of Ama, and Rashiid was
ot pleased with Ama. With a cold sneer he released his
ight hand from the headstall to cuff her across the mouth.
Vith no expression on her face Saara released his other
and from the reins by slicing it off at the wrist.

Rashiid sprang back, stiff-armed, pumping blood like a
arden fountain into the air. The whole household went
till.

Simon the Surgeon had taken no part in the melee, but
ad flattened himself against the house wall as soon as the
orse blew in through the gate. He was paid to do a job,
fter all, not to get himself killed. But as Simon was a sur-
eon he knew what was necessary when a man had lost a
nember, so he took Rashiid, tripped him, dragged him to
he overturned brazier and pressed his spouting arm against
coal. The householder's shrieks reached deafening propor-
ions.

Faces appeared—cautiously—at the gate. They disap-
eared again. There came the sound of a horn from without.
t echoed along the street and was answered by another.

Gaspare looked at Saara. So did Raphael. Saara glanced
rom one end of the suddenly motionless yard to the other.
he shifted her knife nervously.

Then the smell of hot metal and the horrible smell of
Rashiid's seared hand stump mixed with another smell of
urning. A lacy, twisting shadow descended. The carefully
vatered grass withered and steamed as the dragon set him-
elf down. Djoura squatted within one enormous claw, her
ands firmly over her face.

Lantern eyes took in the yard, the pool, the cowering
umans. They lighted on the horse, with its double burden.
So! It seems you didn't need me at all!" the dragon said
rightly.

Like a caterpillar with fluffy spines the dragon rode
hrough the air, the gyrations of his body pushing first
Djoura, then Raphael (who held to her), and then Saara
who held to HIM) upmost. Saara was at the end of the line
ecause she had the least to lose by falling. Gaspare rode on

one of the monster's upturned palms, to be nearer his horse.

"He did well, didn't he, dragon?" asked the redhead, not for the first time. "He cut into that mass of Saracens like . . . like . . ."

"Like a black dragon," prompted the black dragon.

Gaspare thought maybe the dragon was making fun of him. "I am serious. Festilligambe showed the real, heroic soul of a horse down there, regardless of fire, knives, screaming . . ."

"Horses . . ." the great creature rumbled meditatively, "have very different souls, one from another. So have men. Have they not, Venerable Sage? And dragons, too, of course."

Venerable Sage let the wind toss the fair hair from his face. "I certainly cannot deny that." Then Raphael added, "Could you speak in Arabic, please, so that Djoura can understand?"

"Certainly," the dragon replied. In Arabic. "The language of Mecca, or of the south, perhaps?"

"The south."

An enormous long throat was cleared. "The young man has just noted, Child of Beauty, and I have agreed, that horses, men, and dragons are quite various. Within each species, I mean—the other is obvious."

Djoura shifted her three-finger grip at the handholds in the dragon's neck scales. "Men are very different from one another, of course. Some are pink."

Then she lifted her head high and rested back in Raphael's arms. "But that difference is of no importance."

It was a beautiful morning over the foothills of the Pyrenees, with scattered soapsuds clouds over the pelt meadows. The dragon writhed for the sheer feeling of it.

"Where exactly am I taking you all?" he asked, first in Arabic and then in Italian.

"Lappland," answered Saara promptly. "If you are going that far." Gaspare groaned from below.

"I think you're a fool, my lady. But Lombardy for me, signore. Where else?"

"The land of lights is not too far at all," stated the dragon. "And Lombardy is on the way." Again he shifted language.

"And you, Venerable Sage—where would the lady and yourself like to be ferried?"

Raphael was silent. He threw back his head and regarded the blue, uncommunicative sky. "I don't know. All the earth is beautiful, and I'm sure it is my fault that I cannot feel myself to belong to it. It is just that I never expected . . ."

He shook his golden head. "Never mind me. Take us any place we might find a welcome, Djoura and I."

"Lappland," said Saara, who caught the meaning of the exchange through the foreign words.

"Lombardy," insisted Gaspare, who had done the same. "A very civilized place, as Raphael well knows. Besides, I need my lessons."

"There is always Cathay," added the dragon with studied casualness. "In Cathay they know how to respect sages. And spirits."

The blond smiled. "And am I either?" Then his expression softened.

"What can we possibly do for you—uh, Venerable Dragon? I and all my friends owe their lives to you. Prehaps many times over."

The black dragon chuckled steam. "No matter, Venerable Sage. I have a great respect for teachers."

"Do you want me to teach you, then?"

The creature gave a tiny shiver then, which every passenger felt but none understood. "Can you teach me truth?"

"No," replied Raphael gravely. "Just music—the lute, primarily. But in the study of the lute you may find more than you expect."

"Music?" The dragon emitted a long, serpentine sigh. "Truth through tuned strings, instead of through privation, paradox, or long silence? I've never heard of THAT approach."

It was Raphael's turn to chuckle and he gave Djoura a little squeeze. "That is not to say it won't work, however."

The dragon held up one five-fingered, obsidian clawed hand. It was the one that held Gaspare. "It would have to be a rather large lute"

"Very well. You can learn to sing instead," said Raphael equably. "Every type and every individual created has its own music."

Once again the dragon cleared his throat and bobbed diffidently through the sky. "To sing? The thought makes me very awkward . . ."

Raphael chuckled. "The thought makes everyone awkward. But that tension can be overcome. You will find . . ."

"What's that I see?" called Saara from behind them all. "Straight ahead. Coming fast?"

They all looked, but only the dragon's eyes saw, and with an organ-pipe whistling he humped and turned in the air.

Saara clung to Raphael who held to Djoura tightly. The Berber locked her fingers in their grips.

In a few moments they could all see.

It came in the form of a white dragon. It came in the form of a writhing, legless wyvern. It came in the form of a phosphorescent, myriad plague.

It was destruction, dread, the death of hope, and it was coming fast.

"What is it? WHAT IS IT!" cried Djoura, craning her neck around. But she did not need the stricken faces of her fellows to tell her it was terrible. "Why is it chasing us?"

For a moment no one had the heart to tell her, then at last Raphael spoke. "It is Satan—Iblis—whom Saara calls the Liar. It is my brother."

Then Lucifer swept over them. He came between them and the sun, huger than a cloud. His shape was that of a king in rich robes, with a visage of blood.

The black dragon sank crazily toward the earth.

Saara felt the shadow touch her, with paralysis and despair in its wake. She laughed—laughed at the naïveté of her plans for the future. She had no future. But with that single laugh the paralysis passed Saara over, and her despair turned into unbreakable resolve. She let go of the man she had tracked across Europe and took to the air.

"No!" shouted Raphael, as he felt her go. "Saara of Saami! This is not your battle anymore!"

And indeed, as she flung herself at the breast of the hideous king, it vanished in front of her, leaving nothing but cloudless sky. The dove fluttered wildly before an iron hand struck her and sent her falling.

Gaspare screamed.

The dragon vomited fire at the apparition. He grabbed the falling woman with one hind claw. Flicking his snake's tail he flung himself toward the broken hills.

The sound of cruel laughter was all around them. It turned the air poisonous to their lungs. All eyes dimmed.

But the black dragon touched the earth again, searing the autumn grasses at his feet. Gently he shook off his living cargo.

Lucifer alighted before them, and his towering size reduced the Basque hills to clods of dirt. His colors were bright and monstrous. He wore a crown of gold and the face of Raphael.

"Haven't we done as much mischief as we possibly could?" he inquired jovially, looking carefully from Saara to the dragon to Gaspare. "Haven't we?"

The dragon coiled around his tiny dependents as dragons coil around their hordes. His corona of gold and scarlet stood out stiffly from his head. His eyes gleamed as white as an August sun. "Delusion!" he hissed. "Puffed, empty delusion!"

Lucifer regarded him thoughtfully. "It is no delusion that you are going to die, snake" he said, grinning horribly.

But a small black hand gripped one of the dragon's coronal spikes. Djoura's face appeared next to it. She had a stone in her hand. She stepped out.

"No, child!" The creature moved to guard her. "You don't know what it is you are facing."

She opened her lips, which were whitened with fear. "I know," she said. "I have faced slavery," Djoura whispered almost without sound. "I have faced swords. I have faced YOU, great dragon.

"AND," Djoura found her voice at last. "I have stolen the moon. The moon! Did you know that, Iblis?" And with a mad laugh, the Berber woman flung her stone at the Devil.

It soared its futile course. It might have hit the apparition's knee. But instead the small missile hung in the air and grew, until it became the image of a black man in blood-

caked robes. His body was hewed and his head struck off
before them. The open eyes of the head wore an expression
of idiocy.

Djoura shrieked her incoherent rage, and she would have
flung herself at Lucifer, armed with nothing except her
black robes and her fingernails. But Raphael, wordless and
set-faced, came up behind the woman and restrained her
with his arms.

Again Satan laughed. He reached a long arm out. The
black dragon swelled dangerously, like an adder in the
grass, as the hand of Satan came near.

"How is our little woods dove, then?" A gout of acid flame
passed through his arm harmlessly. "I know her from before, I think. I have a weakness, you know, for the small
songsters."

Saara lay white-faced where the dragon had put her
down, her head against Gaspare's narrow breast. She
watched death approaching and she said, "You never
touched me, Liar. You never will."

Gaspare, too, watched the hand descend. Because he was
seventeen years old and Italian besides, he rose to meet it.
Because he was Gaspare, he unslung his lute and began to
play. He shouted, "Here is a small song, then, from a small
songster."

The hand hovered, seemingly more from amusement
than fear. "Gaspare of San Gabriele," said Lucifer. "You are
miserably out of tune. As always."

"Out of tune, certainly," replied the redhead. "But in
time, you must admit. I am told that is more important.
And besides, Satan, if you do not like my lute playing, then
I will be forced to sing for you, instead, and many find my
voice even harder to take."

Then Lucifer tired of the game. His hand swept
down . . .

And found itself between the lance-toothed jaws of the
black dragon. Fire spouted from its nostrils and between its
buried teeth. Both the dragon and the red king hissed.

Lucifer fit the fingers of his other hand around the
dragon's throat. The tiny human atoms fled away—all but
one that stood motionless as a tree on the bare hillside.

Toad-flat, baleful, the dragon's head steamed. He ground his teeth into Lucifer's hand. Ninety feet of black iron struck the ground like a whip. Lucifer lifted the creature, still locked in his hand, and struck again, this time at the speck that was Djoura.

A writhing whip, however, is not an accurate weapon, and he missed. Frustration flushed the perfect face purple. He exposed a swollen mottled tongue as he lifted the dragon again.

"Stop!"

It was Raphael who had stood still on the smoking hillside, regardless of the titanic war around him. "All of you. Satan—leave him. Your business is with me."

Lucifer turned his mountainous head. The gold of his crown shone in the sun.

"You?" he said. "You, little ball of clay: half-witted animal?" His mouth split into a sly snarl.

"You are the only one among these in whom I have no more interest. What more could I do to you, after all?"

But as Lucifer spoke so, he flung the dragon away from him. Like a thread in the wind, the dark length swirled.

Djoura was stalking toward Raphael, her eyes locked on the mountain of dread before him. Saara came up slowly in his other side.

But Raphael stepped forward, putting them both behind him. In his sculpted face was neither confusion nor doubt. "It is not what you could do to me which is at issue. It is what I can do to you. I know you fear me."

"WHAT?" The air around the robed shape wavered. It burst into flame. "Fear YOU? What you can do to ME, you bag of offal? You are helpless!"

Raphael, weaponless and half-naked, stepped toward the mountainous form. "You have no idea what I can do, Satan. You have never known, and that is WHY you fear me. But I will tell you what I can do.

"As you took my hand, Satan, so I can take yours."

Lucifer watched his brother approach, one arm stretched out before him. "Maggot! We both know you have no power to . . ." But the red king seemed to shrink into himself as he spoke, growing smaller, or perhaps farther away.

As he walked Raphael was whispering, though neither his brother nor the friends who stood silently on the hillside behind knew what he said.

He came to the brooding apparition on the hill.

With a hand pierced and bloodied, Lucifer made to push Raphael away. They touched. And at that touch the red king collapsed like a sheet full of wind, and Lucifer and Raphael stood face-to-face: of equal height, two images of the same creation.

"You do not know me, brother," Raphael said quietly. He reached forward. "But now you will."

His fair hand lifted toward Lucifer's face.

Lucifer recoiled. "No!" he cried, and he flinched away. Raphael smiled patiently. He reached out again.

"No! I won't have your tricks! You insipid, cunning toady, it's not you but HIM in you! I won't stand it!"

Lucifer backed off, his voice cracking, but still Raphael walked toward him. The Devil reached out fending hands which became claws. Raphael slipped past them. Satan had turned to flee when he felt Raphael's touch on his shoulder. In blind panic Satan took the man by the neck with both hands and he shook him. Then convulsively he threw him off, smashing Raphael against the ground.

So quickly the fight was over, for Raphael's human body lay motionless at his brother's feet, its mouth bloodied, its neck at an ugly angle.

There was stillness on the rolling hills, and the only sound was that of the smoldering grass.

Saara stared transfixed at the defeat of her last crusade. Gaspare, beside her, held the neck of his lute in both hands and his lips were pulled back from his teeth. He opened his mouth to ask a question of someone, but no sound came out.

Djoura, too, stood without moving for a terrible minute. Then with a thin cold wail she flung herself down at the very feet of the Devil and bent her head to the broken body.

But oddly enough, Lucifer, too, stood paralyzed, staring at the shape of flesh he had himself created. His lips drew back from his teeth in an expression that was not a smile. He lifted red eyes to the sky.

There was a crack of fire in the air above. All looked up to see the black dragon swimming back toward his enemy, flaming along his entire length. In the beast's yellow eyes gleamed no more intelligence, but only bestial fury. Where the dragon passed, the earth smoked beneath him.

Lucifer saw him coming and his hands clenched at his sides. His eyes searched distracted over the hills, almost as though in search of hiding. He took once more to wyvern shape and fled upward.

Ebony jaws closed around the wyvern's serpentine tail. The wyvern shape wavered and a flayed form dripping with pus flapped its wings against the dragon's rococco head. Slipping free in its own mucus, it fled, with the dragon giving chase.

Flame ate through the membrane of one loathsome wing. The dragon caught Satan again, and now it was a creature of many boneless legs which wound vinelike around the black dragon, and pressed a sucking, platterlike mouth against the scales of his neck. The dragon spun, and bit, and burned the lamprey-sucker to dry leather. Both beasts howled.

But the sky around the combatants changed suddenly, deepening and growing more clear. The furies in the air faded to shadows. Their cries were muted.

All the stars came out.

Saara lifted her head to witness the sun and moon shining at opposite ends of a sky grown glorious. Gaspare gazed at the heavens mutely, holding to his little lute as though to a lover. Miles away, a panicked horse slowed his flight, blowing clouds of bloody froth onto his lathered sides.

Only Djoura the black Berber missed the miracle, for she was alone in her world of grief, rocking and sobbing above the cast-off body of a slave.

In the middle of this indigo splendor, one star grew brighter than all others. It swelled to rival the moon. It flickered in shape like the shadow of a bird in flight.

Silver light entered the mad eyes of the dragon, and he let his enemy go.

The Archangel Raphael shone in the sky like truth re
vealed and in his hands was a sword. "Come, Satan," he
called, and his voice was sun striking a field of ice. "See
what your malice has bought you."

The wyvern took to wing again but the brilliant air re
jected him. He sank to the earth and his stiff wings fell from
him to lie like the wings that ants shed in their season and
that one finds in the morning grass, covered with dew.

As Raphael descended, Satan rose once more as the red
king—King of Earth—and he shouted, "You interfere
Again! It is unfair! It is not your right, Raphael, for the earth
is MINE and all upon it!"

Still the angel descended. The burned hillside grew
bright as crystal. "I do not interfere, Morning Star. I am
sent against you.

"For not all upon the earth is yours, nor ever will be."

The sword of light struck once and the Devil's gold crown
went rolling over the turf.

Lucifer lifted his arms in defense. "I am given no weapon
against you. It is not fair!"

But the angel made no reply. His blinding wings drew
forward and round his brother and encompassed him. "Go!"
cried Raphael, and once more, "Begone from this place
and torment these children no more!" and he touched Satan
with his hand.

The Devil was not there.

The heavens lightened slowly and the glory went out of
the sky. Gaspare drew a breath that rattled along his throat.

Saara looked about her at the daylit plain, and she saw
Raphael as she had seen him many times before, a figure of
alabaster and feathers, no larger than a man.

"Chief of Eagles," she greeted him gravely.

But he did not reply, for he had not heard Saara at all, nor
seen her. Raphael's eyes were on the keening Berber
woman, and the body she had covered with her tattered
clothing.

He stepped over to her and went down on one stainless
knee beside her. "Djoura," he whispered for her ear alone.

Through her grief, that was the single voice which had
the power to reach her. She stiffened. Turned to him.

Her sloe eyes widened as she took in what he was. Who he was. "Djinn!" she gasped. "The great Djinn."

And after a moment. "Raphael?"

He cupped his hands around her face. "Your Pinkie. Always." He lifted her to her feet.

Djoura blinked around her. Her eyes were tear-blind. She seemed to wonder where the Devil had gone. Then she glanced at Raphael again and lowered her eyes.

She turned away.

"Isn't that like me," she mumbled to herself. "One man I can stand, out of all the cursed world. One silly pink fellow is all, and he turns out . . . turns out to be . . ." She shook her head till the coins in her hair rattled. "Well, not for me, anyway." She sought again the body of her friend, but it was not to be found, but only the black shawl with which she had covered it.

She kicked the crumpled fabric. She took a step. Another. Tears streaming down her face, Djoura strode away from the scene of battle as though she was beginning a journey which promised to be long.

But Raphael was beside her, and in his face was a loss which did not belong on the features of an angel. He wrapped her hands in his and she was forced to raise her head. "What, then?" she said roughly. "Does the great Djinn want Djoura to wash pots for him?" And she laughed at the idea. Harshly. Like a crow.

Wings flashed back with a sound of cymbals. Raphael threw his arms around the woman and pressed his head to hers. The angel gave a short, sharp cry like that of a hawk and the wings plunged forward, crashed together.

Raphael was gone from under the sky.

So was Djoura.

After a few stunned moments Saara, Gaspare, and the dragon crept forward. There was nothing to be seen on the Pyrenean hill, neither angel, nor devil, nor black Berber woman.

There was nothing to see but burned dry grass. Nothing to hear but the call of a horse in the distance.

"Well," commented Gaspare, fiddling nervous fingers over his tuning pegs. "It's not everyone's idea of courtship."

"No," replied Saara wearily. "Not everyone's. But as long as it suits . . ." She ran her hands through her heat-damaged hair.

The dragon cleared ten feet of throat. "Madam, I would like to suggest we catch our missing cattle and leave this place—before anything else untoward happens."

"Nothing else will happen," Saara replied, wearily but with great conviction. "And if it did, they wouldn't need OUR help!" She let Gaspare help her onto the broad black back of the dragon.

Epilogue

Two men walked up the hill toward San Gabriele. This village was surrounded by a bank of dirt and stones which might once have been a wall, but was now reduced to a mound that harbored grass and wild alpine pinks. Beside the road leading into the village rose a single oak tree much the worse for wear.

The old man, dressed loudly in vestments of Tyrian purple, with sleeve bobbles picked out in silver, stopped to lean against the tree. It was an action appropriate to both his years and the difficulty of the climb, but his attitude along with a certain hauteur in his lean face, gave the impression he had halted only to gaze out over the tilled valley below.

The younger man, perhaps twenty years of age and dressed demurely in black, felt a prick of guilt at having used his great-uncle too hard. His neat, smooth-shaven Provençal face darted a glance at the other's bitter features. But how to apologize, when old Gaspare would never admit he had felt tired?

Great-uncle made it difficult to feel sorry for him.

Now the old man's fierce green eyes rested on his com-
anion. "Why do you call yourself Caspar, when you are
ipposed to be named after me?" he asked. His leathered
iouth pulled sideways, as though he tasted something foul,
id two white points appeared on the bridge of his nose.

The story was that Grandmama and Great-uncle Gaspare
ere the illegitimate children of some Savoyard nobleman.
had always seemed silly to Caspar—the sort of story any
istard might make up—but looking at old Gaspare, he
und it more credible. From where else had the old man
ime by that hawk face and those obnoxious manners?

"Caspar is the same as Gaspare, *Grand-Oncle*, and
imes easier to a Provençal tongue."

The ancient green eyes narrowed. "I didn't want you to
called Gaspare at all." Caspar scratched nervously under
s skintight black jerkin and wished once more he hadn't
ime to visit, namesake or no. "I wanted you to be called
amiano."

Caspar hit one hand with the other and snapped his fin-
rs in the air. His gestures were Provençal, not Italian, and
reat-uncle Gaspare regarded them with suspicion. "That's
The name my grandmother keeps forgetting, of the lute
acher you had as a boy."

Gaspare, through the years, had grown quite a set of un-
ly gray eyebrows. He raised them both. "He wasn't my
acher, boy, but my good friend. And your grandmother
s no business to forget his name. Not with what he did for
r."

Caspar's eyes slid to the packed earth beneath the tree.
;ain that business. Caspar himself would rather have
ime from a family of no pretension, conceived between
vful sheets. "You mean that Grandmama Evienne and
. . . that he might be my . . ."

"NO!" spat Gaspare, glaring at his namesake's small, very
ench features. "Your grandfather was Cardinal Rocault,
rtainly. Almost certainly."

The old man flung himself away from the tree and pro-
:eded with great, gasping energy into the village. Caspar
lowed, drumming his fingers against his thigh uncom-

fortably. He heard his great-uncle mutter, "I could or
wish . . ."

Since there was a hint of softening in that voice, Casp
humored the old man. "You told me about that one whe
was a little boy, hein, *grand-oncle*? He was the one w
talked to animals, yes, and God sent wounds of flame in
his hands, and an angel comforter? He tamed a wolf th
had ravaged the village."

Gaspare's look of incredulity settled into scorn. "That w
Saint Francis."

"Ah. So it was," Caspar replied equably. "I am mistake
But I heard so many stories, you must understand, and a
child I believed them all."

The old man's lips drew back from his imperfect teet
and his angry hand made the swordsman's instinctive ge
ture toward the hilt of his sword. This surprised Caspar
well as daunted him, for to the best of his knowledge, l
great-uncle had never worn a sword in his life. "Delstre
was a man of our times—of MY times, at least. There mig
have been much of the fantastic about him, but he was
REAL person, boy. Born a few days' ride west of here in t
city of Partestrada."

"I rode in from the west," replied Caspar readil
"But . . . I can't recall a city of that name." Then, realizi
he had not spoken diplomatically, he added, "This is not
doubt you, *grand-oncle*. There are many ruins."

Gaspare winced. "Yes, no doubt. Ruins.

"It never really WAS a city, of course. Except to De
strego. A market town.

"Ah! It means nothing, boy. Forget it" The look of defe
on Gaspare's ancient face might have melted the your
man's amiable heart.

But he never saw it, for his great-uncle had turned h
head away. "And forget the stories you heard as a child," th
old man growled. "About dragons and witches and ange
and . . . whatever. It was just to entertain you: not to l
believed. If you could remember only that the man was th
greatest musician of his day . . ."

Gaspare gave a dry snort and smoothed his fashionabl
threadbare, trailing purple sleeve. "Or perhaps even that

o much. Yes, I'm sure it is. It . . . it has been a very long
ne, boy, since I have seen an angel." He turned at the
airs that led to his rooms, and, though he would have liked
 rest before assaulting them, preceded his grand-nephew
).

The cynicism of this last reply heartened Caspar. He did
ot believe, whatever his family in Avignon told him, that
reat-uncle Gaspare was mad or senile. He was just old and
gry (as old men often were), and had his own kind of
mor. Caspar sat down at the other side of the table and
zed at the old man's incredible lute while Gaspare poured
m a mug of rough cider.

Such an instrument. Covered with inlays of shell and
ory, it was almost too pretty to be taken seriously. But
aspare had plucked it for him, and he had perceived that
was of the highest quality, with a true tone clarified by age
 bell-like sweetness. "That is the lute Pope Innocent gave
u?" Caspar asked, a touch of awe in his voice. He smiled
e smile that everyone in Avignon found so charming.

But Gaspare was staring out the window. "The Pope gave
 to Delstrego. I inherited it only." Cold green eyes wan-
red through the room, and though they touched Caspar's
own ones only for a moment, the younger man was
ashed.

"It seems I was born too late," Caspar said.

Old Gaspare's eyes widened, looking at the other's sleek
terior. Remembering the plague. Remembering hunger.

"Too late for Avignon," Caspar qualified. "Since the pa-
cy has been in dispute, most of the good patrons have
moved to Rome. And so has the . . . the thrust of the
usic."

He shrugged and touched both hands to his breast. "So.
u see me on my way to Rome. Following my art."

Caspar quailed as his great-uncle's face went red, then
rple. It clashed terribly with his purple jacket. The old
an's aristocratic hooked nose stood out white in relief.
Vhat do you say, boy? You are going to Rome—after the
usic?"

"Yes," came the answer. "Oh, I know it must sound ab-
rd to you, as it does to my own father (since I am guaran-

teed a place in the guild at Avignon, and that is a thing
man may seek for a lifetime), but . . ."

Gaspare had turned from his namesake and was stari
fixedly again out the window. His hands, laced togeth
were white-knuckled.

"Following the music," he mumbled under his brea
"Without a sou, I suppose."

"No." In truth it had been part of his plan to ask his gre
uncle for provision during his stay, but one look at the
man's worn foppery had caused him to put that matt
quietly away. His innate honesty forced Caspar to ame
his answer. "Not quite without a sou."

Gaspare cast one taut look in his direction. He gestur
at the lute on the table. "Play it for me, boy."

Caspar had been longing to play ever since seeing t
lute. But the voice held more challenge than invitation, a
besides, old people never liked his music.

Yet it was old Gaspare who taught his father to play t
lute and Caspar had learned from him, so Great-uncle ha
right to hear. Caspar cleared his throat. "I am more used
an instrument of six courses," he qualified, lifting the l
from the table. It was almost weightless.

"Six!" cackled Gaspare. "Why, boy, you have only fi
fingers to play them with!"

Caspar's smile twisted under the expected witticism.
found the lute in very close tune.

Gaspare listened to a Provençal folk tune done in ve
pleasant, antique style. In a very few seconds' listening
had granted the boy technical competence. But he cut h
off roughly before the song was done. "Don't humor n
Nephew! God's bollucks, I'm a musician too! Play your o
music for me! Play to your limit!"

Caspar's eyes rose startled and he glared back at his gre
uncle.

Everyone at home thought the world of Caspar and
did so LIKE to be liked. Here he'd come eighty miles out
his way to visit the old man only to be treated like th
Unremitting hostility and scorn.

Of course what Gaspare said was quite true. Caspar HA
been humoring him. He ground his teeth together a

lexed his fingers over the hand-tied frets. "Very well," he
snapped at his great-uncle. "I'll play what I like best. But
don't bother to tell me you don't like it!"

Caspar played. His left hand spread like a spider on the
broad lute neck. His right hand bounced. He played seconds against one another. He ended lines on the seventh
chord. He played melodies that chased each other impu-
lently in and out of a music where structure threatened to
dissolve momentarily into chaos. The lute sounded like a
guitar, like a harp.

But though there was virtuosity in Caspar's attack, it was
not mere show, for the technique worked in the service of
feeling, in a music with much soul and a very playful
rhythm. His unobtrusive chin (nothing like Gaspare's chin)
jutted out as he played, like that of a man who speaks and
does not expect to be understood.

When he was done and not before, he glanced up at his
great-uncle. He was prepared for coldness, and half-
expected an explosion. But to the Provençal's horror, the old
man was weeping. Tears spattered onto the black wood of
the tabletop. Caspar was stricken. "Great-uncle! Forgive
me. It is dissonant, when one is not accustomed to it, certainly. But I had no inten—"

But the young man was no fool, and he read the truth in
his great-uncle's face.

Gaspare reached over the tabletop, shoving pitcher and
mugs to one side. "Boy," he whispered. "Don't apologize.
Never apologize for being what you must be.

"And pay no mind to me, for I can't explain it to you. It's
just the music, when I'd believed it to be all lost.

"But nothing is lost, you see? Nothing. Not even if
his . . . his city is lost, and no one remembers his name."

Caspar's quick brown eyes narrowed. "I don't understand, grand-oncle. But have I finally done something right
in your eyes?" Caspar asked, half touched by the old man's
tears, half still-resentful of his tempers.

"You have," replied Gaspare, grinning at his great-
nephew. "Of course you have, boy. You have shown me an
angel."

THIS IS THE LAST OF THE TALES OF DAMIANO AND HIS
FRIENDS I WILL WRITE. BY NOW I IMAGINE THEY ARE ALL
RATHER TIRED.

I KNOW I AM.

BUT NO CONCLUSION IS FINAL, AND THE READER IS WEL-
COME TO CONTINUE THE STORY IN ANY DIRECTION DE-
SIRED. AFTER THREE BOOKS, HE OR SHE KNOWS AS MUCH
TO THE PURPOSE AS I.

Bertie MacAvoy